AMBUSHED!

With a snap of my fingers, I turned suddenly away.
That same instant a rifle clanged close by. I saw the
finger of red light dart from the muzzle and felt, rather
than heard, the sound of the bullet tearing the air beside
me. The explosion lifted me as if with its own force.
I jumped like a wildcat and landed behind a rock, on
my knees, shaking like a feather. The Colt Special was
in my hand, and I didn't know how it got there. I had
no memory of drawing the thing. But I said to myself:
They're after me. *They're after me. I've got to fight back,
or they'll murder me.*

Max Brand®

Dogs of the Captain

LEISURE BOOKS NEW YORK CITY

A LEISURE BOOK®

November 2007

Published by special arrangement with Golden West Literary Agency.

Dorchester Publishing Co., Inc.
200 Madison Avenue
New York, NY 10016

ISBN 10: 0-8439-5873-1
ISBN 13: 978-0-8439-5873-7

Visit us on the web at www.dorchesterpub.com.

Dogs of the Captain

CHAPTER 1

The wise old Latin advises one to begin in the middle. Captain Slocum was the beginning of the middle, and, in a sense the end, for me. So I start with Captain Slocum.

He was our man of mystery and he lived in our "house of mystery," our "house on the hill." It seems to me as though every town in the West has its house on the hill, if only there is a hill near the town. The house on the hill is always quite old, having been built by the richest man of the pioneer days; it has at least one wooden tower, more ornamental than useful; it has carved scrollwork around its eaves; it has tall bay windows, a large stable behind, a fir hedge trimmed into some sort of imposing design about the gate, a lofty mill, a tank house nearby, almost equally tall, and a general air of mystery for all the inhabitants of the village.

Captain Slocum's house had all of these advantages, and in addition it had a ghost. The ghost lived in the wooden tower that stood up in the center of the roof. It was hexagonal, with a small window in each side, and in the panes of those windows lights glinted from time to time. Some said that it was a reflection from the stars, others declared that the lights were the dim glow of the other lighted windows of the town below, but no one could deny that the gleams were occasionally seen in the windows of the tower on the hill.

At least, that was the rumor.

Such being the rumor, there had to be a ghost, and the ghost was furnished by the Slocum family with great ease. It was the spirit of the aunt of the present owner. She had died young. There had been a missing lover. Still her unhappy ghost returned and, from the windows of the tower, looked out across the four roads to see the faithless lover return. But he never would come, and she would always be watching.

That was the story.

Captain Slocum was just the man to fit into that tale. He was tall, spare, dignified, calm. When he stood still, his long, spare legs seemed to bend backwards at the knees, in a great bow. We used to laugh at that.

No one could say that Captain Slocum was bad. But everyone could say that he was not good. All that he offered to the poor and the unfortunate of our little village was a pair of signs: BEWARE OF THE DOGS and NO TRESPASSERS.

And there never were any trespassers.

The man who cultivated the orchard lands and sowed and reaped in the lowland meadows of the Slocum place was a brutal Swede who never bothered to load his shotgun with rock salt and pepper. Instead, he used bird shot, and he had filled the skins of two or three boys with minute little specks of lead. The villagers hated that Swede so heartily that sometimes the men got together and talked gloomily about organizing a lynching party and giving the Swede the benefit of the necktie. But nothing came of it. Our village had lived past the first splendid free days of easy gold, murder, and lynching parties. It could not screw its courage to the sticking point.

Beyond the dense thorn hedge, therefore, lay the Swede and his gun, and his terrible pair of hands. He could lift 1,000 pounds. I myself saw him do it. In Parton's blacksmith shop a big canvas sack was loaded with iron junk and the Swede picked it up. His knees trembled. His face swelled. I could hear creaking sounds as though sinews were tearing away from the bones. But he put that sack on the scales, and I saw it weighed at 1,007 pounds and a fraction. A tremendous feat!

And the Swede, still sweating, had looked around in a leering, horrible smile to collect admiration from the crowd. He got no admiration, but only black envy and fear.

That seemed to content him just as well, I must say.

The hedge and the Swede, you would think, were enough to shelter any man and his house from the curiosity of the most prying and adventurous people. But that was not all. There were four huge dogs of a strain that was half mastiff and half Great Dane, I think. They had sooty muzzles and were striped like dingy tigers. Their barking—they did little of that—sounded like far-off, melancholy thunder, and their growling was a deep moaning sound. But they did little growling. They simply went for a stranger and made him hop it. Young Tag Evans, coming back from the mountains on a hunting trip, took a short cut across the Slocum place. He came closer to heaven than to home, that day, for the dogs sighted him and went for him, full tilt.

He got up his rifle and fired, but his first bullet missed, and he lost courage to stand his ground. He threw away the rifle and legged it for the hedge. And he got to the hedge one step in front of the dogs. There was nothing for it. He had to jump. So he leaped and came down on the broad back of the hedge. He might as well have come down on a bed of flames, because that hedge was literally filled with thorns as hard and sharp as needles and two or three inches long.

Poor Tag! He was cut to bits. He rolled over the hedge to the street and wallowed in the dust in an agony—and that was the last time that anyone tried to get across the Slocum place, day or night.

The sheriff was a friend of Tag's father. He went up to the Slocum house to make trouble about the thing, but he only stayed five minutes and came away looking as though he had been in an icebox and caught a chill.

The hedge, the Swede, the dogs—they were three barriers against the world. And there was a fourth and a fifth. There was an old hag of a woman, like a witch of a stepmother in a German fairy story. She did the cooking and most of the housework. When she came down the street with her humped back and her outthrusting chin, wagging her head from side to side and grumbling to herself, I can tell you that we didn't hang about to mock and tease her. Her deformity was not ridiculous. It was simply horrible. Her name was Mrs. Ebenezer Grey.

Her husband also worked in the Slocum house. It

was a miracle that such a man should have married such an ugly witch. He looked fifteen years younger than she. He was a straight, well-built, rather good-looking fellow, and he dressed extremely well. He had a face without any expression in it or any color, either. His hair was almost white, not from age but the way an albino is white. He had no eyebrows. His eyes were a pale, pale gray. Still his features were regular and he was quite smart in appearance, particularly when he came down to the station with his master, for he went away on all the trips that his master took—and these kept Captain Slocum away at least half the year.

This fellow, Ebenezer Grey, was the fifth and last line of defense for the Slocum place. It was understood, I don't know how, that he always carried a revolver, that he was a perfect shot, and that he would die in the service of his master.

That was the household of the captain. Those were the only people who ever entered the place. There was no mother, wife, child, or any relation. The captain lived there entirely alone—with the ghost.

There were two daily events of importance in our town. One occurred at eleven fifteen in the morning, when the train came in. The other took place at three o'clock sharp when the captain walked down the hill and went to the post office for his mail. As many people were sure to be on hand to see him as to see the train come in. But he never spoke to a soul. He kept his eyes straight before him, like a soldier, and, when he left the post office, he went straight up the hill again with a long, powerful stride that seemed to make nothing of the slope. In his hands he was sure to have a batch of letters and at least one thick newspaper or journal from the East.

Sometimes he shook out the newspaper and read as he walked, never slackening his pace, stepping always with the same assurance. And in his wake he left, in spite of his silence, a new crop of whispers and rumors. As a matter of fact, we knew nothing about him, and this left our imaginations more room. We did not even know where he went or what he did on his trips to the East. It was rumored that he was a man of large business affairs, that he was a Wall Street shark, but I never heard a word of proof that this was the actual case.

He was our most prized possession. Crow Hollow and Greensburg were bigger, richer, more influential, but they couldn't compete with Merridan because, although each had at least one house on the hill, neither could show anything to equal Captain Slocum. How could we have filled up the long winter evenings or the still longer summer afternoons, if we had not possessed a Captain Slocum as a broad basis and bedrock upon which to build dreamy towers of fancy?

Now, Captain Slocum is on the page, but I must introduce the thing that, eventually, brought me in contact with him. That was a patch of watermelons that the Swede cultivated in the hollow near the creek, on the slope that faced south and collected every ray of the sun as in a broad-mouthed cup.

There were other watermelon patches around Merridan. There were yellow-bellied melons with broad, crooked backs; there were huge green-black cannon balls with hearts of crimson and tissues of sugar-frosting; there were the usual egg-shaped green melons, too; but there was none like the melons that the Swede was raising in that hollow. For these were striped with yellow so that they could be seen afar. Almost every day someone carried to school a tale of how the striped melons of the Swede were growing, how they were plumping out, how some of them must weigh sixty or seventy pounds, at least, and how the yellow stripes bloomed like veins of gold.

I myself sat one afternoon for an hour in the branches of a tree that looked over the thorn hedge and into the hollow; I fed my eyes until my throat ached with yearning. When I thought I had my fill, I got down from the tree and went home. I was sure that the melon patch was out of my mind, but, when a boy is twelve years old, such things have a way of getting into the very soul.

I woke up in the middle of the night with a jump and sat up in bed. I had been dreaming of watermelons, of great yellow-striped beauties that tasted like ice cream soda and watermelon combined.

I stared out the window. The moon was shining like a silver sun, and I could look straight up the winding road that went by the thorn hedge of Captain Slocum.

The moment the idea came to me, I lay back in the bed and covered my face; I was sick with fear that the temptation would be too strong for me. And it was.

In ten minutes I was up, dressed, and walking the whiteness of that road, with the thin dust squirting like warm water between my bare toes.

CHAPTER 2

It was one of those very still nights. The moonlight poured down on everything like so much water, so much shining water, with pressure and weight that drove the wind out of the sky and froze the houses, the trees, the fence posts, and their still shadows. There was no living thing in the world. There was only my small self, raising the dust there under the moon.

I was between an ecstasy and a terror. On the one hand, the delight of the adventure filled me; on the other hand, I felt the great thorns of the hedge bayoneting me to the heart, or the teeth of the huge, silent dogs fixed deeply in me.

What kept me going was the thing that had wakened me in the middle of the night. I had to have one of those watermelons. A thirst possessed me. The scent of the tarweed, the alkali in the wisps of rising dust, a vague memory of salt meat from the day before helped to build up such a thirst as I could not remember having suffered from before—a thirst that no amount of spring water, snow-cold and pure, ever could remotely touch, to be slaked only by the crisp, brittle, deliciously cold flesh of the watermelon—aye, by the red heart of the melon alone.

My mouth now began to water copiously. I broke into a run and went scampering up the last slope. I knew exactly the hole in the hedge that I would use. When I came to it, I got down on my hands and knees and crawled through. Midway, a thorn jagged into the small of my back, for I had arched my back like a dromedary.

I hung there for a moment, tasting the pain, grinning like a wolf, then I wriggled away from that sword point and a moment later I was standing on the dangerous, enchanted ground. Not 100 yards away from me was the magic fruit. The big melon leaves looked like feathers and gilt; the melons themselves fairly glowed at me like lanterns.

I held myself in. I scanned the slope, and above the trees I saw the head of the Slocum house with two attic windows looking out at me in the manner of two eyes, and above the peak of the roof was the central tower.

"Well, ghost," I said to myself, "if you come after me, I'll light out faster than any old ghost ever traveled in his life."

In fact, I felt as light as feathers in a wind, there was so much fear and apprehension in me. As for the dogs, I could, of course, take to a tree if I sighted them in time. But that would be a dangerous business, for I was persuaded that the Swede would come if he heard the dogs bay me and that he would shoot me out of the tree in cold blood. I remembered the dreadfully brutal leer of that man when he had stood in the blacksmith shop after lifting the burden of iron junk. Well, how he would laugh again when he found a life in his hands.

It would all have to be a matter of speed with me.

So I got across the open space, gave a last look at the gloom of the shadows under the nearest trees, and then cuffed the nearest big melon with my bare heel. The rind split; I ripped away the fractured end. I tore the rind apart all down the side and to this moment I can hear the crisp, fresh, tearing sound. There lay the heart before me, glistening under the moonlight. I seized it in both hands. I shook off the black seeds that adhered to it. And instantly my teeth were in it.

Was it very different from the other watermelons of the district?

I dare say that it was not, but to me it seemed different. It seemed as different as the blue of heaven is from the dusky meadows of the earth. In all the universe there was nothing else that could so satisfy the lust of my thirst that was hunger and my hunger that was thirst. I ate, and I ate. Let the juice run where it would, so long as the major portion was coursing down my throat; I blessed the God who created watermelons.

However, my wits began to come back to me, after a moment. I should not make myself heavy with too much, even of this heavenly food. But I must take away with me some proof that I had done the thing.

Now that I had tasted the fruit, I wanted to enjoy the fame of a great and daring sinner. There was not a boy in Merridan who would not look upon me with awe and uttermost respect. There was not a girl capable of looking at me without emotion. I would become, at a single stroke, the foremost boy charac-

ter in the town. I would be the only one in months
or years who had ventured to disturb the privacy of
Captain Slocum.

Well, I wanted to take one of the biggest of the
melons, but some of them were too heavy for me.
There's nothing so bulky and slippery as a watermelon, for its weight. At last, I picked out a good,
firm fellow that was shaped like a football and must
have weighed twenty pounds. That would have to
do for me. I snapped off its withered stem and stood
up, taking the watermelon under my arm.

The next moment I almost dropped it. The terror
was upon me! I had thought of flight, but flight was
impossible. So great was my horror that not even the
idea of running would have come to me, unless I
had been a full hundred yards farther away. For
coming toward me from beneath the tree shadows,
which brushed him to obscurity one instant and let
him step into the full clarity of the moonshine the
next, was Captain Slocum himself, with his four
huge guard dogs at his heels.

"He'll kill me," I remember saying aloud, for the
husky sound of my own voice astonished me.

Captain Slocum came down the brief slope with
his long, regular, unhurrying step. The biggest and
oldest of the dogs walked right under the sway of
his master's right hand, stepping so that his head
would be touched at every stride the captain made.
That brute would be first to fly at my throat.

I looked at the captain more closely, fascinated.
His face was so thin that I could see the shadow that
smudged his cheek below the cheek bone. His nose
and his chin were more prominent, and he had
seemed to have a death's-head grin. The people of
Merridan were fools. Not only was this man far

from good, but he was a paragon of evil. It was stamped too deeply into his face. I would as soon have encountered death itself as that long, lean form, striding toward me from under the shadows of the trees.

When the dogs saw me, the great fellow that walked under its master's hand kept straight on and paid no heed to me, but the other three drove at me in a single volley.

I tried to run. I could not. I tried to scream. I could not. I closed my eyes. I waited for their teeth, but, instead, I felt the monsters nosing and sniffing at me.

Suddenly they were gone. I heard the pound of their galloping feet almost like the sound of a running man, and, when I looked after them, I saw that their owner had gone on. He had not paused. What difference did it make to him whether his dogs tore an intruder to pieces or not? The law could not touch him for it. He could pretend total ignorance. And what could the law attempt?

But the dogs had been a little baffled by the very motionlessness of my fear. And so they had gone off to follow the captain and left me behind them, untouched. I saw one of the brutes stop and look back at me, as though he doubted the statue might be made of flesh, after all. But then he went on again, galloping, and I saw the last of them melting among the trees.

What was the business of this man in strolling across his woods and meadows with the four great brutes? Why was he out, when the honest men were home, asleep? Why, above all, had he seen a thief among his watermelons and yet chosen to stride on past him and leave him unnoticed? All of these questions combined to make the picture of him more dreadful than ever, in my mind. Pity, amusement, sympathy for the pranks of the young one never would expect from such a creature as Captain Slocum. But there he was, gone away, and I with a good chance to get back to the hole in the thorn hedge.

I got to it. When I had to turn my back on danger while crawling through the hole, I felt one nightmare pang, but then the thing was done, and I was walking down the street toward my home. My arms began to ache. I found that I had been unconsciously lugging the stolen watermelon with me all that distance.

When I reached home, I put the melon under the drip of the windmill, which was the coldest place about the house, then I went in and got to bed. I remembered the curious way my heart raced and stopped and raced again as I lay flat on my back, staring at the ceiling. Then I began to tremble violently. A hot fever burned my skin. I had a sense of weakness; I was falling into a frightful pit.

Of course, it was shock, but I couldn't realize it at that age. I simply thought that Captain Slocum had put the evil eye on me and that the reason he had not harmed me when he found me was that he preferred to kill me by a slow torment after I had got to a safe distance from his place.

I sat up in the bed, sick with this thought, and I was about to call my Aunt Lizzie. But something stopped me. She was never very amiable and her temper was particularly short at night. I lay back again in the bed; in a few moments a good perspiration began, and in another instant I was asleep.

Two things, in the morning, told me that this had not all been a dream. One was the thorn cut on my back and the other was the sight of the watermelon, misted over with coolness and beaded with shining water drops.

I went to the fence and called my neighbor, Charley Mace. Charley was a year older and a year larger than I; he could run farther and faster, dive from a greater height with a smaller splash, shoot marbles straighter, jump higher and farther than I. Besides, he lived in a larger house. His people had money—a vague term. Charley Mace wore at least two new suits a year. In short, in every way Charley was my envied superior.

Now, however, I went to the fence and called him, and a deep, poisonous joy was working in me. I intended to wipe out in a single stroke the envy, the heartaches of years.

Charley came out on the side porch, holding an open book in his hand. The book had a cover design in red and black and I guessed, hungrily, at a tale of pirates.

"C'mon over and help me eat a watermelon," I said.

"Aw, I dunno," he said. "I been eating so many watermelons lately that I feel all kind of soggy."

"All right," I said, "you think you've eaten watermelons, but you never have. You go on back inside. I'll holler to Jack McGuire and he'll come and eat it with me."

"Aw, hold on," said Charley Mace. "I didn't say I wasn't coming. I only was thinking." He shied the book through the door, which he had left open behind him, and thirty seconds later Charley was permitting the drip from the windmill to fall unheeded upon his tousled hair while he stared at the yellow-striped melon. He grew rather pale around the lips.

His eyes became enormous, and he raised his glance incredulously toward me.

"Jiminy, Don," he said. "You didn't go and do it? By golly, you did. You went and got it!"

I stood by in an attitude of profoundest indifference. But I could have begun a song and dance, for I knew that now I was the uncrowned king among the boys of Merridan.

CHAPTER 3

My attitude was very far from moral perfection. When he said—"Didn't you see nothing?"—I replied casually: "Yeah, all the dogs." This fairly rooted him to the ground. He grew pale in sympathy with that dreadful moment.

"And you, Don . . . look-it, what did you do?"

"Why, nothing," I said. After all, that was exactly correct.

"You didn't do nothing?" he said.

"No, I didn't do nothing."

"They didn't see you, maybe?"

"Why, there I was, right out there in the moonshine, as plain as day."

"And they didn't pay no attention to you?"

"I didn't say that. Sure they paid attention to me."

My casualness began to drive my friend mad.

"By Jiminy, Don," he shouted, "ain't you goin' to tell me what happened?"

I pretended to be surprised. "Why, of course, I am," I said. "I'm not holding anything back."

"But my gracious heavens," he said, "why don't you tell me what happened when the dogs saw you?"

"I told you."

"No, you didn't."

"Don't get so jumpity, like a boiling teakettle," I said.

He blinked. He accepted the remark of criticism with a mildness that amazed me. "You go on. You tell it your own way," he said.

"Why, there wasn't anything. They just came for me and I stood still."

"You did what? You didn't even run?"

"No," I said in a superior tone. "Of course, I didn't run. They would've torn me to pieces. Of course, I didn't run."

His mind suddenly grasped at a great idea. "You just stood there and looked them in the eye," he suggested.

I had not been intending to say that. But since he fathered the idea, I thought that it would do as well as the next one. I merely said: "Well, there's no use in running away. Look at elephant hunters when an elephant charges. They just stand out there and fold their arms and look the elephant in the eye."

"Do they?" he asked.

"Sure they do," I said as carelessly as ever.

He fairly groaned with self-abasement. "Well, I never could do it," he admitted sadly.

"Well, you know the way that it is," I said. "You know that some people are born hunters, and some people are not."

His sigh was another groan. "Oh, I know," he said. "I guess that's the way with it. But you stood the dogs off and came away with a melon, too?"

"You wouldn't want to go that far and come back without anything, would you?" I said.

"Hey," he said, "have you told anybody?"

"No. I haven't told anybody. There's not much to tell . . . just stealing a watermelon. I guess every boy in town has done about that much, one time or other."

"Do the McGuires know nothin'?"

"No, they don't know nothin'."

"Lemme call 'em over."

"Why, sure, if you want to. I've got to go downtown for Aunt Lizzie, now I recollect. You and the McGuires polish off that melon. After all, I stuffed myself last night, and there's plenty more where that one came from." I grew more magnificent as I went along.

"Great holy smoke," said Charley, "you wouldn't mean that you'd go back to the Slocum place again?" He was agape, drinking in my greatness.

"Well, why not?" I said. "I guess that's Aunt Lizzie calling me now. So long, Charley. I hope you like the melon."

Aunt Lizzie had not called me. But I wanted to be alone and away from the boys for a time. In that way, the innumerable reiterations would be avoided, and I could trust the hearty imagination of Charley to repeat the story in due order. In fact, I had never had a more helpful listener than he, and I hoped that he would have a stimulated imagination.

I was correct. He kept the main skeleton of the story, but after he had finished embroidering it, I was such a hero that I should have been sent to a reform school. The boys of Merridan wakened to find that a star was shining in their midst; it was the sensation of that year, and, when I went down to the post office to get the mail that afternoon, I was hailed from all sides along the way. The youngsters sang out to ask me how much I liked watermelons, and what they tasted like with moonshine sauce. I could feel the electric excitement in the air behind those remarks. Wonder and admiration pursued me. I was the happiest young liar that ever walked the street of a small town, and in small towns liars are more expert, vigorous, ingenious, and talented than in the greatest cities. They have to live every day among their deceptions, so to speak.

When I got down to the post office, the clerk grinned at me broadly as he passed a single envelope for my Aunt Lizzie through the window. "I hear you've got to be kind of a sleepwalker, Don," he said.

"Me?" I stated innocently. "I don't know what you mean."

He laughed loudly. Two or three more standing by laughed heartily, also. Then they were suddenly silent, and I turned from the window to find myself confronting the tall form, the lean face, and the bright eyes of Captain Slocum.

He did have some snake-like power of hypnotism in his glance for me, at least. I was frozen as still as I had been the night before when he came striding out from the scattered shadows of the trees. He looked straight at me, pausing a noticeable second. Then he went on to the window and I started for the door and the open air.

The terror, I was sure, was on my face. My little day of life as a hero was ended, and I wanted to get home with my shame, but, as I got to the door, I heard one of the loiterers at the stamp window saying: "Did you ever see anything like that?"

"No," said another. "The kid never turned a hair. He's the coolest brat I ever saw . . . outside of jail!"

They both laughed, and I went through the door more revived than if I had inhaled pure oxygen. They seemed to have seen nothing.

I loitered about for a moment, patting Dick Bower's half-breed setter, which has a better nose than any thoroughbred. Really, I wanted to enjoy the electric eye of public attention and favor that was shining on me now.

The captain came out again. I stood by one of the verandah pillars and put back my head and looked casually, steadily at the tall captain, but this time he went by without giving me a glance.

Yet I knew, when I sauntered up the street that afternoon, that he had recognized me as the interloper on his premises of the night before. I knew that he had recognized me, and, as I remembered the glance that he had fixed upon me in the post office, I wondered whether it was rage, malice, or plain curiosity in his eye?

Suddenly I felt more kindly toward him, as one does toward those who one has exploited. From that moment, my position in the town altered. So did my position in the house of my Aunt Lizzie. She said to me: "I didn't know that you had that much gumption . . . I dunno but something might come out of you, after all."

It was her nearest approach to optimism in the five years I had been with her, an unwelcome addition to her lonely household.

Captain Slocum left town the next day. The story of my midnight adventure grew more and more polished in the hands of time and the village gossips, and my own position was that of a promising young adventurer who was absolutely fearless.

The boys could have told that I was not fearless by remembering my past. But they didn't remember. Boys never do. They feel that youngsters must be capable of change. They swear by change, for each youngster hopes one day to be witty, profound, physically powerful, and heroic, the adored of millions. They simply took it for granted that a fortunate change had come in me. I was simply growing up.

If the reader believes that too much space has been given to the stealing of a watermelon, I have to say that this narrative deals almost entirely with my troubles in life, and every one of them, in a sense, sprang out of that unlucky midnight adventure. This will be seen quite clearly as the history continues.

The very next day of school the first trouble came upon me. Alec Moody, a youngster of about my own age, had the broad face and the stout heart of a fighter. Besides, he knew something about boxing, and he used to bowl us over like ninepins when it came to fighting. He didn't like my new prominence and so he picked trouble with me by tripping me up as I went by the corner bench at the noon recess. When I saw that it was Alec, I would have pretended to find a hidden humor in the thing. I would have laughed and accepted my shame, but instantly it was clear that the other boys were keenly expectant. They expected something of me.

Suddenly I knew what it was. If I were the hero of the stolen melon, the dangerous dogs, and all the rest, then I certainly would not endure an insult from another boy. I saw this in a flash. Then I turned on Alec.

"Did you mean that, Alec?" I asked in a superior way.

"What if I did?" said Alec. "You don't need to try no airs on me. I ain't a dog or a watermelon."

My fear was terrible. I saw the big, red fists of Alec, so famous among us all. I was so frightened that, to keep from showing fear, I relied on loud bluffing. "You're a fool, Alec," I said. "I don't want to hurt you, but I'll wait for you at the vacant lot down by Tom Green's place after school." I favored him with a sneer and a smile, dexterously commingled. Then I walked off.

I heard one of the lads say: "Gee, Alec, I guess you'll get about killed, pretty near."

"I'll bust his jaw for him," said Alec. But his voice was full of indecision, and a sudden wild hope arose in me.

All that afternoon, since Alec was in my class, I avoided his eyes, until it was about a quarter to three, the end of the day. Then I turned deliberately in my seat and looked across the room at him.

He felt my eye. He jerked his head toward me so suddenly that I knew at once he had been covertly watching me most of the time. He seemed pale and tense. He sat stiffly in his seat and his eyes were very big.

It was exactly what I had hoped to find. I smiled at Alec, and nodded my head toward the door, by way of reminding him that he had a meeting with me after the hour struck.

Alec made no sign of understanding. He slowly turned his head and stared straight ahead.

And I knew that he would not keep the appointment. With a vast relief and a lightening of the heart,

I understood that my tactics had won for me. After that my spirits rose every instant.

When three o'clock came, I walked slowly down to the vacant lot that had been named in the challenge. A crowd of the boys went with me. Every lad in the school was gathered there to see the terrific encounter, and there I stood idly and cheerfully chatting with them. I had taken off my coat and rolled up my sleeves, but I talked of the swimming hole and other matters, and said not a word about the battle to be.

How they admired my casual attitude, my cheerfulness. I saw astonishment and pleasure in their faces. Many, incredulous, stood and stared at me for a long time. For, mind you, the fists of Alec were famous weapons among us. But where was Alec?

"He's not coming!" shouted a very small boy suddenly. "He's got cold feet. Alec's showing the white feather. He's given up!"

There was a dead silence, in which I said to the little boy: "Look here, Bobby, don't you go saying things like that about Alec. Alec never ran away from a fight."

"He never fought you!" cried Bobby.

There was undeniable truth in this. And, as the slow minutes increased to fifteen, to twenty, it became clear that Alec was not to appear. The truth of the matter was that he was shamed.

In the meantime, there was the swimming hole waiting for us, and the sun was hot, and the air dry as an oven's breath. The temptation was too great.

Away we went to the cooling waters of the pool, and raced Alec out of our minds.

It was a fresh triumph for me. No boy was ready to stand up to me from that moment.

CHAPTER 4

I did not stay long at the swimming pool. I began to grow thoughtful although the air was warm and the water delightful to the touch. It was all very well to have other lads there who could outdive and outswim me. There were plenty of them with physiques that made mine seem very spindling, indeed. But that mattered nothing, if I were their acknowledged master when it came to fighting.

Well, I was acknowledged, but my superiority was only an attitude of the mind. Presently I got out of the water, dressed, went home, and spent a long time till dark in the little barn behind our house, where we kept the cow and the buggy horse. I had a little manual of boxing. There in the loneliness of the barn loft, I studied that manual with an intent interest and began to practice blows. I went downstairs, got a strong canvas bag, filled it with sand, and, carrying it up, I tied it by a rope to a rafter. Then I practiced pummeling, tugging, twisting at this bag, executing the strokes as well as I could.

That kept on until dark. I determined that I would do the same thing every day. But, oh, for a trained teacher in the manly art.

You might say that the iron of ambition was now entering my soul. I was like a man in high public position, having to appear with a certain dignity. But I hardly expected what followed within two weeks.

Captain Slocum had returned to town with his right hand bandaged. Dr. Lewis attended him to dress the hand, and the word went out that the wound seemed to have been made by a knife—a dreadful wound that would cripple the hand for life, it appeared.

The very next day a new blow fell on me.

We sat about during the morning recess. It was too hot for the usual running games. Some of the boys were playing marbles, but marbles were a shade beneath my new dignity.

"Say," said one, "I seen the light up in the Slocum tower again."

"I seen it, too," said another. "I guess the ghost is there again."

"The ghost showed up to make the captain feel at home, and keep him company," said a wag.

"Say, Don," said Charley, my neighbor, "you ever seen the ghost light?"

"I don't believe in ghosts," I said.

"He don't believe in ghosts," said Alec, laughing a little.

They all looked coldly upon Alec. He was a discredited lad now.

"Well," said Alec, "if you don't believe in ghosts, why don't you go up there and get into the ghost tower some midnight?"

I said nothing. The mere thought was too dreadful to be kept in mind.

Then I saw that all eyes were turning on me expectantly and a chill of dread went through me. Did they actually think that I would attempt such a thing? Why, not even grown men would like to spend a midnight hour in that grisly tower.

"Sometime I might do it," I said. There was a stir, an intaking of breaths.

"By Jiminy, Don, would you really do that?"

"Well, why not?" I argued faintly. "Ghosts are only air, I guess."

"If you're going to do it sometime, why not tonight?" argued Alec, his little eyes filled with malice.

I refused to look at him. I drew a small design on the ground with the toe of my shoe, but I said, as though in thought: "Well, maybe I will. I don't know."

"Some of us will go up there and see you climb to the tower," said Alec.

"Sure we will," volunteered many voices.

My heart sank into my shoes. I moistened my dry lips. "What's the good?" I protested feebly.

"Yeah, he's getting cold feet," said Alec.

I would have overlooked the insult, but Charley said stoutly, full of a great belief: "He's not afraid of anything. He'll go if he says so, won't you, Don?"

"Sure I'll go," I said. I saw that I was drifting with a fatal black tide, but I did not know what to do or say to stop the current.

"Well, at twelve o'clock, about, I'll be waiting outside your gate, under the elm trees," said Alec relentlessly.

"I'll be there, too," said Charley.

"And me! And me!" said others.

Oh, yes, there would be plenty of them ready to see me attempt the thing.

Suddenly I could see that lonely tower and its blinking, mysterious windows as they appeared at night. I tried to speak. No sound came. I cleared my throat.

"I'll meet you under the elms, then," I said.

So the thing was done. I was trapped. I knew that I could not go through with the affair, but I had given my word.

That afternoon I spent pursuing my homemade course of boxing lessons. But the dreadful future came between me and my work. I wished, now, that I had remained the same unnoted, insignificant lad I had been a month before. The terrible cold load of fear sickened me. That night, at supper, even Aunt Lizzie noted that I barely touched my food.

"You gotta have some sulphur," she said. "It's high time you had some. This time of year the blood gets to changing."

I wiped the dishes, after supper, hardly knowing how my hands were employed. And then I got to my bed.

I had made up my mind. I would go to sleep and forget all about the appointment. Let the boys come and waken me, if they wanted me. Let them come and waken me, if they dared to risk the dreadful wrath of my aunt. Eventually, unwilling sleep came over my mind. I slumbered like the dead and dreamed strange dreams.

Suddenly I wakened, as I had wakened that other night when I had set out to rob the melon patch of Captain Slocum. I lay for a time listening to the heavy, sickening pounding of my heart. Then I scratched a match. I hoped it was nearly morning; I found to my horror that it was only a quarter before midnight.

I lay back again on the bed, shaking from head to foot. But the impulse was stronger than I. Presently I found myself dressing. I left off my shoes, as I had that other night. Shoes were no good when it came to climbing, and what a climb I might have to make this night!

But a vague hope remained in me that the boys would not be there. There were too many reasons against that. They would not be awake when the grim middle of the night arrived. They would be sound asleep or else, rising, they would be ordered back to bed by stern parents. Mothers and fathers with the eyes of eagles and the ears of wildcats—these appeared to me the most sensible, useful, and ornamental creatures in the world. It was a new viewpoint for me, but I adopted it heartily.

I had no expectation of finding the waiting group under the elm trees across the road from our house. But, when I went down the hall, I fervently hoped that Aunt Lizzie would wake up and catch me. She had the power of a giant when she was armed with a whip, but I would gladly have taken a thrashing, if it could give me a rational excuse for abandoning this enterprise.

Then I heard deep, half-groaning sounds from her room, and I knew that she was sleeping. I never was very fond of Aunt Lizzie. I hated her, then, for her snoring, and purposely I stumbled and recovered myself noisily.

I waited, but there was no cessation of that organ-deep snoring. My stumble had been to her no more than the noise of a falling leaf. So I went on to the front door. It stuck fast, even after I had turned the key, and I wrenched it open carelessly, so that a loud, shattering sound went past me down the hall.

That should have fetched Aunt Lizzie from her slumbers, but it didn't. No, she kept right on. I could hear her plainly as I stood there in the open door, as one lashed to the mouth of a cannon.

Peering hard among the shadows under the elm trees across the street, I was left not a moment in doubt. Out of the shadows, as I appeared, came a dozen forms of youngsters who waved their arms and danced with a frantic joy. The moon shone on them. I could even see the dust that they raised.

So I looked behind me into the deep-mouthed darkness of the hall and felt that I was saying farewell to my life. In fact, that was correct. To my old life I was saying good-bye forever.

CHAPTER 5

I drew that front door shut with a spiteful slam. I had just about given up all hope that Aunt Lizzie would waken. I suppose I was about the only boy in the history of the world who reluctantly bade adieu to the hopes of a heavy flogging.

Now I was opening the front gate, which I allowed, carelessly, to slam behind me. Here I was, at last, surrounded by the crowd, and not a sign of intervention from my aunt.

The boys were in a high state of excitement. They were delighted and seemed a little hysterical, also. There was hardly a moment when someone or other of the lot was not suppressing a nervous giggle.

"You've got your nerve, Don," said one of them. "You're going through with it, eh?"

"You're gonna have your fun, too," said another. "Right now, Jimmy Sanderson, here, when he was coming down the hill, he saw the flash in the window of the tower. I guess your old ghost is waiting for you, all right."

I stopped short. I could not breathe or move.

"He's got cold feet, all right. He's only bluffing. He'll never go through with it," said Alec.

I managed to say: "I'll tell you what . . ." There my breath failed me.

"Tell us what?" insisted Alec. "Tell us why you ain't going to do it?"

I made a last desperate cast into the depth of my mind, but I found nothing that would serve as an excuse. So I forced myself to sneer, saying: "Look at here . . . what do I care if there is a ghost up there in the tower. What can a ghost do to me? A ghost has no flesh or blood."

"That ghost can make lights shine," said Alec.

"Leave him alone," said Charley. "You can see that he's going through with it. You wouldn't have the nerve to do it."

We were walking up the road. I measured the distance, and it seemed a frightfully short way to that looming silhouette of the Slocum house on the hill.

"Sure I wouldn't have the nerve," said Alec. "I wouldn't be such a fool. Everybody knows that it was a ghost took the wits out of old man Hale. He's been a doddering, slavering idiot ever since the night he saw the ghost."

"Bah," said Charley, "that ghost of his, he found it in a whiskey bottle."

I listened to this discussion with a sinking heart.

"Aw," I said, "you can't tell me. I know that ghosts can't do anything. I don't know, even, that there are any ghosts. A lot of pretty wise people say there aren't."

Alec laughed derisively. "Wise, are they?" he said. "Well, I know about how wise they are. You can't tell me. Ain't it in the Bible? Ain't it in Shakespeare?"

How did he know that it was in Shakespeare? However, those two names convinced me. Half the things in books of quotations, which I had seen, were signed "Bible" or "Shak." If ghosts appeared in both works, ghosts there must be. I returned to an earlier theme.

"Well, nobody ever heard of them doing anything."

Alec laughed again, in his sneering, brutal way. "They can't do anything, eh? Then what about the man that dug up the grave and robbed the man of his silver arm? What about him?"

"Well, what about him?" I asked weakly.

"Well," said Alec, "they found the robber dead right in the middle of the road. There wasn't no sign nor trace about him of the way that he was killed, only he had a mighty terrible face to look at. The people that seen it, they had nightmares all the rest of their lives."

"Aw, I don't believe it," I said.

"Don't you? Well, sir, they traced the robber back to the grave he'd opened. He'd shut the grave after him, again, mind you. He'd piled all the earth right back on top. And on top of that piled up fresh ground, there was the silver arm lying. Now, whacha think of that?"

I thought a great deal. I felt even more, but I found not a single word to say. The little breath that was left to me, I had to use in climbing the hill, slowly. The rest of the boys respectfully measured their steps by mine. They seemed to take my slowness for a dignified determination.

Alec had more treasures in store for me, however. He went on: "And then there's other things. Look at Sam Whipple over in Laurel Creek."

"I never heard of him," I said truthfully.

"You never did? That's funny. 'Most everybody has. I'll bet Charley has."

"Maybe I have," said Charley. "I'm not saying."

"You could say, though. You could say that you know how Sam Whipple went to bed one night as big and strong a man as you ever heard of. And the next morning he was laying out there in his night-shirt as dead as a nail. You could say that, if you wanted to, and it would be true."

"You look at here," I argued. "There's aplenty of people that die in the middle of the night, and no sign on 'em."

"Ah! And what makes 'em die?" demanded Alec in a dreadfully significant voice.

"What was Sam Whipple's ghost?" I asked.

"Nobody seen her," said Alec with great satisfaction. "But everybody knows that Sam's wife up and died on him, ten years back, and, when she was dyin', she swore him never to marry another wife, or she'd come back and haunt him. Everybody knows that. And everybody knows that Sam Whipple was engaged to get married all over again, when he was found dead. And ever since then, there's been funny sights and sounds around the Whipple house, and there ain't a man in Laurel Creek that would spend a night in the place, not for a million dollars, they say. I wouldn't, for one!"

"Say, what you trying to do to Don? Scare him?" asked Charley.

Two or three others told Alec to shut up. "Once he's put his hand to a thing, I guess nothing would make Don draw back from it," said Charley.

I felt only a faint sense of gratitude to my defender. I was too nauseated with dreadful, cringing, dizzy fear to feel any other emotion.

Now we stood in front of the Slocum house, and there was the terrible thorn hedge and in the opening appeared the gate. Behind the gate and above it, the long, narrow windows of the house looked down at me with a sort of blank malevolence, like the eyes of a fish.

"Which way you gonna start?" asked Alec. "Right through the gate, maybe?"

I hated that boy with a great hatred. I wondered why a stroke of lightning did not drop out of even that clear sky and wipe out Alec. But there was no sign from above, and I had a chance to remember that there were other difficulties, besides ghosts, in connection with the Slocum house. Yes, there were plenty of them.

There was that devil of a Swede, ready to shoot, ready to kill in cold blood, people in the village said, so wrought up was he over the report that his melons had been stolen. And there was the evil witch of a housekeeper, and the pale, clapper husband, who was such an expert with a pistol. And there was the terrible captain himself. Then, finally, I could count on the dogs, again.

So I lifted up my head and stared at the tower. I could see only the upper portion of it, and the top part of two of the windowpanes. At that very moment, I could have sworn that I saw a dim light rise, glow faintly behind the black gleam of the glass, and then go out. Suddenly the other dangers became nothing. There was only that unknown frightfulness in the tower room.

Well, men have marched to their death because they were ordered to. I suppose that some of those old senators in the days of the empire's tyranny in Rome had no more courage than I, and yet they took their own lives at the bidding of the emperor. They simply sat in their baths and opened their veins. I was the subject of tyranny, also, the tyrannical power of boy society that enters further into the souls of its subjects than any power of matured men.

I started for the gate when suddenly Charley grasped me.

"He can't go," said Charley in a choking whisper. "He might be killed. He might be . . . I don't know what! He can't go. I won't let him. I'll yell and raise the house on us all and . . ."

I did not resist Charley. I merely blessed him with all my soul. I was most willing to be wax in his generous, friendly hands.

And then the devil inspired young Alec again. He said, with his sneer: "Look how they've got it fixed!"

"How who has got it fixed?" demanded someone.

"Why, how the two of 'em has got it fixed. Look at Don, the way he marches up here as big as you please, but he never meant one minute to try the job. He ain't that much of a fool. He's got it fixed with Charley first, to stop him at the last minute. Look at Don, will you? He ain't fighting none to get away from Charley."

"You speckle face! You slimy frog!" gasped Charley.

He would have made a leap at Alec; he moved far enough in that direction to make Alec jump, but I caught hold of him.

"It's no good, I've gotta go," I told Charley. It helped me, vastly, to have my friend near me. I respected him more; I respected myself more for having such a friend. My heart grew warmer and my brain a little more clear.

"You can't go," said Charley earnestly. "Anything might happen to you, and . . ."

"What would happen to me worse," I said, "than for everybody to say that I'm a bluff? There wouldn't be no use living, after that happened, I guess. I've made up my mind, Charley. I'm going to go. There's only one thing I want to do first . . . I want to shake hands with you."

How he wrung my hand, and how I wrung his. The strength of him—doubt it not—ran up my arm, and into my cold, quaking body.

For one instant I almost forgot my fear. Then I found my eyes stinging with sentimental tears of self-pity. So I turned on my heel and started head-long for the gate.

CHAPTER 6

When I got started for the gate so quickly, nothing stopped me even mentally until I was through it. Once in the garden path, however, it seemed to me as though I could see the burning eyes of the great dogs staring at me out of the shadows, ready to leap at me. I could not very well turn back. Instead, I ran forward.

My feet were bare, as I have said, but even the naked, tough skin made a good deal of sound, scuffing across the gravel. I got to the porch quickly, however, and I climbed up one of the pillars like a sailor, until I was sure that I was out of the jumping range of the great beasts. But not a sign of those dogs did there appear.

It did not occur to me that we villagers might have exaggerated the ferocity and the omnipresence of the big beasts. I simply thanked whatever power rules our fates when, getting to the roof of the front porch, I looked down and saw that none of the monsters was in sight.

I remember, to this moment, how the shadows of the trees fell like ink upon the white of the sanded and graveled path, and how the group of the boys in the street seemed to me absurdly small, clustering together as if for mutual warmth or protection. I could distinguish Charley, though, standing well to the front, his hands gripped into fists and one leg advanced as though he were about to start in pursuit to join me and share in the honor of my task. Somehow, I knew that Charley was hardly more than a stone figure and that the advanced foot would never stir farther in the race.

Then I looked about me, over the slanted roof of the porch, where the rough, thick shingles made excellent footing for me. And I stared still higher and saw the wall of the house mounting like a cliff above me, a naked and unapproachable height at first glance.

Afterward, I saw certain advantages. There were, for instance, the sills of the windows, the carved brackets that set them out from the wall, and the projecting mountings above them. There was a drainage pipe, a good big one, which took down the water from the eaves. And that pipe I determined to make my road, with the sills of the windows as resting places.

As for what lay in wait at the end of my journey, I shut it out of my mind, as a room is shut out of sight when a curtain is drawn down. There was this immediate violent work lying before me, and it took all my mind because I chose to put all my mind upon it. I simply dared not look forward to the tower and its mysteriously lighted windows.

So I went to that drainage pipe and put the full strain of my weight upon it, and tugged back and forth, but it was fastened and supported so strongly that the weight of a big man would not have budged it. Then I started to climb and found that I went up easily enough. For the angle in the corner of the house was a help, and so was the succession of projections about the windows. With the aid of these, I went up in bounds, as one might say, and suddenly I was reaching out to grasp the corner of the eaves.

When I realized that, I grew dizzy. I turned and, looking down, I saw beneath me two interesting things. One was the group of my companions standing there in the middle of the street, their small shadows lying black about their feet. Their heads were tilted. I saw the flash of their faces, even of their eyes, I thought. And suddenly I said to myself: *I've cheated you. I've lied to you. I've made you all think that I'm wonderfully brave and strong. I'm a great liar and a knave, but now I'm going to pay for my cheating, and I'll probably pay for it with my life. So everything is absolutely square between us.*

Then I looked sheerly down—hanging out from the wall of the house as I was—and I saw on the broad gravel walk, about which I've spoken, I saw there, squatting on their haunches, all four of the great dogs of the captain. Of course, the first glimpse of the brutes frightened me, with their mouths hanging open and their tongues working a little as they breathed, but, on second thought, I only hoped that I'd have a chance to get down there to their teeth.

I freshened my grip on the eaves and took a good swing to the side. I swung again, whipping my body with a snap, so as to increase the momentum on which I depended to swing me up and, as I did so, I heard a *creak* and a tearing sound above me. At the next swing, I hooked my left heel over the edge of the roofs gutter. The next moment, I was lying there panting, stifled by the tremendous beating of my heart.

I remained still, although I heard the gutter *creak* and give ominously beneath me. I remember thinking that I would not be able to come down again at that point, and it would take perilous exploring to find any way down as good as the ladder I had used for the mounting. Finally I got to my knees.

There were the other youngsters, as before. But they were farther beneath me and looked smaller than before. Perhaps it was because of my excitement, but I no longer distinguished one from another. I could not pick out Alec, my enemy, from Charley, my friend, and it hardly mattered a great deal.

When I turned around, I saw the terrible windows of the ghostly tower just before me, and I knew that I would have to go forward. It was almost easier to go forward than to turn back, because once I started to flee, the sinister, the malicious power that was behind those windows would rush forward, invisibly, and cast me headlong to the ground. People would say that I had simply slipped.

I got up to my hands and knees, then, like one of those Romans I've spoken of before, went to my death. My death it was, because when I came down to the ground level again, I was changed for life. But of that I had no thought. I dreamed of only one sort of danger, mysterious and hard to name, but the thought of it was able to curdle my blood.

So I crawled up to the nearest window and tried it. I hoped that the lock would be fast and strong. But it was not. That window went up with a faint, deep groan, and I was looking into the pitchy darkness of the interior. A warm breath came out at me. I suppose that it was only the sun-heated, imprisoned air, but it seemed to me like the breath of a beast in my face.

There was very little left of my strength when I forced my leg over the sill and entered the room. I had to let myself down farther than I had expected, and, once I was standing on the floor, I felt the dust of it smooth and slick as oil, almost, under my bare feet. The boards seemed warm, as though there were a fire burning just beneath them. Then I wanted to look out and down again, upon my companions in the street, but I dared not turn my back on whatever presence was invisibly there in the midnight darkness of the room. I felt it. Distinctly as one feels a waiting eye upon one, I felt that dreadful, waiting presence in the little chamber.

I crouched in a corner. No, everything was not entirely darkness. I saw, at last, as the dimness caused by my own terror lifted from my eyes that the moonlight entered. I could make out what looked to be a large chest in one corner, and then I could see the skeleton of the upper part of a balustrade, mounting from the lower story into the tower room itself.

What I saw eased my nerves a little. There is nothing worse than the void of total ignorance. My breath began to come more easily. I could feel that the stifling labor of my heart had eased a little. I was able to stand up quietly and take a closer stock of what was around me. Most of all, I remember how the head of a lofty cypress tree stood up outside of the easternmost window, a broken, black, skeleton triangle against the moon-flooded sky.

I remember thinking that, before long I would be

out there under that sky, walking with the cool, water-thin dust of the road under my feet again. After all, I had not been a very good boy; I had done my share of fighting, lying, and other things. But I had not done anything deserving my death, I felt. There was a God. He would watch over children. There was something in the Bible about that. At least, I thought so.

In fact, I was almost beginning to feel at home when the horror struck me. Actively and actually it struck me.

From that farther corner in which the awkward mass that I took to be a chest was reposing, a single ray of light was loosed and fell full upon my eyes. I hardly realized what it was. I saw light; I expected to see the gleam of it expand and grow into a vision.

And, by heaven, into a vision the ray grew!

Yes, as I looked, unable to dodge the frightful, unphysical finger that rested upon me, that touched me to the soul, there appeared behind it, and behind the big mass of shadow a standing form that looked like a shrouded human being. And it was shrouded in white!

Had there ever been any real doubt in me as to the truth about ghosts? It left me then. I knew that there were ghosts, and that this was one of them. Had there been any doubts as to what power ghosts could obtain over living flesh and blood? That doubt left me, also. I did not reason what the harm could be. I simply expected that the cold agony of fear in which I stood would increase until, with some monstrous revelation, the life would be struck headlong from my body, and my soul would be dispatched to the region of unending torture.

There was no sound. Yes, there was a faint whispering outside of the window that I had just opened. Was it the wind? No, not to me. It was the commencement of a ghastly summons. It was the arrival of unheard of legions of lost spirits, flying on their almost soundless wings, waiting to receive me. There was no sound beyond that faint whisper. But there was movement.

Yes, one white-mantled arm of the ghost rose slowly, with a deadly certainty. That hand, mind you, was not included in the single ray of light that shone into my eyes. It was visible, but it was visible by its own power. It was clothed and invested by a ghastly brilliance that showed to me a long finger pointing toward me, a finger that seemed as skinny as the finger of a skeleton. All brightness ended with the hand itself. It was not spread over the hanging sleeve of the robe. Rather, that was seen by the light that shone from the unearthly hand.

Could I flee? No, not through that window, with the demon ready to leap on me from behind. Instead, I did what any cornered rat will do. I ran straight at the inescapable horror.

CHAPTER 7

Then, from that white, mysterious figure before me, came the voice of Captain Slocum himself saying: "Stop where you are!" The world of ghosts and ghostliness crashed literally about my ears. I came up with a stagger and stood swaying from side to side, as dizzy and bewildered a boy as ever lived. The white robe, at that instant, fell from him, a glove was drawn over the glowing hand, and a bull's-eye lantern was completely unhooded. The light of it bathed me from head to foot and a sufficient illumination was reflected from the walls to show me the captain's figure and his lean, stern face.

I said nothing for the good reason that I could not speak.

"Go before me down those stairs," said the captain.

I obeyed him. Only, at the top of the stairs, looking down into the fathomless blackness beneath, I hesitated one instant. But my fear was passing. Compared with the horror that I had had before my mind the moment before, no other danger mattered. Suppose that he were taking me down to throw me to his four huge dogs? Well, even that was less terrible than the blinding instant of horror in the tower room.

So I walked down those stairs, and, after I had taken a few steps, the light from the lantern shone behind me and made my footing secure. My own shadow, swelling big or shrinking to a wide-shouldered dwarf, wavered and bobbed before me.

So I went down into the lower room of the tower. It was used for storage, I suppose. The boxes and trunks were gray with dust that had accumulated on them. I had to wait here for Captain Slocum to open the door for me. I saw his gloved hand fit the key into the lock and turn it, and I noticed that it was the left hand that he used. Only then did I remember the wound that he had received in his right hand, according to the doctor.

Then he took me down into a library, and there he made me sit down in a big, leather-covered chair, so much too large for me and so slippery that I kept sliding all the while I sat there. After that he went out of the room.

I wondered if other mysteries were about to be practiced on me. In the meantime, there was something else to take up my thoughts, and that was the room itself, for it was furnished with a very lofty ceiling, and around the walls marched rows and rows of books. A fire was dying on the hearth, and the gleam of it pulsed like regular breathing on the leather bindings.

It was a perfect room for a murder, I thought to myself. And where was the captain? And why had he left me?

If it had been any other than Slocum himself, I would have felt that this evening's performance was very silly, indeed, like a Halloween trick. I mean that the whole business up there in the tower, the waiting ghost, the hand lighted with phosphorus—it must have been that—and the sepulchral gesture of the captain himself were childish in the extreme.

But Captain Slocum was not a fellow one would accuse of lightness of mind or action. I wondered if he had chosen that preternatural role because he wished to make people think that some secret of his house was watched over by spirits?

At any rate, the problem now was entirely one of earthly fact. I could live and breathe in this atmosphere. I could be on my guard against danger. So I sat up in the chair, with my elbows braced upon the slickness of the leather upholstery, and waited.

I waited there for perhaps ten minutes before the captain returned. I shall never forget this entrance of his. I did not hear him open the door, and the first I knew was the approach of a dull light. It was a big lamp with a circular burner that cast the glow and, with the wick turned down very low, the light of it hardly spread at all. Only, above and behind the chimney, I saw the face of the captain, apparently floating there in mid-air, without a body attached. His eyes were turned down. He looked ghastly pale. It was like the face of a corpse.

Well, this was very eerie and unpleasant, but I could endure a great deal more, after my tower experience. So I did not stir, but watched him as he softly and slowly approached a table and put the lamp down on it. He turned up the wick, and the room was suddenly blazing with light. It seemed to me that I never had seen such a brilliant illumination.

Then he told me to put some wood on the fire, and pointed out the hamper that contained it. I did as he told me, working with a good deal of care. The splintery feeling of the wood, I remember, was a kind and homely thing to me. I found some fine-chopped kindling that I laid first on the coals, and over this I put smaller and then bigger wood. After that I leaned and blew through the wood upon the coals until a dense white smoke rose and thickened, began to form in billows through which a detached yellow flame glittered, died, came again, died again, and at last, multiplied a hundredfold, went rushing up the chimney with a roar, knocking the smoke galley-west. Then I got up and dusted my knees and turned to the captain for further orders.

He merely pointed to the chair I had sat in before. I obeyed him and got back into it. It was so deep that my legs stuck out straight before me. I wiggled about a bit and faced the captain. He had placed the lamp so that most of the light shone on me and very little came to him. Between us there was a bearskin rug with the head pointing toward the fire. The head was mounted with shining red-stained eyes in the most realistic manner. The jaws were wide open, and one of the long, yellow canine teeth was broken off. On the table near the captain's hand was a book with a long-bladed ivory paper knife thrust through it by way of a marker, I suppose. I remember feeling that the captain would as readily skewer a human being as a mere pad of pages, if there were need for such an act.

He said at last: "So you're not only a melon thief but a housebreaker, Don?"

I was glad that he used my first name. It seemed to soften his accusations. "Well, I stole a couple of watermelons," I said.

"Doesn't bother you, though?" said the captain in his harsh, dry way.

"You see, about everybody around here will steal a watermelon. I mean . . . the boys," I explained.

"You mean the boys, do you?" he repeated. He sneered at me and the whole community, I felt. "None of the grown-ups would, though?" he suggested. "None of the great, hulking, idle, worthless, lying, gossiping, treacherous sneaks . . . none of them would steal a watermelon, I suppose?"

"No, they wouldn't," I said. I met his eye more easily. It seemed to me that this sneering, bitter attitude lessened him, made him more feminine and capable of being worsted. I believe that your hardbitten pessimist generally gives that effect. People avoid him because they detest him, and he is flattered by taking the detestation for fear. The critic is the coward almost every time.

"They wouldn't? And why wouldn't they?" asked Captain Slocum.

"Because a grown-up stealing watermelons, he'd have to go to jail. Nobody wants to go to jail for watermelons, I guess."

He began to nod very slowly, like a pendulum working up and down, as though he found something surprisingly profound in my remark, something over which he wished to pore for a long moment, agreeing more and more deeply all the time.

"People don't like to go to jail for watermelons," he pronounced at the last. "Now, you tell me something, my son."

"Yes, sir," I said, very startled by the familiarity of his last speech.

"You tell me," he said in the same tone, "what happens to people who break into the houses of others?"

"I didn't break in," I said. "I just pushed up a window. There wasn't no lock on it that I noticed."

"Burglary," said the captain, "consists of pushing open gates, even yard gates, and then entering houses unannounced, by stealth, in the middle of the night, in the darkest hour."

"There was a moon shining," I said.

"Ha?" he exclaimed, his voice a sudden roar.

"There was a pretty good moon shining," I explained. "Right from the eaves, I could look down and see the faces of the boys that were in the road."

"Ah ha!" said the captain. "And who were those boys?"

"Who were they? I wouldn't exactly know, sir," I said.

"You wouldn't know!" exclaimed the captain. He lurched forward in his chair and stopped himself from rising by placing his elbows suddenly on the arms of it. "You wouldn't know. As a matter of fact, they were your scalawag friends!"

"No, sir," I said. "Not all of 'em."

"What?"

"No, sir. There were enemies, too."

"And who were the enemies?"

"I wouldn't want to say, sir."

"You wouldn't want to say, sir," he mocked me angrily. "Do you think that it's right and sensible to stand up for your enemies?"

"I don't know, Captain Slocum," I said.

"You don't know, eh? You don't know that if a man is your enemy, he's a bad man?"

I grasped largely and vainly toward this idea. At last I got hold of it. If a man was one's enemy, he must be a bad man. "Well, sir," I said, "I suppose you're right, but . . ." I thought of Charley. I never had liked him in the old days so very well. Now he was my dearest friend. He was sealed to me by something more than blood and bone.

"But what?" said the captain.

"Sometimes only the worst part of me has hated people."

"Ha!" said the captain. "And what do you know about hate, young man? Who do you hate most in the world?"

"Me? I don't know, sir, exactly."

"Come, come! Out with it. Who do you hate most in the world?"

"Aunt Lizzie," I answered. I jumped out of my chair and clapped my hand over my mouth. My hair stood on end. My eyes strained at the face of the captain.

"Ha?" he said. "Your Aunt Lizzie."

"I didn't mean that," I said.

He stretched out his wounded right hand, swathed in bandages like the hand of a mummy. "Sit down, sit down," he commanded. "For now we're going to get at the bottom of something."

CHAPTER 8

I was terribly upset. I had turned on my own flesh and blood!

"Why do you hate your Aunt Lizzie?" asked the captain.

"I don't hate her," I said. I sweated with haste. "Only . . . that word kind of popped out. I didn't mean that I hated her. I didn't mean that at all."

"Ha?" said the captain. "You didn't mean it, eh? What did you mean?"

"I don't know. I guess I was thinking about whippings or something. No boy likes them very well."

"No boy likes them? I suppose not. But you wouldn't hate a person simply for a flogging, now and then."

I leaned to him a little, nodding eagerly. "Yes, I would," I said.

"Well, well," replied Captain Slocum, "now we'll go ahead and forget about your hating Aunt Lizzie. By the way, was she your mother's sister?"

"She's only a kind of a cousin or something," I said.

"Ah, only a kind of a cousin or something," repeated Captain Slocum with gravity. "Then she's a mighty kind woman to lay out her time and her care on a rough lad like yourself."

I blinked a little. But I was willing to do Aunt Lizzie more than justice, considering what I had just said before. "Yes, sir. I guess that she's mighty kind."

"One of those big-hearted women who never can do enough for others. I know the type," said the captain.

"*Hmmm,*" I said, beginning to think.

"The finest creatures in the world," said the captain solemnly, "are the good women, the charitable women who ask no return for the good they do to others."

"Well," I said, feeling that enough had been said, "I guess she gets a kind of a return in a way."

"What sort of a return? Affection from you, I suppose?"

"My father gave her some money to take care of me."

"How much?" said the captain.

"I wouldn't know, quite."

"You wouldn't, eh?"

"No, sir."

"I'm more and more interested in this fine woman," said the captain. "I believe I've seen her. She's a fine, big, handsome woman, Don, is she not?"

"She's on the biggish side," I admitted. I thought back to her, unhappily.

"And I suppose that she's busy from one day's end to the next with her household work?"

"Her?" I said. "Well, she does some cooking and shopping. Mostly she lays around a good deal."

"What?" said the captain. "Lies about?"

"She reads a lot . . . newspapers and things. She's mostly always reading," I assured him. "She's not very well."

"What's wrong with her?"

"It lays kind of betwixt and between," I stated.

"Betwixt and between what?" said the captain.

"Betwixt her nerves and her liver," I said. "Her stomach's not very good, either, except at meal times, and she gets swimmings in the head."

The captain said: "And still the poor, good woman makes a home for you and keeps your clothes patched and all."

"She leaves the patching to me," I corrected. "She says that it's a poor man that can't take care of himself and his clothes."

"She's right," said the captain, giving me an odd look. "She has the great Spartan idea. She may make a man out of you one day."

"I hope so, sir," I said, and waited, for I could see that something more was to come.

"But in the meantime," said the captain, "you seem on a fair way to become a thief . . . a fruit stealer and a burglar who breaks into houses."

He kept his fixed eye upon me, while I squirmed and grew hot.

"It was only a kind of a joke," I said.

"Stealing watermelons and burglary?" he asked.

"Well, I looked at those watermelons until I could hardly get along without them. It woke me up in the middle of the night with a thirst, and I came out . . . and you saw me there."

"Yes, I saw you. I should have turned the dogs on you, I suppose, but I had something more than watermelons in my mind. And the burglary was a joke, too?"

I squirmed again. "They dared me to do it," I explained. "I sort of had to . . . after they dared me to."

"They dared you because you'd built up quite a reputation after stealing the watermelons. Was that it?"

"Well, that was about it."

"You had to do it because you didn't want to lose that big reputation you'd built up . . . of being a thief?"

I saw that he had cornered me. "Well, sir," I began, "I suppose you can put it that way."

"Yes, that's the way I'll put it. Was it hard for you to shinny up the front of my house and get into the tower?"

"It wasn't hard," I said, "only I was scared to death all the time, so that my hands were shaking."

"What were you afraid of?" he asked.

"Why, getting through the hedge. Then there's Missus Ebenezer Grey, and her husband, and the dogs, and the Swede with the shotgun, and finally . . . there's you, sir."

He nodded at me, stern as a face carved from rock. "And it was I who you met at last," he said.

"Yes, sir," I said. Then curiosity gave me the courage to ask: "What made you do it, sir? I mean . . . be a ghost like that?"

"What made me do it? Why, you were speaking of jokes, and perhaps that was one of mine. And perhaps I merely wanted to discourage thieves, young and old, for the future. I might have had several reasons. But the real one was none of these."

"Can I ask what it was, then?"

"I was curious about a young fellow in this town," said the captain. "I had heard a good deal about him. The Swede, as you call him, had said that he was going to cut that young fellow's throat for him the next time he showed his face on the place. And then I learned that he planned to come tonight."

"You knew about it?" I gasped.

"There's very little that goes on in the town that I don't hear sooner or later," he said. "And I wanted to see what the nerve of the young burglar would be like. I wanted desperately to find out. It took me back to my youth, I believe. So much so that I still feel as if I owned youth and two good hands." He leaned back in his chair for the first time. "Push that bell by the door," he said.

I did as I was told. Almost instantly the door was opened by Mrs. Ebenezer Grey, and I thought, when she saw me, there was a look of recognition and of hatred in her face. I never had seen her so closely before. Her hideousness was increased by the nearness, as the frightfulness of an insect is multiplied under a microscope.

"Tell your husband to come here," said the captain. "And tell John to come and to bring all the four dogs . . . at once."

She said nothing. She merely closed the door as soundlessly as she had opened it. All the time I knew her, she never answered a question if she could avoid it. She gave the impression that speech was poisonous to her—that to breathe out words was like breathing in a deadly gas, so far as she was concerned.

"Go back to your chair," said Captain Slocum to me.

I went back to my chair and sat down, feeling rather green about the gills. I remember, at that moment, I could hear a mournful and distant music, and I knew that it was old Tom Masters moving out his herd over the southern hill and down the Mexican trail.

But what would happen when the two men and the four dogs came in? Was I to run the gantlet? Or was I to be given a sporting start and hunted down to the thorn hedge, across the fields of the Slocum place?

They came. You could hear the feet of the dogs pounding almost as loudly as the heels of men, those brutes were so big. They came swarming in through the door.

"I hear you got him," said the Swede with great satisfaction, "and I'd like to have a mite of him before the dogs get the rest!"

"Bring those dogs to him," said the captain. "And make them take his hand."

I saw the Swede turn his huge, ugly head toward me and then back toward the captain. Amazement and rage shared equal parts in his expression. After that instant of hesitation, he did as he was told. He brought those four monsters up to me, and each of them looked as though it would like to have the swallowing of me.

But the Swede made them sit down, and I went up to each of the brutes and patted the leonine heads, one by one, and learned their names: Hans, Tiger, Red, and Butcher. I spoke those names to them. I asked for their paws, and the great paws were lifted solemnly to shake hands with me. Butcher was the youngest of the lot. He actually wagged his tail with a swishing sound over the carpet as he gave me his paw.

"Now, you, John, and you, Grey," said the captain. "Shake hands with my young friend, here."

John made the face of one tasting vinegar, but he gave me his vast hand. Grey smiled coldly on me and shook hands in turn.

"Now where's Missus Ebenezer?" said the captain. "Come here, Missus Grey, and shake hands with Don."

But that witch of a woman, who had remained close to the door, now backed out without a word and shut the door behind her. The captain did not turn his head, but he seemed to know what had happened.

"She'll be brought to time later on," he said. "In the meantime, this lad is free of the place. Do you hear me?"

"Yes, sir," Grey said.

"Aye, aye, sir," said the Swede a moment later in a surly rumble.

"If you find him any place, from the tower rooms to the cellar, you find him where he has a right to be," said the captain, "or in the garden, or the fields, or . . . the melon patch, John."

The Swede uttered a faint groan of anger, but he said no word.

"That's all," said the captain. "You may go now."

They started away, when he jerked his head about at me with a scowl.

"Why don't you go with them?" he demanded. "Aren't you late enough home as it is?"

CHAPTER 9

I jumped up and was about to make for the door, when something caught in my mind, as impulses will catch now and then, and I whirled about and went back to the captain. I held out my hand.

"I'd like to say good night, sir," I said.

He looked down at his bandaged hand, then he looked up to me, and the iron in his face never relaxed for a moment. "I've never shaken hands with my left hand in my life," he stated. "And I don't intend to commence the practice now. As for my right hand, I shall never be able to use it again. Good night, my lad."

"I've gotta thank you," I said, dragging out the words. "You might've put me in jail or reform school. I've gotta thank you a lot. Good night, sir." Then off I went, as fast as I could go.

At the door, I found that both the Swede and Ebenezer Grey were waiting for me, and just behind them was Mrs. Grey.

"You may think that you've got somewhere," said

the Swede to me, in the most savage manner. "But you ain't. You ain't got a spot with me. You ain't got nowheres at all."

"I'll show you to the gate, sir," said Ebenezer Grey, with his faultless manner.

And then, as I went through the front door, the voice of Mrs. Grey snarled breathlessly at me: "If ever you dare to show your face . . . if ever you dare!"

I went on past her, as the trembling malice choked away her words, and I walked with Grey himself toward the front gate. The big dogs came swarming about me, but they were not hostile. That one introduction was enough to take the edge from their ferocious temper, it appeared.

"It's gonna be the ruin of the dogs," said the Swede. "It's gonna pull their teeth."

He spoke from the steep shadows of the porch, his voice thicker than the gloom that surrounded him. But I patted the heads of the dogs, and looked up to find Ebenezer Grey waiting stiffly for me at the gate, which he held open.

As I went through, I thanked him, and he bowed as though to his own master. So I looked up to him, half hoping that I would be able to find in his face some sign of kindness and real friendship but, instead, there was that faint, cold smile. Suddenly I felt that the open surliness of the Swede and the hideous malice of Mrs. Grey were less dangerous than the cold courtesy of this fellow.

So I went out into the street and heard the gate *click* shut with a discreet softness. I glanced back, and there was Grey standing part in the black shadow of the hedge and part in the silver bright moonshine. When he saw me looking, he bowed a little again, and turned back to the house, while I passed down the road.

I had hardly gone ten steps when two boys came darting out at me from the shadows of the brush across the street. One of them was my newly made best friend, Charley. The other was my profoundest enemy, Alec. They pushed up to me and crowded close. They were full of questions.

What had happened? After I passed into the tower room, what was the light that had glowed there faintly, then with a great flash went sinking away to nothing again? The sight of that illumination had sent all of the other boys scampering home, for they thought that I never would be heard of again, and they didn't wish to be in on any later questioning. Besides, there was the sheer uncanny terror of it that had unnerved even the two who waited—one of them because he was my friend, the other because he hated me profoundly.

These things I gathered partly by inference, of course. Then they wished to know how I had descended through the house and by what magic arts had I subdued the four big dogs, for they had seen me pat the heads of the mastiffs. Above all, how had I worked a spell on John, the Swede, and Ebenezer Grey, that cold and cunning man?

I answered them, honestly, that I was too tired to talk. For a great lassitude had come over me, like the effect of a drug. My legs were limp and numb about the knees. I had no will to walk or to speak. That effort that I had made, prolonged so long from the time I left my home until I got safely back into the roadway, had taken every scruple of my energy. I put a hand on the shoulder of Charley and leaned heavily.

He took on himself to understand, at once. "You shut up, Alec," he said fiercely. "Look at what he's gone through, account of you and your dares. Look at what he's gone through that no other boy would ever want to even think of. Now you expect him to talk. Have a bit of consideration."

Alec was silenced. But he was in a frenzy of excitement. He kept twisting from side to side as he walked along with us, an unwanted companion.

Charley said: "I'm pretty low. I guess that I'll never be much good. When I saw you climbing, I wanted to rush in there and follow you. I wanted to, and I got as far as the gate, but then I saw the four dogs. If I'd been like you, I would've gone smashing straight ahead and got through 'em, or else got myself ripped to pieces, trying. But I'm not like you. One of them turned his head and gave me a look, and that finished me. I went back to the rest of 'em, there in the road, and watched you.

"I tell you what, old-timer, when you got up to the eaves and turned and looked down at us, I felt pretty sick. I despised myself. I despise myself now, but I'm mighty thankful to have you back again. You've been through something big, Don, and you're tired . . . I've been through something mighty small, but I'm tired, too. I'm pretty near shaking. I never saw anything so awful as when you opened that window and stepped right out of sight into the darkness. And then, when you came out of the door of the house again, it was like seeing somebody come out of a grave. That was what it was like!"

I loved Charley for this talk of his, but I could not answer him. There were too many things to say. My mind was burdened down by the future, also. For something told me that for manifold reasons I should keep away from the house of Captain Slocum, and yet I knew inwardly that I should never resist the temptation of going there and making myself at home, as he had said I could. I was like a man who is afraid to get on a horse, because he knows that he will ride it too fast over hill and dale.

When we came into the town, we separated from Alec. He gave me a parting shot.

"I don't care what the rest of 'em think," he announced. "Fact is, you knew the folks in the house all of the time . . . you knew that there was no spooks there. That's why you were so free and easy."

"Get out of here," said Charley, "get out of here or we'll punch your head for you!"

Alec went off down the street to his house. Charley and I went on to the gate of my Aunt Lizzie's house. There we paused for a moment, speaking softly.

I said: "One of these days, I'm going to try to tell you all about it, Charley. Right now, I can't. I'm all fagged out."

"You don't have to tell me nothing," said Charley.

"There's one thing, though, that I'd like to tell you."

"You tell me black is white, and it's all right with me," he said.

"No, it's not that way. I wanted to tell you that when I looked down from the house and saw you standing there in front of the rest, with one foot out, like you wanted to come to help me, why, that did me a lot of good. It made me feel that I sort of mattered to somebody. I felt you were a friend of mine."

"By Jiminy," said Charley, "I'd like to be big enough and right enough to be your friend."

I took hold of his hand. Suddenly I felt old and overwise in the ways of the world. "Ah, Charley," I said, "you're a lot bigger and better and braver and stronger than I am, really."

I left him standing there as one stunned by a revelation from the sky, while I went through the gate and up the path to the house. When I got to the front door and opened it, a specter stood in the dark before me. The specter caught me by the nape of the neck. It dragged me in, slammed the door, and brought down the lash of a black snake across my shoulders. The cutting end of it curled about and raised a welt on my side and stomach. But I seemed to have taken a narcotic against pain. I merely laughed, rather feebly.

"You big, worthless blatherskite, laugh at me, will you?" Aunt Lizzie cried, and she fetched me a whack with her open hand that knocked me sidelong against the wall.

While I recovered myself, she brought down the whip again, with an extra force. I felt the pain, and yet I did not feel it. I should have howled and begged for mercy, as I often had done before, but somehow it was different this time, and I was able to say: "It's no good, your flogging me, Aunt Lizzie. I don't mind the whip. I don't mind you, either."

She went into a heightened fury. She dropped the black snake and grabbed me by the shoulders. The force of her big hands was like the force in a man's grip. "You don't mind me? I'll teach you to mind me. You night thief, you night wanderer! Where you been? What you been up to?"

"I've been up calling on Captain Slocum," I said.

She had relaxed her grip for a moment. Now she caught me again and shook me until my teeth knocked together. "You lying little wretch! You brazen-faced, good-for-nothing scoundrel. You tell me that you been up calling on Captain Slocum? I'll captain you. I'll fix you. I'll fix you so's you'll never lie to me again. Laugh at me, will you? I'll laugh you, you wretch! I'll tell you what you'll do. You'll die in jail. You'll die the way your father died before you. They'll hang you up by the neck, the way they hanged him, and a good riddance to rubbish." She let go of me suddenly.

I leaned back against the wall with both of my hands spread out against it. A touch, and I would have fallen to either side. Through the darkness I could hear her panting, dragging in her breath with a faint rattle.

Then she gasped: "I wouldn't've said it . . . only you drove me. I didn't mean to say it, Don. You come along, and I'll get you into bed, and . . ."

She came up and put a hand on my shoulder; my flesh crawled under the touch, and her hand fell away again.

"Oh, great guns," said Aunt Lizzie, "now what've I gone and done?" She hurried down the hall.

I heard the slamming of her door, then I heard her heavy, man-like sobbing begin. It seemed to shake the house. But still I could not move from my place in the dark.

CHAPTER 10

When I got into my bedroom, I dropped on the bed without taking off my clothes. There I lay with my arms thrown out widely from my body because it seemed to me that in this posture I found breathing easier. The darkness pressed down into my face, stifling me, and in that darkness, when I strove to arrange my thoughts, I could only see the picture of a man standing on a platform with a black death cap drawn over his face and his hands bound behind his back.

Someone asked him what last words he would speak, but he answered nothing. I lay there harkening desperately to the voice of my imagination, hoping, with what desperate eagerness that he would cry out: "Innocent! I am innocent!"

But there was always no answer, no matter how often my mind went over the scene. There was always that deep and frightful silence. Then someone said: "God receive his soul."

After that, the trap on which he was standing

dropped—he hurtled through—and I heard and felt, in the base of my brain, the shock as he came to the end of the rope—came to the end of it and rebounded a little, then settled, spinning slowly to one side and then unwinding in the opposite direction.

There my vision ended, only to begin over again.

How I furnished myself with all the details, I don't know. Newspapers cherish such items, and newspapers doubtless had filled my mind with the necessary details. But I was not conscious of searching my memory for probabilities. All came to me as by revelation.

Dwelling morbidly on the subject, I seemed to see the trial commence. I saw the witnesses, I heard them attest against the prisoner. I saw my father listening, grave and attentive. The condemnation I heard. I felt the voice of the judge quivering with righteous indignation as he denounced the guilty man. And always it seemed to me that my father was listening with that curiously polite, attentive, analytical air of his with which he was so associated in my memories of him. In such a manner he used to listen to my childish lies about this and that.

I saw him in the death cell, where the condemned may have anything they choose, and I could see him perfectly, smoking a very sweet Havana and turning it slowly in his mouth, looking carefully into the pages of his book and smiling with delight at what he found there. I saw the fumes of the smoke rise; I breathed of it. Then the vision went forward again to the horror of the death scene.

At last I fell asleep and wakened with that guilty start, that spinning brain that one has who has overslept his usual time. A hot pain crossed my shoulders, ran down my side, and curled across my stomach. I put my hand against it. Even through the cloth I could feel the welts and remembered the flogging I had received from my aunt.

It was high noon. I looked out the window and saw the shadow beneath the fig tree falling straight down under the broad leaves. The brown hen and four of her scraggly chickens were scratching about among the fallen leaves, occasionally finding a fallen fig or a bit of one. Then they would all run together with beating wings and struggle over the prize.

I undressed, poured some water from the pitcher into the basin on the washstand, and gave myself a good sponging with soap and water. I soaked a towel and bound it around the back of my head and neck. That, by degrees, drew out the heaviness and left me normal-minded once more. There was only a slight tremor of the hands and weakness in the elbows when I dressed and left the room.

The singing of Aunt Lizzie guided me to the kitchen. She was frying potatoes and cold ham together, with butter to grease the pan. The big coffee pot was steaming. I recognized the smell of the ham and the potatoes. It was a favorite dish with my aunt because it was so easily made ready.

When I appeared in the doorway, I hoped that some compunction would remain to her from the night before, but the sunshine has a way of turning all the actions of the night into mist and moonshine. The scowl she threw at me over her shoulder was enough to settle my doubts.

"Up at last, are you?" she said. "I thought you were dead, maybe. Reach me that salt off the shelf . . . the rheumatism has got me beat again. Then cut some bread and lay the table. What's the matter with you, standing around like an oaf?"

I did what I was told, and afterward we had lunch—the potatoes and ham, the bread, a smear of rancid butter, and coffee like lye. But I ate of everything. I was hungry as a wolf and despised myself for it. I felt that a really great and sensitive soul, after learning what I had learned, would have been unable to touch food—for days, perhaps. Even dogs would mourn longer for a master.

When we had finished, Aunt Lizzie told me to get her book from her bedroom. She was going to sit there for a while and drink another sip of coffee, she said, and read, and try to forget her pain. So I got the book and cleared off the table, all except the coffee, her cup, and the platter of potatoes, which she was finishing, chip by chip, eating them from her fingers, reaching out absently as she turned the pages of the book.

I washed the dishes and dried them, then hung out the dishcloth and the dishrag on the line near the back porch, to dry and sweeten in the sun. After that I went indoors and found Aunt Lizzie still at the table over her third or fourth cup of coffee. She had found an exciting place in her story, and she was devouring it with a frown of concentrated interest. The title of the story was *Diana and the Lord Marquis*, or some such rot.

I stood in the doorway for a moment.

After a time, she turned her head a little, went back to her book, glanced around a little farther, and finally looked over her shoulder at me with a jerk. "Now what are you up to?" she shouted at me. When she was stirred, she always raised her voice. When she got into an argument, she used to beat the table, like a man.

"I wasn't up to nothing," I told her. "I was only here."

"And why are you there?" she demanded. "Why ain't you out breaking windows, or stealing water-melons, or calling on your friend, Captain Slocum?"

I swallowed hard, but I controlled my voice. "I wanted to ask you," I said, "why they hanged him. What had he done?"

"Him?" said Aunt Lizzie. She shrugged her shoulders so hard that the fat under her chin wobbled up and down. "You better hear it from me than some-body else," she said, meaning, I suppose, that she would break the news to me with a more expert gentleness. "He killed his brother. That's what your father done, and that's why they hung him. Now you know!"

Well, I got out of the room to the back yard and there I slumped down with my head between my hands. A calf was bawling mournfully from the cor-ral. It was being weaned from Old Grey, our best cow.

In the nakedness of my soul, I looked into the thing and could not understand. A brother was what I had always wanted, somebody to fight for or to fight for me. Other boys held over my head, like a club, their "big brother." Other boys championed the youngsters of their families. But my father had had a brother and killed him with his own hands.

I jumped up and ran to the screen door that opened on the dining room. I flung it open with a bang and I screeched: "It's a lie! It's a lie! He never done such a thing!"

Aunt Lizzie looked at me with bulging eyes, like a person going mad. "You ungrateful, horrible, de-testable brat," she said, and she flung her half-filled coffee cup straight at my head.

It sailed past me, and I went down into the yard again.

Somehow, I could breathe more easily now. I walked around to the front of the house. The windmill was at work with a busy and cheerful rattling; I heard the water plumping into the half-filled tank, and I found myself speaking in soft rhythm with the sound: "It's a lie. It's a lie. I'll prove it's a lie."

The house of Aunt Lizzie was a burden on my eyes and on my soul because it made me think of her and what she had said, so I got out into the street.

The two McGuire boys and Joe Purchass came by. They shouted when they saw me and came flocking about. They wanted to know everything.

"Charley told us. Is it right? Did you really get into the tower? Did you really come out through the front door? Did Mister Grey see you to the gate?"

I looked at them with far-away eyes. "It doesn't matter," I told them. "I don't care what you believe."

So I left them behind me and walked up the hill, not because I wanted to go in that direction, but because it was opposite to their own course. When I was at a little distance, they shouted an insult or two to show that my indifference had nettled them a little, but I walked on. For I felt that nothing that boys could do would hurt me, after what I had suffered at the hands of grown people.

Presently I found myself, with a start, in front of the hedge that walled in the Captain Slocum place. I walked down it, thoughtfully, pretending to pluck at the steel-sharp thorns, my mind in a haze, until I came to the gap in the hedge. There I hesitated a moment but, after all, that hole through the hedge seemed to me an escape from the wretched world in which I was living. So I got down on my hands and knees and crawled through.

Once inside, I stood up and stretched and looked

about me. The meadow was at my right, sloping down. The face of it was bright and sweet with wild-flowers and the captain's four horses were grazing there. They were four beauties. When he drove out with a span of them hitched to his rubber-tired sur-rey, and Ebenezer Grey erect on the front seat, Mer-ridan forgave him all his imagined sins, all his pride and haughtiness, so great was its satisfaction in hav-ing such a man among them.

I looked at those horses now and wished that one of them had the wings of the fable, and that I were on its back, for then I would fly out of that green meadow, across the hills, and across the desert, far away to a place where I could find a new life and a new name, unbranded as mine was.

I looked up from this thought and saw the Swede, with a digging fork in his hand, standing in silence not six steps from me.

CHAPTER 11

John, the Swede, was watching me with the same expression of disgust and hate with which he had looked on me the night before.

"I was right," he said. "They all said that you wouldn't, and I said that you would."

"That I would do what?" I asked him.

"That you'd come back here, like a beggar."

"I'm not a beggar," I said.

"Then why'd you come back?"

"Because I wanted to see the place, maybe."

"That ain't it," replied the Swede, shaking his head, and he freshened his grip on the handle of the digging fork so that the sunlight shivered and blinked along the tines of it. "That ain't it. You come back here to see what you could get out of the captain."

I was about to fly into a rage, but I knew that rages were foolish in the presence of a grown man, so I controlled myself and laughed at him.

"Maybe I came back here to badger you, John."

His passion swelled his forehead and his very cheeks. "Maybe yuh came here to get your neck broke!" he roared at me.

"Not by you," I said, measuring the great bulk of the man. "You couldn't get your hands on me."

"Couldn't I? Well . . ." Suddenly he lurched at me, but I knew by the swagger of his body that he was no runner. I waited until he was fairly reaching out his hands to seize me, and then dodged to the side. He missed by an arm's length and went thundering past me like a train on a downgrade. When he pulled up and turned about, I laughed at him again.

"You see, you're no good," I told him. "Come on and try again."

"I ain't a runner," said John, puffing, pink-purple in his fury. "I stand to do my fighting. And if it's brats like you, I have dogs to catch 'em."

"The dogs'll never catch me," I said. "They wouldn't hurt me, now that I know 'em. They're more apt to eat you, if I sent 'em at you."

"Hey?" shouted the Swede.

He reminded me, suddenly, of Aunt Lizzie. Like her, he was big, strongly made, clumsy, and passionate. This similarity sent me off into a peal of real laughter that soon had me staggering, for I thought of how furious she would be when I told her of the comparison. Once every month or so I treated myself to the liberty of making some sharp remark to her. I generally suffered for it during the following week, but the sweetness of the moment always offset the afterpain. The sight of this true mirth overcame John, the Swede. Besides, he saw me staggering, so he gritted his teeth, his great mouth making his cheeks bulge against his ears as he grinned with fury, and then he came charging again.

I was so unsettled with laughter that I barely was able to avoid him. And the sight of his clumsy miss made me laugh harder than ever. He swooped at me again and again. But he was like a clumsy-winged eagle, trying to strike a shifty swallow. Once I tapped him on his bulging shoulder as he dashed by me. This sobered him. He stopped and jammed the digging fork into the ground up to the hilts of the tines. I could guess that he wished it were in my body.

"Well," he said, panting, his face streaming, "I'll have you one day. You just think of this . . . 'John never forgets.'"

"No," I said, "you're like the elephant. I could see that the first time I looked at you."

This quip he understood only on second thought; his anger became so great that his red face was patched with white, like a quilt.

"You'll send the dogs at me, will you?" said John.

"Why not?" I asked him. "They don't like you!"

"That's a lie," declared John.

But he blinked a little, and I went on, feeling my way with guesswork. "It's no lie. I know all about it."

"Those dogs, they love me," panted John. "They love me because I always take care of them. Why for should they not love John?" His eyes popped. He seemed actually to be pleading with me.

"Those dogs, they hate you," I told him. "They hate you because you always beat them and shout at them. Dogs like quiet voices. You got a voice like a sea lion. Maybe that comes from always eating fish."

He wrenched the digging fork out of the ground; I almost thought he would hurl the thing at me, like a javelin, and I stood light-footed, ready to jump to either side. But John controlled himself.

"Dogs are fools. They got no sense," he said, "and why should I care what they like? Me or no? I don't care. Them dogs, they jump when John speaks . . . maybe sometime one boy will jump, too."

"Maybe," I said, imitating his scowl, "sometime John will jump when I speak."

"Hey?" he shouted.

"Yaw," I said. "Maybe sometime John, the big Swede, will jump when I say . . . 'do this!' or 'do that!' Maybe he'll jump over sticks, like a trained dog."

At this, it suddenly seemed to occur to John that he was no match for me, at least in the English tongue, so he shouldered his digging fork and went off, fairly trembling with his rage. And I was still quaking with triumph and with laughter when he whirled about and shook his fist at me.

"One day you know John never forgets!" he shouted.

I only laughed the harder. It was a perfect triumph for a boy of my age. I had tormented a grown-up almost to madness, and now I was able to go on my way, rejoicing. The trouble that was in my mind now eased away and I went on through the woods.

I wandered for an hour, enchanted. There were other ranches about Merridan of five or even ten times the size of the Slocum place, but most of them were swept bare of timber. The winter storms whipped the cattle over the naked hills and the flats and pressed them head down against the strong lines of barbed wire. The timber had been cut down with a reckless axe to make room for more grass. And now the undelighted eye could sweep over 5,000 acres in a glance and find it always monotonous.

Here all was different. The trees had been left standing in the natural patches where they had always grown. Only they had been thinned out, the underbrush was cleared away, and the plantations were given the full benefit of as much sun and rain as would come to them. Every year a certain number of mature trees were cut down, and there were always saplings ready to be planted in place of the old trees. To be sure, the trees occupied a great deal of space that might have been grazing land, but the timber that was cut yearly almost made up for the loss, besides the invaluable shelter for the cows in winter, to say nothing of the added beauty that one viewed at every turn.

I walked through those timber patches with delight and continual wonder, remembering, as I could not help doing, that the entire landscape might have been like this in all directions.

I felt a great admiration for the Slocums, seeing that they were willing to trust so much to time. It might take 100 years for the new trees to grow to a full height. But the Slocums were willing to wait for the 100 years; they trusted the soil and the century, and wagered silently that a Slocum would still be on that soil.

There was something noble and touching about this, I thought. Men were working for the sake of people who would not yet be born for two generations. It changed my attitude toward Captain Slocum, for one thing. He was taking as great care of the place as any of his predecessors, and yet he had no direct heir to whom he could leave the ranch. There would have to be some obscure cousin, some distant dwelling nephew or niece or someone still more remote.

For all his sternness, he had a feeling for his blood, then. Well, there might be many other interesting things that I should discover about him later on. With every step I took through that well-tended farm, I determined to know him better, since, by his own permission, he had given me the key to enter his life.

Now I got down to the thorn hedge that closed off the limits of the farm proper, setting it apart from the broad sweep of the outer ranch, which comprised by far the greater part of the acreage. From a little hummock that gave me sufficient height, I could look over the sweeping hills of the outer ranch and see that all was as on the farm itself very largely. There was the same growth of trees, spotting the hills. There was a repetition of the thorn hedges, making a stout fence between fields, and the chief difference was simply that there was no irrigated ground, no green patches of vegetables, no orchards, and the whole sweep of the land looked to me wilder and rougher.

There had been a Slocum, I remembered, who fought the Indians and received this land for a reward. Well, his services had need to be splendid, because it was a magnificent spot. It made all the rest of the ranches seem stupid and worthless by comparison and yet a single generation of ordinary ownership would reduce it to the same condition the others were in—a treeless, wind-swept, storm-driven waste.

I turned around from this observation and was startled to see Ebenezer Grey immediately behind me. He was walking up to me with no more sound than the shadow of a leaf makes as it slides over the grass, back and forth.

When he saw me turn, he halted. I wondered if he were confused to be observed, but he showed not the slightest indication of this in his face. It was pale, as calm and as politely indifferent as ever.

"Good afternoon, sir," he said.

"Good afternoon," I replied. "Why do you call me 'sir'?"

"Why," said Grey, "a servant ought to use that term in addressing people who are above him . . . or who are about to be above him."

"I'm not above you, Mister Grey," I said.

"You will soon see," he said, with his faint smile. "And from now on, it would be better if you called me 'Grey,' without any title of respect. Since I'm a servant, my feelings won't be hurt."

I shrugged my shoulders. I felt, once more, that the clumsy, open hatred of big John, the Swede, was nothing compared with the cooler malice of Grey.

"Well," I said, "I'll try to do whatever is right. But probably we won't see much of one another."

"On the contrary," said Grey, "we'll see each other every day, I take it. Captain Slocum has just sent me down here to ask you to the house."

"How in the world did he know that I'm here?" I asked.

"A bird, no doubt, told him," Grey said, with the first show of open sarcasm. "He understands their language, it appears."

CHAPTER 12

I went along with him, biting my lip, and not at all at my ease. As a matter of fact, I could not tell what to say, and he kept "sir"-ing me all the way and making me hot around the collar. I was glad to get to the house.

Two of the dogs came rushing out to me. Then they recognized Grey and stopped. When their noses found the scent of me, I was delighted to have them come to my hand, wagging their tails. There's nothing that makes a small boy feel better than a touch of power over the great guard dogs. And there's nothing that's better for the boy, I'm convinced, if he can learn to use his authority with the proper balance.

We went into the house and Grey took me to the library door.

"You will find him perhaps a little nervous," said Grey. "The master is learning how to write with his left hand, and that's a difficult matter, it appears." He then opened the door, spoke my name, and I entered.

Captain Slocum did not look up for a moment. He was busy at a table with a big mirror in front of him and into this mirror he stared, while he traced great, clumsy letters on a pad of paper, holding a pen in his left hand. It was plain that he was making a great effort. His forehead glistened. His jaw muscles were tensed.

"Well?" he said, and repeated impatiently: "Well, well?"

"You sent Mister Grey for me, sir," I said.

"Don't call me 'sir,' and don't call Grey 'mister,'" said the captain. Then he jerked himself abruptly around in his chair and glowered at me. "You've been badgering John, the Swede, again," he said. He struck the arm of his chair with his left hand. "I won't have it," he declared loudly. "I won't have him teased and badgered any longer."

"No, Captain Slocum," I said.

"But you tell me what happened," urged the captain.

"No," I answered. "There's no good in that. John is older than I am and you know him a great deal better than you know me. Of course, you'd believe him."

"Don't tell me what I'll believe or who I'll believe," insisted the captain. "Tell me what happened!"

"Why, it wasn't much. He called me a beggar when he found me inside the thorn hedge. Then I told him that I wasn't a beggar and I began to tease him. I told him he was no good because he couldn't get his hands on me. He got pretty mad. He got pretty wild. That was all there was to it. After a while he went off."

Captain Slocum looked at the ceiling, and then he looked at the floor. "You laughed at him, did you?"

"I laughed till my sides were splitting," I answered frankly.

It did not occur to me to attempt to deceive this wise man. "Well," said the captain, "you shouldn't laugh at John. I don't want you to do it again. I forbid you to do it again. Do you hear?"

"Yes, Captain Slocum," I said. "But I won't be seeing very much of John after today. So there's no use worrying."

"Why won't you be seeing much of him, if you please?"

"Because I'm going away, sir."

"The mischief you are!" exclaimed the captain. He stared at me as though I had insulted him. "Where and why are you going?"

"I've got to go away. I've got a job on my hands," I informed him.

The captain leaned back in his chair.

"You're being farmed out to work, are you?" he asked. "Is that the way of it? Well, I suspected before that your aunt was not only an honest but a very shrewd woman. She knows how to handle boys. So she's sending you away to work on some ranch or other, is she? Well, she's right enough, but this is the ranch that you're to come to. Do you hear?" He struck the arm of his chair again and frowned at me.

"What, Captain Slocum?" I cried, astonished.

"Don't stand there bawling out exclamations," he told me, "but go home and pack your clothes and come up here this same afternoon. We'll make room for you, and we'll find work for you, plenty of work. Keeping out of John's hands, for one thing."

I looked at him in the most utter amazement. Some of the things that Ebenezer Grey had said to me recurred to my mind. I could understand them better, now, when he talked of my becoming above him in position. He meant this very thing—that the captain wanted me to come and live in his house. On what basis? Well, that would have to be seen—but my mind was set on another matter. I shook my head.

"Ha?" said the captain.

"I can't come, sir," I told him.

"I see . . . I see," said Captain Slocum, frowning. "We're to make ourselves rare and special and diffi-cult. We're to be teased and entreated, are we? Is that your scheme, young man?"

I blushed at the thought of such a thing. "It isn't my aunt who's sending me away," I told him. "I'm sending myself. I think I must have come up here to look at your place for the last time."

"Pathos is the present theme," suggested the cap-tain with an ugly sneer. "Well, get on, get on, and tell me where you were sending yourself."

"I don't know," I admitted.

"What nonsense is this?" he asked me.

"I've got to get away. That's all I know."

"And you don't know where you're going?"

"No, but on a back trail. I'll find out where."

"Who from?"

"From my aunt."

"Will you talk sense that a reasonable man can follow?" he asked me hotly.

I felt my face grow cold. I shook my head again. "I can't talk about it," I admitted.

He leaned his head forward and looked up at me through his bushy brows. "You look as though you had a pain somewhere," he said. "Is that what's the matter with you?"

I put my hand on my stomach. "No. It's a kind of an empty feeling," I said.

"Because you're going away or because you're not coming up here?"

"I couldn't come up here, anyway," I told him. "Because I'm not the kind of boy you'd want in the house."

"A watermelon thief, is that it? And a burglar?" he demanded.

Somehow I had to tell him. I fought against it. At last I said: "It's because of my father."

"I thought he was dead."

"He is, sir," I said. "It's the way he died. My aunt only told me this morning. He was . . . hanged!" When I brought out the terrible word, my brain spun like a top. It was like receiving a blow. My knees buckled, and I only kept on my feet by gripping the back of a chair and holding on tight.

My mind began to clear again. Through the mist I heard the captain say: "Some of the best men in the world have been hanged." He spoke sharply and quickly, and I blessed the sound of his voice. It restored me to myself. "What was he accused of?"

"Murder," I answered. "He . . . killed . . . his brother!" I got out the whole of the ghastly business, and then waited for something to happen.

A moment dragged by so slowly that I began to hear the ticking of the old-fashioned marble clock on the mantelpiece.

Then the captain said, with a snap: "Your aunt told you this?"

"Yes."

"I don't believe he ever did such a thing," said Captain Slocum.

"Good bless you!" I cried, from the bottom of a very tormented heart. "I don't believe it, either. And that's why I'm leaving. I'm going to find out."

"Ha?" said the captain. "You? You're going to find out?"

"Yes."

He leaned back, watching me as though I stood at a great distance from him, instead of in the same room. "What do you propose to do first?"

"To find out from my aunt where the . . . the thing . . . where it was supposed to happen. Then I'll go there."

"Where's your money to travel?" he asked.

"I'll get from Aunt Lizzie what's left of my father's money."

"And suppose that she's used up all of that money on your living expenses?"

I shook my head. "My father would never give her so little as that," I insisted. "He wasn't a man to leave me to charity to bring up."

"*Humph!*" said the captain. "Now, suppose that I'm right, after all, and that all the money is gone . . . I make my bet that it is . . . what would you do then?"

"I'll steal rides on trains," I said. "Then . . . I'm big enough to work, here and there."

"At what?"

"I could sell newspapers in cities. I could milk cows and help with housework . . . and a lot of other things. I could do most kinds of ranch work. I can use a rope pretty good, too."

"Now, then," he said, "you let me take this matter into my own hands, and in my own way."

"Thank you," I said, "only, I don't see—"

"I don't suppose that you do," he told me. "And

neither do I, but we'll soon find out what can be done. Ring that bell."

I did so, and in a moment Grey appeared.

"Grey," said the captain, "take the surrey and the bay span. You used the grays yesterday, I think?"

"Yes," said Grey. "But they're still fresh, sir."

"Take the bay span," said the captain. "They need a bit of exercise. Drive down to the house of Don's aunt and bring her up here to me at once."

CHAPTER 13

It was a full hour before Aunt Lizzie arrived. I waited on pins and needles, while Captain Slocum returned to his work before the mirror, tracing out the letters with his left hand, sweating with the most determined application to his job. He acted as though I were not present in the room, but now and again I could hear him murmuring his impatient annoyance.

It was a very sad thing to see a grown man at work in this manner, like a child learning to work at a thing that it already has mastered. Like a child he was, laboring over his letters, shaking his head, and biting his lips. Once or twice he threw a glowering look at me, but I guessed that this was due to his anger with the work rather than to any dislike of me.

At the hour's end, the door opened, and there was Grey, ushering in Aunt Lizzie.

She had put on her brown taffeta dress. It had been let out twice and needed another freeing at the seams, all around, but there was no more of the material to serve. The color had faded a little, and one could see the two lettings out, if one had half an eye for such matters. That dress had puffs at the shoulders and a skirt that fitted snugly around the hips and then flared out toward the bottom in a surprising way. There was a neat collar of yellow lace, which was the only real treasure and prize in Aunt Lizzie's life, I think.

As for the dress, I knew, in a way, that it was old-fashioned, but it was so accepted as a thing for state occasions that it never occurred to me to criticize it; it was a household institution. Aunt Lizzie had on her high-heeled slippers and silk stockings, and she wore gloves a good deal mended around the tips of the fingers, her hair was done high on her head, and she was set off with her amber beads, which made two turns around her neck and dropped in a long, wide loop across her chest. When she came in, holding her head up so that the fat under her chin would not hang, I was struck with admiration—she had such dignity, her smile was so lady-like, and there was so much of her. To this day, I never see a woman dressed up without remembering Aunt Lizzie and feeling that hers was the greater triumph.

Captain Slocum, I was glad to see, seemed impressed also. For he got up hastily from his chair and went forward to meet her. It was quite wonderful to see his stiff back unbend and to watch his smile and his courtesy to her. I never had seen anything like it. He appeared to have only one thought in the world, and that was for her comfort. At the time, I even felt that there was a trifle of the servile in his actions.

Well, I stood by and watched the two of them, and admired them both, and was very glad to be in the same room with them.

When the captain got Aunt Lizzie seated, he excused himself a moment while he brought up a chair for himself, to be near her. In that interval Aunt Lizzie shot me the most curious glance in the world. It seemed to say, all in a flash: *How in heaven's name do you happen to be here? What have you done to the captain? What does he want with me? And is anything important going to come out of this talk?*

Then she said aloud: "Don't be sitting there like a lump, Don. Help the gentleman with the chair."

Of course, I jumped to do it. But the captain shook his head at me. That chair was a reasonably ponderous affair, but the way he managed it with one hand was a thing worth watching. I could tell that he still had iron in that wrist of his.

Now he was seated, and I was back in a shadowy corner again.

"I have been hearing a tragic thing from Don," said the captain, in a voice so gentle that I never would have recognized it. "I have been hearing what he just learned from you . . . the unfortunate circumstance of his father's death."

I thought that was a very tactful way to go about the thing. I must admit that I thought very little about my father just then. I was too absorbed in the maneuvers of the pair before me. When Aunt Lizzie heard the statement, she tipped her head a bit to one side and looked up to the ceiling, and gave a sigh that made the taffeta seams of her dress creak dangerously.

"Ah, yes. Ah, yes," was all she said.

It made me a little hot. I hoped that the captain would not be taken in.

"A man you were fond of," he said, "or you would

not have spent so many years of effort on his son, *madame*."

"Years of effort! Years of effort! Ah, ah," said my aunt. And she put one gloved finger against her cheek and tilted her head to that side. She gave her head a little shake, too, as though the annoyance of those years was coming up in her mind and she would not give it place, just then.

"And now do you know," said the captain, "what this foolish boy is determined to do?"

She shot me another look. I could see, by it, that she would have given a month of her rheumatic pains for the sake of thirty seconds' explanatory talk with me. "And what does poor Don intend to do?" she asked.

"In the first place," said the captain, "he wants to find out where the trouble took place."

"What trouble, if you please?" said my aunt.

"Between his father and . . ." He paused.

"Ah, that?" she said. "That was at Chalmer's Creek. I never could bear to think of it. You know how it is with a woman, Captain Slocum. The mere thought of such a thing will give her bad nights for a six month."

"I can plainly see that you're very sensitive, my dear *madame*," he said gently.

"Too much so, I fear. Too much so," said my aunt, with another creaking sigh. Again she looked at me with a most pathetically inquiring glance, as though she were a fox, asking the way into a hen yard. But I could not even give her a sign, because I didn't know what was coming next.

"Well, then," said the captain, "if the trouble took place at Chalmer's Creek, that's the place our Don is bound for at once."

It did me good to see the way she started when he said "our Don." She looked down at the floor suddenly. I thought that I saw her bite her lip.

"I don't quite understand," she said, looking up at him again.

"I don't, either," he said, "except that Don is bound to get out there . . . and it's a goodish distance to Chalmer's Creek, as I happen to know . . . and that he wants to hunt about until he's found evidence that his father was innocent."

My aunt allowed a faint smile to appear on her lips. "And who'll take him out there?" she asked.

"He doesn't want taking. He'll go by himself, it appears," said Captain Slocum.

"Oh, indeed. Oh, indeed," said Aunt Lizzie. "And where will he get the money to travel on? That's another question."

"That, he presumes, will come out of whatever is left from the money his father gave you for his support."

It was really as if my aunt had been struck, such a quiver ran through her. She stiffened in her chair and flashed one cold, quick look at the captain, and then at me.

"Whatever is left," she said scornfully. "A precious lot, to be sure."

"Ah, but money runs away," said Captain Slocum, nodding his head and closing his eyes, very like a doddering old idiot. "I know how it runs away."

"Indeed, it does," she said, "and with the prices going up and the quality of everything going down. Just to keep him in shoes . . ."

Suddenly she saw my bare, brown toes, which

were wriggling into the soft nap of the carpet, and something made her end her sentence quickly.

"Yes, money runs away, and I don't suppose the original sum was very great."

"No, it certainly was not, considering."

"How much was it, then?" asked the captain.

"Twenty-five . . ." she began. And hastily checking herself, she said: "Two thousand five hundred." She flushed; she stirred with angry impatience.

"A precious lot to leave for the rearing of a boy."

Well, it was a mere trifle, to be sure, on which to rear a boy, but, although it was a lot more than my aunt had expended on me to date, I could not help feeling that my father never would have made such a small provision for me. He never had been exactly poverty-stricken. I usually had what I wanted, and the ghostly memory of my mother was of a lovely woman dressed delicately as a woman cannot dress unless she has plenty of money. My recollection of our home, too, had been one of spacious rooms, with servants about. I could remember one grinning, polished ebony face of a Negress, for instance. However, all of these memories were so dimmed with years that they would never have done as evidence—not even one startling picture of my father riding an exquisitely beautiful horse that was bucking and pitching in a fiendish temper.

Altogether, those recollections of my father made me get up out of my chair and stare fixedly at my aunt when she said that I had been left such a beggarly sum. I was an only child.

Captain Slocum did not seem surprised. "However," he said, "on twenty-five thousand dollars a youngster can be raised with reasonable comfort, because the income ought to be at least a hundred dollars a month, and—"

"Twenty-five thousand!" cried my aunt. "And whatever put such an idea into your head? Twenty-five hundred, I said, or meant to say. Good heavens! Did I make a slip of the tongue and say twenty-five thousand?" She looked wildly at me, and she turned a deep crimson.

Suddenly I was sorry for her. Her meanness, her guilt, her fox-like trickiness were all so patent in that fleshy face of hers. I had to look down at the floor.

"Why, yes," said the captain urbanely, "I believe that you did say twenty-five thousand."

"I must have been mad," she said. Little beads of perspiration had started out on her forehead and across her upper lip. She got out a handkerchief and rubbed them away, but, in so doing, she made a little red streak across one cheek.

Her high color was explained to me, now.

"One makes these slips of the tongue," said the smooth captain, "and, if it was only twenty-five hundred, I suppose the money has been gone for some time."

"As a matter of fact," she declared, "he's been living with me on my own poor little fortune for years." Hastily she added, with a small and pathetic smile: "Not that I complain. Oh, no. I don't complain. You know that blood is thicker than water, as that old saying goes."

"I know it very well," said the captain. "But now I wanted to broach an idea to you. I don't want to steal Don away. But the fact is that I'm fond of the lad, and I wondered if you would allow him to become my boy and live here with me, as my son."

CHAPTER 14

My poor Aunt Lizzie, when she heard this, nearly fell out of her chair. For an instant, she forgot her attitudinizing and, leaning forward, gave Captain Slocum a stare that must have searched the farthest corners of his soul. When she could read nothing in his face, she favored me with a back cut, as it were, but I was as blank as the captain.

This invitation was fuller than the one he had given to me. To come there to work was one thing, to live there as "his boy" was quite another. I saw before me a prospect of a heaven of gold and blue. It opened until my eye was dazzled.

My aunt took up where she had left off, but on a slightly different key. "Captain Slocum," she said, "I can see that you've a mighty big heart. A child could see that. Compared to what you could do for Don, why, what I can do for him is nothing at all. But you know how it is. As we were sayin' a while back, blood is a good bit thicker than water. I lead a lonely

life, Captain Slocum, a lonely and a hard-workin'
life, and I won't say that the boy hasn't been a trouble to me. But the house would be only an empty
shell, with him out of it. I'd kind of have to go away
and start a new life, and I ain't got the means for
that."

She put a gloved hand over her eyes, so that one
could see the patches on the fingertips. I suppose
she thought that she was covering emotion, but,
while her eyes were covered, the captain permitted
himself a smile. It was only a ghost of a smile. It
came and went and I could hardly be sure that I had
seen it. But I stopped being ashamed of Aunt Lizzie
and the almost open begging of her last speech. I
stopped being ashamed for her and began to pity
her, after I saw that smile of the captain. Whatever
might be in her mind, I felt that she would hardly
win against him. He saw through her, as a needle
can see its sharp way through the whole of a big,
soft, clumsy eider-down pillow.

"But there's the other thing," he said. "There's the
removal of the expense, do you see? After all, that's
a consideration. Of course, you don't put money
ahead of the affection you have for Don. But on the
other hand, one must be practical."

"I'm trying to be," said Aunt Lizzie. "Only, it's a
terrible wrench that you've giving my heart, Captain
Slocum. I dunno when I've suffered like I am now."

"Ah, well," said the captain, "I can guess how it
is. And perhaps we can arrange matters so that
you'll be able to go away from Merridan, if you'd
rather, and start up that new life?"

My aunt tried to sigh, but her eyes glittered, her
breast rose and fell; she looked as though she were
going to shout with joy. However, she managed to

control her voice. "Well, Captain Slocum," she said, "I see how it is. I see that you're a man likely to have your own way. I suppose that a poor woman can't stand up against you, once you've put your mind to an idea."

"I'm very heartily glad," said the captain in a very simple and genuine tone, "that you can agree. Then, to get down to the first steps, I presume that you have some position as his legal guardian?"

"Legal position?" said Aunt Lizzie. "I dunno that I have. I've got a letter from his dad, putting the poor boy in my care, if that's what you mean."

"I mean that, in a way. And then, if I take over the position which you're occupying now in relation to him," said the captain, "I must also be in a position to give an accounting of the monies which were left to him by his father."

"Of the which?" said my aunt, her voice growing a little sharp, and her head canting to one side like a bird that sees, or thinks it sees, a worm in the plowed ground. "What would you want an accounting of?"

"You must understand how it is," said the captain, smooth and explanatory as before. "Suppose that some relative turned up and asked me for an account of my stewardship."

"You could tell him that he ain't got no money," said Aunt Lizzie, "and that's as true as I live."

"I've no doubt it's true," he said. "But you must see what an awkward position I'd be in if I had to make a complete explanation without having any accounts to offer. If you will give me some sort of a statement clearing my hands . . . that's all I'd ask for."

I pricked up my ears. Perhaps I was more than usually sensitive at that moment, but I felt, underlying the captain's words, there was a trap that Aunt Lizzie was likely to be caught in. She seemed to see nothing, however.

"Why, of course, I'll give you a statement that every penny of his is spent," she said. "That's easily done."

"Of course, it is. I think I can tell you the little formalities you'll have to go through."

"All right," she said. "I don't understand legal lingo a bit myself. You just give me an idea of the tune, and I'll manage to put in the words." She smiled at her pleasantry. It was plain that the sorrow that had been wringing her heart a moment before was pretty well forgotten.

The captain lay back in his chair, closed his eyes, and puckered his brows. "It would begin by stating that you had received through a certain bank a sum of money." He paused, as though continuing his thought.

"That was the New York Brace National." She nodded. "Go on, Captain."

"You also state when you received the money, how much it was, and where you deposited it. Then you produce canceled checks, vouchers, or something of that sort to represent the sum expended, and—"

"Canceled checks, vouchers!" exclaimed my aunt, gaping a little. "What would I be doing with canceled checks and vouchers? I never was no kind of a businesswoman, Captain, if that's what you mean."

The captain looked almost equally amazed. "You don't mean to say," he said, "that you've nothing to show?"

"Why should I have?" she said.

"Why," said the captain, "because it would be extremely awkward for you if anyone decided to ask you for an accounting. They might even say"—he laughed the thought away as he uttered it—"they might even say that you had spent the money on yourself and not on the boy." He allowed his glance to drift, for an instant, to my bare feet.

My aunt was not a fool. In spite of the laughter, she saw that the captain meant something, and she jumped suddenly out of her chair. She gripped her big hands into fists, and one of the overstrained fingers of her glove burst with a pop. "It'd be nobody's business," she said, "and, besides, nobody could ever find out how much was sent to me. I guess that settles that." She put her chin up into the air, but the captain brought it instantly down again.

"My dear lady," he said softly, "anybody could find out, if he had a touch of influence. Anyone could find out from the Brace National just how large was the check they sent you after the death of Don's father."

I saw that it took down my aunt's high chin. As a matter of fact, it set her down again in her chair so hard that the chair gave a sudden groan. She said not a word. She looked straight into the captain's face and suddenly she saw the trap that I had guessed at before. She saw it too late and knew that she was lost. Her big, fleshy face wrinkled with hatred, and changed color.

"I don't quite know what you've got to do with this business," she said, "or what right you got to interfere. Has he been talking to you about me?"

"Don has been discreet," said the captain gravely. "But, as a matter of fact, what did you do with the twenty-five thousand dollars that were entrusted to you in a sacred trust on his behalf?" And he pointed toward me.

There was nothing melodramatic in his gesture, but it brought the scene to a high spot, I can tell you.

Poor Aunt Lizzie actually weakened so far that she glanced over her shoulder toward the door, and then realized that there was no escape and that she'd have to sit and face the music. The tune that the captain started piping was not very sweet. At last she said: "You've wrote to the Brace National already. They've told you." She sagged in her chair, half sullen, half sodden in defeat.

"They've told me nothing," said the captain, "but when I first spoke to you, a few moments ago, you mentioned twenty-five, and then changed it to two thousand five hundred. Why did you change? It would have been as easy to say twenty-five hundred as to say two thousand five hundred. Even then, you could have covered yourself up, perhaps, if you hadn't given me the name of the bank. But now, *madame,* I think that I have you in a bag, and that the top of it is securely sealed."

Aunt Lizzie looked at him, and quailed. She looked at me, and all at once she threw out her heavy arms toward me and cried out: "Oh, Don, Don! You ain't going to let him touch me? You ain't going to let him ruin my name and my life, are you? Not after all the jolly times we've had . . . particular, right after you came to me."

My heart softened instantly. "No, Aunt Lizzie," I began, but the captain broke in, with a new ring in his voice.

"Don, be quiet," he said to me, without looking in my direction. "As for you," he said to Aunt Lizzie, "you've committed the most despicable crime on the calendar. You've stolen from a defenseless child. You've abused him, as well. You've dressed him in rags. You've beaten him . . . with a black snake. Tut, tut, don't make denials."

"You little rat!" gasped Aunt Lizzie, turning on me. "You've been whining to him and lying about me. I always knew that you'd be the wreck of me."

"It's the common talk of your neighbors, *madame*," said the captain. "They've heard the boy scream, and they've heard the blows fall. I have you now, neatly, in the hollow of my hand. But I won't close the fingers if you do what I tell you to do."

Aunt Lizzie did not answer, because she could not. She had lost her voice and could only make a gesture of pitiful surrender. Still, with a side glance, she fixed her loathing and her hatred upon me in an unforgettable way.

Said the captain quietly, making a pause between phrases: "You will return to your house, and there you will write out a complete statement, including names and dates, to the best of your ability. You will declare the sum of money given to you, above all, and you will conclude your statement with a just estimate of what you have spent on the boy and what you have spent on yourself. In concluding your statement, you will call God to witness, solemnly, that you are telling the truth and the whole truth. Then you will bring or send that statement to my house, and with it you will enclose the letter written to you by the boy's father."

My Aunt Lizzie still could not answer, but, when he came to the end of this quiet speech, she got out of her chair and went to the door of the room, staggering. She opened it, passed through, and then, as though a panic like a child's fear of the dark had seized on her, she slammed the door behind her, and we could hear her running, heavily like a man.

CHAPTER 15

When Aunt Lizzie was gone, the captain said nothing, but he took two or three turns up and down the room, frowning a little, so as not to show his satisfaction. Then he halted and said to me: "Look here, Don. The name of Slocum is a pretty good name, and a pretty old name. If you come up here to live with me, I would like to have you take it." He paused not long enough for me to answer, and then continued: "I would really like to adopt you formally."

One becomes numb to shocks, after receiving enough of them, but I was still capable of feeling a thrill. I felt one now.

"That's a great big honor you offer me," I told him.

"But?" he said, lifting his brows at me in an odd way. "But?"

I bit my lip. The thought of staying with the rich Captain Slocum fairly made my mouth water. I saw the finest fishing rods, the best ponies, the huge dogs, hunting equipment, shotguns, and everything that a boy's heart could desire. I saw them all, and they were mine, and yet I had to draw back from them in this foolish manner.

"But," I answered him, "I'll tell you the way that it is. My father was as proud as punch. I remember him saying to somebody, once, that there never had been a stain on the name of Grier." I blushed. "Well," I admitted, "I can't say what he said, but, still, it's a name that I would kind of hate to change. Though I guess it would be enlarged, all right."

"What would you mean by that?" asked the captain, his brilliant eye fixed steadily on me.

"Well," I said, "they hitch a pair of names together, once in a while, I believe."

"I understand. How would you call it? Grier-Slocum or Slocum-Grier?"

"Slocum-Grier, I should say, sir," I answered.

"*Hmmm*," said the captain. "I understand perfectly. You begin with the hyphen and finally you drop it. Slocum becomes a middle name. Then it becomes an initial. Then it withers and drops off the Grier tree."

I was amazed to see him read my mind so clearly, more clearly, even, than I had thought it out myself.

"By the way," said the captain, "are you Griers Scotch or are you Irish?"

"I think we're a mixture of both."

"I thought so," said the captain. "Now, Mister Donald Grier, will you spend the week with me in this house before you dash off into the Wild West?"

Of course, I told him that I would.

He did not send me upstairs with Ebenezer Grey. He took me up himself and bade me take my choice. There was a great big room that looked to the south. There was another huge corner room, facing east and south. They were so large that I felt rather lost and ill at ease in them. The ceilings lifted high above me, and, looking up at them, I had my inspiration. I would live in the ghost tower of the Slocum house, and then the people of Merridan would be able to see a light, in fact, up there, crowning the hill at night.

The captain was delighted. He laughed heartily and said it was the best idea in the world. Straightway he set the household to work installing me. When I say that he set the household to work, I mean just that. Every soul in the staff was employed helping, in one way or another, to fix up my room. Mrs. Ebenezer Grey, looking like an Indian on the warpath, ordered the proceedings, and I drove out with the captain in the surrey to see the fair at Bannerville over the hill.

Grey sat on the front seat, driving the bays at a spanking gait, and I was back there in my tatters and my bare feet beside the immaculate captain. I shall never forget how we drove down the main street of Merridan. As we went by, people stopped whatever they were doing and turned to gape, and my brightest picture was of Alec, sweeping the sidewalk in front of the butcher shop. He dropped the broom. An apple could have been popped into his open mouth.

It was a real fair at Bannerville. I mean to say, there were all sorts of booths with all manner of things for sale, from Mexican wheelwork to Mexican saddles, heavy with silver work. A gunsmith had set up an establishment there at the fair, and he did a whacking good business, offering a fine Colt revolver at twenty-five cents a shot, the gun to go to the fellow who managed to hit a red ball that bounded on the top of a dancing column of water.

Some of the best shots in the countryside were there, taking their chances and pouring out their money, but not a one of 'em got the gun. I saw two of the most celebrated barroom heroes in the West, each with many notches in his gun, fire six shots at the dancing ball, but all they succeeded in doing was to break the column of water and cause the ball to fall off.

"You try," said the captain to me.

I smiled, thinking that he was joking, but, when I saw that he was not, I tried and failed, of course. Then the captain picked the gun out of my fingers, and, holding it in his left hand, he studied the irregular jerking movements of the ball for a moment. Then he raised the gun, took a very brief bead on it, and fired. The red ball disappeared from the top of the water column as though a fairy had plucked it away into invisibility.

There was a good deal of shouting and applauding, when this happened. The awe with which people looked upon the captain was immediately multiplied by three at least, and as for that handsome Colt revolver, it was straightway presented to me, the handsomest, the most glorious present I ever had received in my entire life, so far as I could remember. From that moment, I could hardly keep my feet on the earth. I might have risen and floated at any moment, I felt.

I kept fumbling at the gun. It was a Special, hard-shooting and true, but light all over. One doesn't like to say such a thing, but I always felt that weapon was particularly designed for people who needed to be fast on the draw.

The captain took me down a few pegs as we wandered along through the crowd.

"Whenever you shoot again," he said, "no matter what the target, no matter whether it's a tree or a red ball on a fountain column, remember that you must see one picture in your mind's eye. Then you will never miss."

"What is the picture, sir?" I asked.

"A picture," said the captain, "of your bullet going home between the two eyes of a fighting man. Feel that you've either got to kill or you'll be killed, and you'll never miss the mark."

I looked up at him askance, and began to feel that the most I had guessed about this man of mystery fell far short of the mark. But I took that lesson home and never have forgotten it. If you doubt the truth of it, go out with your gun and practice. It takes concentration. In three tries, your mind is tired. But the results are remarkable. Such an effort of the will sends the shot flying true to the mark. That, of course, goes for people who are familiar with weapons.

But now the captain was striding on through the crowd until we came to the corral where horses were being judged, and there was a class of range-caught and range-taught mustangs being shown at that moment.

Other people may love the Arab and the thoroughbred. But give me one of those rare mustangs that have been hammered iron-hard by a few centuries of prairies and mountain ancestry. Give me one of those that have been toughened, but that throw back to the old picture of the Spanish barb that was their ancestry. There were half a dozen of these animals in the corral, and they were dancing, throwing their beautiful, small heads, stamping their steel-hard hoofs into the corral dust, and looking, through the rising mist of dust, like things made of metal.

Old Mr. Samuel Lawson, the ex-sheriff, was standing there in the center of the ring, looking over those six horses with a smile such as a man wears when he sees valuable things that he loves. You simply couldn't pick among that lot. They were all small. The tallest wasn't a hair's breadth over fifteen, one, and most of them were a shade under fifteen hands. But they were dancing beauties, dancing devils, too, from the look of them.

There was a good-size crowd gathered to watch this judging. The cowpunchers stood up on the rails and whooped and waved their hats, until Lawson gave them a dressing down, and said that, if he were still sheriff, he would have them in jail in no time. Still, you could hardly blame them for getting their blood up. The sight of those mustangs made one want to jump on the back of one of 'em and go flying away.

In the midst of things, the gate of the corral was unbarred again and in came an old man with a cadaverous face and two hollows in his skull out of which dull blue eyes were glimmering. He led behind him something that made the rest of the picture disappear. It was a dark, dappled chestnut, with black points and a single fleck of white, which was the star between its eyes. It neither danced nor pranced. The old man simply led it out into the center of the corral and stood there. In a moment, the others stopped leading their mustangs about to show off their flawless action. They stopped and stood in a group. They were not there to criticize. They were not even envious. They were simply admiring.

Now, I don't suppose that the chestnut was much

more beautiful, in muscle and bone, than the others. It was fifteen hands. Its color was that exquisite dappling of leopard spots printed into the grain of a dark chestnut coat—one sees the thing now and then, but not very often. When I looked over the horse, I could not see where it excelled. It was about perfect, but so were some of the others. It was the spirit that made it different. The mare was a lady, a queen. The fire was there, but not the fire that leads to kicking and bucking. Her sweet and quiet eye said simply: "I will die for you in the time of need."

Well, Mr. Lawson simply walked up and gave the old man the blue ribbon, then laid his hand on the mare's neck and smiled at her; we all smiled and choked a little except the captain. He stopped the old fellow as he came out of the ring, and wanted to know how much the mare was worth. There was a shake of the head for an answer, but the captain bludgeoned down that sentimental defense. "I'll give you five hundred," he said.

"I couldn't take it," said the old man, who seemed frightened.

"I'll give you seven hundred and fifty," said the captain.

The other moistened his white lips. He drew the head of the mare closer to his shoulder. But before he could speak, the captain said: "She has no blood in her. She has no pedigree. But I'll give you a thousand for your little picture horse. Don, take your pony."

CHAPTER 16

The old man had a wisp of white beard, and, when this last offer of the captain's was made to him, he knotted his fingers in his beard and looked like a man sentenced to death. He looked at the beautiful head of the mare, and then he looked at Captain Slocum's stern face. I was looking at the captain, too, and I distinctly saw his lips framing the words: "One . . . thousand . . . dollars."

Well, the weight of that sum carried the day, and decided that the pony should be mine. Money was not then what it is now. It was about three or four times more precious than it is today, in its power to buy the necessities of life, and it was ten times as rare. When the old fellow heard the $1,000 offered, he was stunned, but he could not resist. Once or twice more, he rolled his eyes, and then his glance fell on me with a sort of relief, as though he had been looking for sympathy and at last he had found it.

"Is she gonna be for you, my son?" he asked.

"That's what Captain Slocum just said," I answered. And I glanced aside at the captain.

He nodded in the most careless manner, and, taking out a checkbook, he began to scribble out the amount of money due to Jim Wayne, for that was the old fellow's name.

Jim Wayne, when he had made sure that the mare belonged to me, told me to jump on her back, which I did. Then he directed me how to manage her. The horse had on nothing but a halter, and Wayne simply tied the free end of the lead rope into the ring of the cheek piece. Then he gave the loop of the rope into my hands, like the reins of a proper bridle. After that, he walked at my side, and talked in a low voice to me.

"This here mare," he said, "this here Cherry, was named after a girl that I had, and the girl, she up and named her, and the mare was raised for her, and she was raised so's even a baby could handle her, because my girl was kind of sickly. Now, then, son, it seems that Cherry was never to ride that hoss. Cherry is in her grave, and here's the mare, son, that was raised for Cherry to ride."

He sleeked her neck with his big, withered hand as he spoke, and the mare turned her head and looked at him with luminous eyes. No wild deer ever had so lustrous an eye, or one so still and deep with affection. There was no fear in the mare, only love, and old Jim began to explain at once what had happened.

"She was gentled from the first," he said. "She could've walked into our kitchen and ate our Christmas dinner and kicked out the windows and smashed up the furniture, but there wouldn't've been a hard word said to her. Me and my wife and our girl, we all three spent hours a day with her. From the first, she was a picture. When she was a little foal, folks used to prick up their ears and watch her runnin' in the fields like a dog-gone' little antelope. When she was a yearlin' . . . well, sir, she's a handsome animal now, some of the folks tell me, but there never was a creature put on the earth that had the beauty of her when she was a yearlin'. The pride of her, too, it was something wonderful. The look of her was like she was goin' to jump right off the earth and into the heaven that she'd dropped from. And the ways of her was a thing to watch . . . the way that a woman watches her child, son.

"Now, the way that she was raised, it took a while to work on her and get into her nature. She was a kind of a mean and naughty youngster, but after a time that side wore off. She begun to come when she was called. She learned to guide over the neck, and then just by pressing her with your knees. She learned to jump and to change step, to pace and to single-foot. She learned to kneel and to sit down like a dog, though I guess there ain't much use of that.

"While we were teachin' her those things, she learned a pile more on her own account, about how to open doors and lift all kinds of latches, how to slide back the bar of a gate and lift the heavy top of a grain box. The ways of Cherry got to be mighty long ways, and she needed a pile of watching, and she still does. She'll climb a mountain for a piece of sugar, and, if she smells apples, the box ain't made that will keep her out.

"Well, sir, that's the kind of a mare she is. She's five years old. There ain't a flaw or a fleck on her. There ain't a real streak of meanness in her. You could gallop her over men lying flat, and she'd never touch hide nor hair of 'em. She don't know what it means to kick or to strike or to bite. She's sound from head to heel. And she's iron. Mind you, there ain't very much of her. But look at her bone and hindquarters! She looks at least a hundred and fifty pound lighter than she is.

"And him that tires her in a day's march will be a weary man in the saddle, I'm telling you, before he pulls out of the stirrup leathers. She'll never say no. She'll jump any fence she can get her chin over, and she'll run till the heart dies in her, and that will mean a dead mare, because her heart will live longer'n her body ever will.

"Now, mind you, if you treat her like a lady, a lady she will be. Treat her like a fraud, and a cunning devil is what you'll make of her, the way that frauds are likely made in homes where they pet the children. Be mighty firm with her. Make her do your way and not her own, but never wear a spur or a whip on her . . . what you can't get out of her with a word ain't in her to give. And never hit her harder than with the flat of your hand, because the hand that strikes her is whacking something more than just horse hide and hair. Now you listen to me, and I'll show you just how to put her through her paces."

He showed me. It was a most amazing thing to see that lovely mare do all that he had said she would and more. She seemed to be reading his mind, guessing at what he wanted before he spoke. 300 people were gathered in no time, watching, admiring, applauding.

And what that mare could do—the beauty!

Wayne buried himself in the crowd and turned his back to her, but when he called out—"Cherry!"— she came to him, stepping daintily through the crowd, never giving any man the irresistible weight of her shoulder, which could have found room for it soon enough, but rather feeling her way through with snorts and shakes of the head, putting her soft muzzle against the shoulder of the man who had to move, until at last she came up to her master.

Then the mare caught the hat from his head and went off flaunting it and shaking it, flinging up her heels, and frolicking around like a colt. It was a delight to see her perform, and poor old Jim was alternately so pleased and so touched that I shall never forget the picture of him standing there, laughing, while the tears ran down his face. I heard a man say that it was a shame to take what was as good as a second child from the old fellow.

Finally the repertoire of even Cherry was exhausted, although old Jim warned me that the mare would replenish it with new additions, for she had the wit that teaches itself. At last, he said good-bye to me.

"You don't look like a mean boy or a careless boy," he said. "But be good to the mare. Be good to her, and stay good, and the day'll come when you'll bless that horse for the return that she'll make to you. There's no love and no kindness that a man can throw away in this world, for what ain't wanted never falls to earth. God Almighty, He leans and picks it up, because He can use it. He never has enough to go around."

He shook hands with me again, and I could not help promising that I would take the very best care that I knew how of the mare. And then I went off dizzily with the captain.

The same day had made me the possessor of a revolver and a mare. But that was not all. We stopped at the saddlery booth of the fair and we bought a beautiful saddle. It wasn't the heavy Mexican type. I don't suppose that its weak horn ever could have sustained the shock of a 1,200 pound steer coming lickety-split against the length of a forty-foot rope that was snubbed around that pommel. But the whole affair was arranged so as to be light and easy on the back of the horse. It was just a trifle under the usual size, also, and therefore it fitted me to a T.

Well, I came home from the fair, riding Cherry and loving the mare so much I couldn't keep my hands still from patting her. She was the most extraordinary creature in the world. She was like a dog and a horse and a cat all thrown together—I mean she had the strength and the speed of the horse, the sense of the dog, and the cat's way of loving petting. If I stopped stroking her neck or rubbing my hand down her silky shoulders, she would begin to shake her head impatiently and look back at me.

I tried out the mare in a good many ways. Several times I popped her over a fence and galloped her for a detour through the fields. Jump? She loved to jump. She took to the air as though she had wings. Fences were her chief delight, but a chance to jump across a ditch half a mile high but no bigger than a gutter was a thing not to be overlooked by her. The mare had other ways. She enjoyed shying at any sort of nonsense, from a flutter of paper to a blaze on a tree—when you were sitting straight in the saddle with the reins in your hands. But if you were leaning, or bending to the side, or turned about in the saddle, or in the slightest degree unaware of her and what she was doing, then Cherry would not have shied or pranced a single step for all the paper and blazes in the world.

I never saw such a mare and no one else did. She lives in my mind today, enshrined with two or three others. Those others were human beings, but they were no more to me than Cherry. May all men be somewhat kinder to dumb brutes when, in the end, they read the story of what Cherry did for me, when nothing else could have served me.

Well, but I must not get on to that so soon. I must continue with the day of the fair, which ended properly, when we got back to the house on the hill. We paraded, as it were, up the main street of Merridan. The boys were out playing. When they saw me, they lined up as silent and as grim as Indians when strangers come about 'em. I saw Charley and galloped the mare up to him.

I just let the reins dangle on her neck. But she stopped when I spoke and kneeled on one knee at a mere gesture from me. Then I stepped down into the dust of the road. I had started, intending to be very grand, but I caught Charley by the hand, and we danced and jumped around Cherry, and Cherry stood there turning her head to keep track of me in all that madness, I being the only human in whom she could trust for the moment. I think that the boys stopped envying me, for a moment, they were so astonished and delighted by the sight of the mare and her accomplishments. Then I jumped on her back again and raced her to catch up with the carriage of the captain.

I saw the mare into the stable, unsaddled, and fed her, then I groomed her. I sat in the manger, teased and bothered her so that she could not get at the grain. Another horse would have snapped my foolish head off. But Cherry, instead of trying to get at the grain, finally gave it up and stood there as quietly as a lamb, watching me with bright, contented eyes, for all the world as though she were content in my enjoyment.

At last I tore myself away. I went to the door of the barn and there I turned back and called into the thick gloaming: "Cherry, will you remember me in the morning?"

And by all the bright heavens, she answered with the softest of whinnies, surely saying: "Yes!"

CHAPTER 17

When I got to the house, I remembered that I would have to climb all the way up to the tower in order to get to the room of my selecting. It had been a great and bright idea during the brilliance of the day, but now, in the dusk, it was a very dubious and different matter. I looked up toward that tower, in my mind's eye, as toward a new hazard, and something shrank inside me. You might call it my soul; you might call it my stomach.

Mrs. Ebenezer Grey caught me going through the kitchen. I mean to say, as I was slipping through that room, where the linoleum shone softly upon the floor and where the stove heaved its broad, gleaming back in the corner, holding up pots of copper and brass and aluminum as bright as silver, Mrs. Grey lifted her head from cutting fruit for a compote and stabbed me sidewise with a look that might have done injury to flesh and blood. But I got through the next doorway, feeling her look fixed upon the dusty bare soles of my feet like hot pitch.

Presently I was climbing the stairs to the tower, giving myself a good pull on the banisters, to freshen my courage. When I reached the door of the upper room, I hesitated a moment before I could pull it open. When I got it open, I remained rooted to the spot. With a little time, I think that I could remember every detail of that room in all its alterations and all its contents, so deep did each item sink as I stood there and stared from side to side, for it had been turned into a boy's bower of bliss.

First of all, I saw a narrow bed made up at one side of the room, with a little round table near the head of it, and on the table there was a lamp lighted, with the flame turned down low. Near this, in a corner, two streaks of gold caught the light and carried it sheer up into the shadows of the ceiling. That was a pair of jointed fishing rods, assembled. I knew at a glance what they were by the delicate bend in them; I could almost feel the hard octagonal sections in my fingers without coming an inch nearer, and I could guess at the exquisite neatness of the joints. Well, when I got to work with those rods, whipping flies across the face of Smith's Creek and the Wynham Pool, something would happen to certain trout that I knew of, the sleek-sided, fat, insolent bullies of the stream!

Hard by, a double-barreled shotgun rested against the wall, the light tangling softly on its metal arabesques. That steel would be as strong as a rifle barrel and light as a feather, of course. A rifle stood beside it—instinctively my hand went out to grasp it. But, my glance lifting, it ran along a double bookshelf that hung against the wall. All of those books were fresh and bright and new, and somehow the dangerous adventures that filled them reached across at me and lifted my heart.

Under the bookshelf was a fisherman's outfit complete—hip waders, pannier of framed canvas and all. I even saw the heavy boot socks folded neatly on top of the basket. The face of Charley arose beside me. He would go with me on those fishing trips, which I brightly and instantly planned.

On the wall there were several pictures hanging between the windows, pictures with plenty of blue sky in them, a richness of blue that even Italy never could show the eye, and with such gold as no brilliant sunset ever furnished. On the floor there was a good, thick rug that a person could lie on—lie on his stomach and elbows and read for hours without cramp or fatigue.

But why should I be looking at rugs when, just beside the door, there was a camping outfit to moisten the very eye with joy? There was the light tent, the set of knives, hatchets, cooking utensils, everything complete, everything the best. With such an outfit a boy could go out and conquer the wilderness. Charley and I would do it! I could not help leaning over and picking up the mallet; it seemed to me specially made, fitted and balanced for my hand.

However, I cannot go on with all of the other details, because on a chair beside the bed I saw what called for immediate examination. It was a full outfit. Yes, there were boots and shoes, a blue suit and a white blouse, a cap and a hat, a belt and in big cardboard boxes beside the chair I guessed that I would find other essentials.

I got to that chair in two steps and found a small

white envelope lying on top of the heap of things. It was from the captain, a note that read:

My Dear Grier-Slocum or Slocum-Grier:
Try everything. Handle everything. If there's the least trifle that isn't just what you want, let me know. These things are not presents. They are only a welcome home from your obedient and humble servant.

He had not signed his name, but, of course, there was only one person in the world who could have written it, and tears filled my eyes when I saw the big, sprawling, clumsy, formless letters that he had worked out with his left hand, his right being injured. A child in the first grade could have written better.

Well, I tried on all the things, and they fitted wonderfully! How had he known my foot size and my exact measurements all over? Well, I could not tell that. To this day I don't exactly know, for he never volunteered the information, and I soon learned not to question him idly. He liked to surround himself with small mysteries, just as he had enjoyed keeping himself behind closed doors from the village all of those lonely years, until I robbed his watermelon patch. I left him to the enjoyment of those mysteries.

I found a bathroom and took a tubbing, rubbed myself down with such a snowy vastness of toweling as I never had seen before, and then went back to my room, scampering up the stairs in soft slippers and a silken dressing gown—silken, mind you, with a silk belt that went around it, with crimson tassels to tip off the circuit of the belt.

I was so happy that I laughed all the way up the

stairs. Then I dressed with all possible care and came down again, wondering at the soft, neat way in which these shoes fitted one's feet, without grasping the toes or sliding at the heel. They were so light that they were hardly like shoes. One felt even lighter in them than barefoot.

When I got down into the lower hall, I had a glimpse in the dimly lighted mirror of my sun-blackened face, and the sight of the grin on it halted me. Besides, I hardly knew what to do or where to go, now that it was approaching my first mealtime in the house of Captain Slocum.

I walked up and down on the muffled, soundless carpet that covered the hallway, dizzily trying to grasp at the treasures that surrounded me and that were mine. At that very instant, I determined that I never would ask the captain questions of why and wherefore. His wound in the right hand, for instance—I never would ask him where he got it, or what hand bore the knife that had stabbed him, or what fracas he could have been in that had led to such a result.

A soft, regular tread came down the carpet on the stairs. I looked up, and it was the captain descending, his figure as erect as ever, even a little more so, and, as he passed under the light at the turning, I saw that he was smiling as I never had seen him smile. I mean to say, there was a light in the eyes and a real stirring of the lips, instead of the usual half sneer that accompanied his expressions of pleasure or of amusement.

This look of his was that of a contented man; he looked younger, gayer, as if there were something before him. After seeing him in this way, I did not want him to know that he had been observed in secret. I shrank back beside the big grandfather clock that stood against the wall, and I saw him go by me with his long, regular stride. Just at that moment, it fell into slow rhythm with the heavy ticking of the clock. He turned his head. I thought for a freezing instant that he recognized me, but then he went straight on and opened the door to the library and disappeared.

After that I waited for a few more minutes, but finally I stepped out, straightened my tie, and went to the door of the library, which I opened with some diffidence. I saw him sitting by the fire with an open book upon his knee. Even so quickly as this, he had become absorbed in the contents.

"Do you wish me to come in here, sir?" I asked.

He merely frowned, lifted his glance for a fleeting instant, and said: "What's that? What's that?"

I saw that his mind was not on my remark. So I went quietly over by the fire and sat down on the hearth bench close to one of the dogs. It was Tiger. He lifted his head, turned his wrinkled brows toward me, and then dropped his head on his paws, without shifting his glance. But his tail, as thick as a child's arm, began to stir a little and slowly to *thump* upon the rug.

That was my welcome to the library.

Suddenly Captain Slocum closed his book with such a slam that it was almost a gun report. "Don," he said.

I leaped to my feet, my heart racing. "Yes?" I said.

"Now, what do you think?" he asked me.

"About what, sir?"

"About this infernal Don Quixote business?"

"I don't know what you mean."

"I mean," he said, "about this matter of starting

West for the sake of getting at a thing which was ended over ten years ago."

I waited for a time. Before I could answer, he continued: "The thing for you to do, Don, is to settle down here to a pleasant life. That chestnut mare will need attention. Great Scott, what would she do with no companionship except that of John, the Swede? Or do you expect me to handle her? As a matter of fact, you must wait until you're older before you tackle such a job as the one that you've set for yourself."

It was clear, now, that he had piled up this mass of gifts in order to overwhelm me. When I thought of leaving those fishing rods and guns and all that, I was staggered and heartsick.

Then an inspiration came to me. I cried out, as it entered my mind: "But I won't leave Cherry, Captain Slocum! I'll take her with me. I'll ride her all the way to Chalmer's Creek . . . I never could leave her behind me."

CHAPTER 18

For a long time the captain said nothing. We went in to dinner in that silence, and there I sat up stiffly, ill at ease, for I never had eaten in such surroundings as these. Grey served the food. I always had passed my plate, before, and been helped by Aunt Lizzie to what she thought fit for me. Now dishes were served and I helped myself, and I was continually fumbling and dropping things, getting redder and redder, while my eyes popped out farther and farther.

The captain began to talk, to cover my embarrassment, I thought, and, when Grey was out of the room for the first time, he said to me: "Now, Don, after a time you'll become accustomed to such ways at the table and elsewhere. And here's a lesson for you. Never think a man's a fool because he doesn't know how to meet new situations. I don't care how you tackle your food. This happens to be the way I have it served, that's all. Wipe that red off your face, and never let me see you blush again except for something cruel or cowardly that you've done to others."

I listened to him with a good deal of relief and wonder, and the words he spoke sank so deeply into my mind that I have reproduced them here with exact accuracy, I'm sure. I feel that there was a great deal in them, and that, if the captain never had done another thing for me, in that moment he gave me the equivalent of a liberal education.

After he had spoken, a great part of my diffidence naturally disappeared, and I finished dinner comfortably enough. Then I went with the captain back into the library. As he sat down, he pulled an envelope out of his inside coat pocket. He began to tap the edge of the envelope on the arm of his chair.

"Now, Don," he began, "when you say that you are going to Chalmer's Creek, you mean that you've definitely made up your mind and that nothing will keep you from going?"

I fell into a sweat, biting my lip and looking at the bear's head on the floor, with its wicked red-stained eyes. "No, sir," I said. "I don't think that I'd go if you absolutely forbade me."

"Ah, ha!" he exclaimed. "But you know that I have no legal position as your guardian and that I have no right to command you in anything."

I considered this. "Well, sir," I finally answered, "you've given me Cherry and a lot of other things, and I couldn't do a thing that you said no to, sort of with all your might."

"Ha?" said the captain, scowling at me. "You couldn't?"

"No," I assured him. I shook my head. I felt that I was saying the truth and would have to stick by it, although he seemed tremendously displeased.

Then he said: "It's the project of a fool. A boy, a twelve-year-old boy."

I could not help breaking in with the fact that I would be thirteen in a day or two. "Don't interrupt me," said the captain, "for nobody but a fool, old or young, would attempt such a thing. Ten years covers even a house. What will it do to the memory of a man? Chalmer's Creek is a wild place. Ten years ago it was wild. Today, with the striking of new gold higher up the creek, it's wilder than ever. Ten years ago there were killings every day. Today it's just as bad. Do you think that anybody in his senses would go out there and try to dig into the confusion of the past and discover evidence about a thing that everyone has forgotten? Who cares about your father now? Nobody! All that they care about is the strength of the new field that they're working on. Do you realize that?"

"Yes, sir," I said. "I try to realize it."

"Is there any sense in your proposal, then?" he asked.

I admitted that there probably was very little sense in it. "But," I told him, "it's the sort of a thing that I can't argue about. I only know that I've got to go, and I can't say why. You never knew my father, sir. But I can't forget him, day or night."

"You don't forget him, eh?" exclaimed the captain in his harsh and sudden way, making his voice roar out at me.

"No, sir," I said. "I don't forget him. If he were alive, he wouldn't forget me. If there were ten years in between us, he wouldn't care. He'd start to cross over and get to me." I stopped. I felt that I had been talking in a very confused and foolish manner. And I looked up to find that the captain was scowling at me more blackly than ever. "I suppose that I seem to be talking like a fool," I admitted.

"Don't tell me what's in my mind," said the captain. He tapped the envelope on the arm of the chair and looked more furious than ever. At last he said: "Well, if I were your age, in your position, with everything to lose, including my life, with not one chance in a thousand of doing what you want to do . . . I would feel exactly as you do, I hope, and I would never rest, night or day, until I had got myself out to Chalmer's Creek."

It fairly lifted me out of my chair to hear him speak in this manner, exactly the opposite of what I had expected.

"But now," he went on, "I want you to understand what I have learned today, through what your . . . precious . . . Aunt Lizzie has sent up to me." With that he shook out from the large envelope two pieces of folded paper, and he went on as follows: "Here are two letters from your father. They explain themselves. We'll read them over, and then strike on a plan of action." He unfolded one paper. "This is the first letter."

Dear Lizzie:

You won't understand the postmark, unless you've been reading in the papers about the big strike and the gold rush to Chalmer's Creek. It's a typical mining boom town, full of crazy shanties and crazy men, and everybody is sure to be rich before tomorrow. I am here with Will. You never knew my brother Will very well, but he's a grand fellow, and we're teaming it together. Between you and me, we've made a strike that looks like something important. And we have the financial backing of about the finest man in town, Judge Hugh Carrol. We start tomorrow up the creek to open the work on the claim, and I hope, within a short time, that I'll be able to send you some very exciting news. I certainly shall, if all goes as I hope it may.

In the meantime, however, there's another side to the question. That is this: I have reason to believe that my life is in danger. I hope this doesn't sound too melodramatic, and I won't go into the matter any further or give you any of the proofs. They're of such a nature that I haven't even confided them to Will my brother. So you'll understand that I don't want to write at length to you about such tenuous matters. However, I am convinced that I'm walking a very narrow road among very real dangers, and I'm as likely to find my death as to find gold up the creek.

That's the immediate reason why I've written to you. I want to tell you, Lizzie, that I never should have written the letter at all if it weren't that I know you're a splendid woman, with the courage of a man, as you showed on that unforgettable day when you rode the gray stallion at the Fairbank's place. And, having such courage as that, you must have the other and more unimportant virtues. That's why I confide and trust in you, though I suppose that you and I are rather friends than actual relations.

Here the captain lowered the letter, and, getting out of his chair, he walked up and down the room with his long, exact stride. Whatever might have been in his mind, he said not a word about it, but sat down again. For my part, I couldn't help remembering how Aunt Lizzie had sat in the room, this day, and revealed herself as an evil, vain, and wicked woman. I could not help wishing, too, that my poor father could have seen her. No, it was better that he should not.

The captain resumed his reading:

There are a good many ways of looking at this matter, but I can't find a better solution for my problem, which is, if I die tomorrow, I leave behind me a small boy and only $25,000. $25,000 is not a great deal. On the other hand, with proper care, it ought to be ample to give the lad the best sort of an education. For that purpose, I need to put the sum into the hands of a trustworthy person and . . .

The captain dropped the letter again, this time, quite to the floor, and he exclaimed: "So the infernal idiot entrusts his little fortune and his boy to your precious Aunt Lizzie! Not even an aunt, not even a relation at all, as far as I can make out, but simply a girl who impressed this father of yours because, on a day, he had seen her ride a horse in a powerful and courageous way. Why not marry the fat woman of the circus because she has an honest smile, or believe the poet because he sometimes tells the truth?" He began to mutter to himself.

Although I wanted to read the rest of the letter, I could see that the main point had been covered. My father, feeling that he was in great danger of death, had planned to turn over me and the money that went with me to what the captain called my "precious Aunt Lizzie."

He now picked up the other letter and read from it.

Dear Lizzie:

Of course, you will hear that I found death up the creek, though not just as I expected to find it. They accuse me of murdering my brother Will, and for that crime I'm to be hanged tomorrow.

In the meantime, I have waited here in the death

house, turning the question of my poor little boy back and forth in my mind, and I've determined that I cannot leave him in better hands than yours. You won't mind my confession that I've hesitated. Such a matter is the most important thing that I'll ever be called upon to decide, and certainly I could not lightly hit on any one being and remain contented. However, I've made my decision. And I have your answer to my first letter, saying that you'll be willing to take charge of the youngster and his money.

I trust you absolutely. And I would far rather have him in your hands than in the hands of some cold-blooded legal adviser. I know that I am asking you to crucify yourself when I ask you to take him in hand, but the self-sacrificing sweetness of your letter sets my mind at rest. I am certain that even the fact that his father is to hang as a murderer will not hold you back. You will do your duty, and God bless you for it!

This letter, in turn, the captain laid aside.

"He goes on," said the captain, "to say that he hopes that you'll be reared to be familiar with horses and an outdoor life, and the best he hopes for you is that you'll be worthy of the great West in which you were born. A lot of sentimental rot! A sentimental fool is what your father was, and he hanged for it. He hanged for it!" The captain struck his hand violently against his breast. "To think of that poor innocent nailed on a new cross," he said, "for the sake of what? Well, that we shall see. That we shall see."

CHAPTER 19

I was of two minds, when I heard the end of this speech. I could not tell whether I should be more furious with the captain for calling my father a "sentimental fool" or for evidently feeling convinced that he was an innocent man. Rather naturally, the second feeling predominated. My eyes were wet. I wanted further confirmation.

"Captain Slocum," I said, my voice trembling up and down in a foolish manner, "I wish that you'd tell me really whether you think that my father was guilty or not?"

"How do I know?" thundered the captain, with one of his sudden outbursts, to which I never grew accustomed. "He may have been as guilty as sin itself. A judge and twelve honest men apparently thought there was evidence enough for the hanging of him. I don't know any of the facts. But I know my own heart . . . I know my own heart, and in that I find there's no possibility of believing that he was guilty. The man who wrote those letters was a fool, a trusting fool. There's plenty of material there from which a man can draw a full-length portrait of him. He's the product of our idiotic westernism . . . schoolbook rot. All women are good . . . George Washington never told a lie . . . truth will triumph, and such nonsense. Idiots like him flower, now and then, and die on the stalk, mind you, die on the stalk. But they go to heaven. That's the difference. They go to heaven by the shortest route."

A good deal of this outburst I did not understand, but the gist was plain. Captain Slocum called my father a fool, but his belief in the innocence of my father was even more passionate than my own. Suddenly I loved the captain. The strength of my emotion brought the tears to my eyes again.

He saw them and exclaimed: "You may be another of the same ilk! There you are, sentimentalizing. Getting tears in your eyes. Self-pity or pity for him, mixed together. A ruinous mixture, I say, a weak mortar to hold together the resolution fit for any action of importance. You've got to change that. You've got to be ready to go West with the determination to look a scoundrel in the eye and slap his face. You've got to go West determined on finding out the truth!"

"Yes, sir," I said. "I'm going out to prove that he was innocent."

"If you start with that intention," said the captain, "you'll never get anywhere. Believe me, because I know. I'm not going to help you. I'm going to send you out there alone. I'm one of the credulous minority that believes in a personal God, a God who guides and helps us, and punishes, also. So I'm going to let you go out there and try your hand in the matter. But I warn you in the first place, if you start out to look at only one side of every bit of evidence you may find, you'll wind up in the dark. Say to yourself . . . 'I am going to learn the truth about the murder of Will Grier.' Then you may have a chance. I don't know, but I think that you may have a chance. Try on any other basis, and you fail. But truth is a great goddess, my son. She will help you if you keep your face directly toward her. She leaves you and trips you up if you're only worshiping her over your shoulder, so to speak."

I understood him perfectly. I was old enough even to see to the heart of his advice. If I tried to prove merely that my father was innocent, and blinded myself to the real facts of the matter, I could succeed only in gathering darkness to darkness. But, if I hardened my heart and hunted for the truth, I might learn enough on both sides to piece an answer together.

"There's only one thing," I said. "In his letter, he doesn't tell Aunt Lizzie that he's innocent."

"Because he was not a weakling," said the captain instantly. "A poor weak coward would have cried over that letter and sworn that he was innocent. Your father leaves her to make up her mind for herself. He says that he is being hanged, and that's all he does say. Why, there's a man I would have liked to know. I hope that there's something of him in you. Perhaps there is. Only, cut out all sentimentality. Never let another tear come in your eyes as long as you live."

I tried to remember that injunction. You'll see, before the end, how far I was able to succeed in my attempt.

Well, then, the captain went on: "Not entirely alone, however. I couldn't send you out there without some protection. Not a guiding mind, but a force able to protect you . . . and who will that be? Why, who but the Swede." He struck his hands together and began to laugh softly to himself. It was quite a thing to see the captain so amused, so delighted with himself. But I, gradually understanding what he meant, was chilled with horror.

I got up from my chair. My voice was no more than a whisper. "You don't mean, sir," I said, "that you'd send me out there . . . alone with John, the Swede?"

"Why not?" he barked at me.

I moistened my dry lips. "I'd a lot rather go alone, sir," I said. "I'd a lot rather go alone, just with Cherry."

"Ha . . . you would, would you?" he said. "And how long do you think that you'd have your pretty Cherry once you got among that choice collection of rascals? Not a day! They'd have her away from you and pay you for her with a rap over the head. I know mining camps. Next to racetracks, mining camps collect the choicest selection of bad men in the world. Once they saw Cherry and how she's put together, they'd soon have her. Believe me. And that would be a black day for you, wouldn't it?"

I shook my head. I sighed. "I couldn't hardly stand it," I admitted. "But John wouldn't—"

"John will do what I tell him to do," said the captain. He nodded and smiled in a manner that was not altogether pleasant. "John will do exactly what I tell him to do," he said finally. "And you'll have him for your escort. Ring that bell!"

Well, the short of it was that presently John came into the library and stood there before the captain, gripping the brim of his hat with both hands. He looked red and uncomfortable, like a man who expects to be kicked from behind, for he was continually turning his head a little from side to side and glancing backward. I almost felt pity for him. I remember that there was a small draft that caught at the hair on the crown of his head, where it stuck up in a long, pale tuft, and set it fluttering like feathers in a breeze.

"Now, John," said the captain, "you see Donald Grier, do you?"

"I see him," said the Swede.

"You know him, do you?"

"I know enough of him," said the Swede, getting still redder, but not with embarrassment now.

"You're going to know him still better," said the captain.

The Swede stuck out his big, square jaw. There was a glint in his eye that even a child could have understood.

"He's going on a trip," said the captain. "He's going on a long trip, and you're going to go with him."

"I'd rather," said the Swede, "go with a one-eyed calf with the string halt and blind staggers. I wouldn't go a step with him, except to the whippin' post, sir."

The captain tapped on the arm of his chair and smiled at John. He was not in the least impatient or angry. I have noticed that rebellion doesn't trouble masters unless they think they will be unable to quell it.

"You're going to go with Donald Grier," persisted the captain.

"Yes, sir," said John.

My hair bristled. It would be better to travel with a bear than with this ugly fellow. But I did not see, any more than John did, how the captain's determination could be turned aside.

"You're going to take care of him," said the captain in continuance.

"Yes, sir," said John. "I'm to take care of him." He turned his head a little and gave me a baleful eye.

"You're to see that not an atom of harm comes to him, day or night. If he's sick, you stay by him and nurse him. If he's tired, you carry him, by the eternal, if he's thirsty, you go without water for his sake. If he's hungry, you steal for him. You understand?"

It was almost like one of those intense speeches that a hypnotist makes to a patient under the influence of the charm. Poor John had almost a similar expression, his eyes being fixed in a vacant stare, his mouth stupidly agape.

He nodded and said: "Yes, sir."

I had a sudden picture of John striding across the ridges of the Western mountains, bearing me in his arms.

A new light came into the captain's eyes. "In the meantime," he said, "you will have many duties on your outward journey. The boy is young. He's soft. He knows little about horses and guns and such things. He will have to know a great deal in order to face the sort of duties that he may have to perform at the end of the trip. You, John, will school him in those things."

"Hey?" said John.

"Yes," said the captain. "You will be his schoolmaster. You will teach him everything that has to do with the trail. You will teach him how to go hungry and thirsty, how to ride day and night, how to find a trail and follow it. You will, above all, teach him how to shoot and find his target. Do you hear me?"

"I hear you," said John sullenly. "But what power'll I have to make the brat do exactly what I tell him to do?"

"You have power," said the captain, "to beat him until the bruises reach the bone, if he doesn't do what you tell him to do. You have power to leave him in the middle of the desert that you will have to cross, if he won't understand and obey you."

One side of the picture had been rosy for me. Now I was showed the reverse, and my heart grew as small and as bloodless as a withered almond.

As for the Swede, he needed more time to soak up the full meaning of what he heard.

The captain went on: "He enters the ride, a boy, at this end of it. On the other end, I expect you to have made him a man."

By this time, John, the Swede, understood. He broke out in a hearty roar: "Captain Slocum, I'll make a man of him, or I'll wear myself clean out trying!"

"That's all," said the captain coldly.

John left the room, but he left it with a light step, while I was weighted down with lead.

"Do you mean it, sir?" I asked.

"I mean it," said the captain. "It may be that I'm a sentimental fool myself in letting you go out there, a child, to do what men would shrink from. But I'm not going to be such a fool as to let you get there soft-handed and soft-headed, as you are now. By the time you're through with that march with John, you'll find yourself a man."

CHAPTER 20

That was how I happened to make the long journey by horseback and in company with John, the Swede. The captain gave us exactly twenty-four hours to get ready, and he delivered marching orders to John that were as brief as the orders that a military commander would issue.

John was to conduct me to Chalmer's Creek. I was to be under the Swede's direction in all things until Chalmer's Creek was reached. The moment that we came to the creek, the position was reversed and I was actually put in command of John.

I thought that John would fairly choke when he heard this part of the directions, but from that moment I hardly thought at all about what might happen when we got to the creek.

My first taste of what was to come came when I prepared my pack, and John, looking it over with a sneer, threw out nine-tenths of the stuff I had accumulated. He left me, of course, horse and saddle, a Winchester, the light Colt Special, a length of lead rope for various purposes, some tough cord, a hunting knife, a short-handled, light-headed axe, an amount of ammunition for rifle and revolver, a slicker, a blanket, some salt, and very little else except one change of underwear and three changes of socks.

The captain looked over these arrangements, and even he had to remark that it seemed to him we would be traveling light. John, the Swede, made no answer, except to sneer. It was plain that he hated his present job so thoroughly that he would have thrown it up and left the service of the captain for good, if it had not been that the latter held him on some mental tether.

That afternoon, I saw John stalking about the farm, looking at his vegetable patches and the flower gardens around the house. He loved his work with a devoted love, and it was bitter for him to leave it. Another man was to be hired from the village to take his place while he was away, but John would not let the stranger come onto the place until he was off it. I never saw such jealousy. He was like a mother about to be exiled from her child.

That night I slept very little. I had gone down the evening before and said good-bye to Charley. My eyes stung with the tears that came into them. And Charley silently wrung my hand. He followed me out to the gate of his house and stood there until the turn of the street took me out of his sight. Then I went up to Aunt Lizzie's house and rapped at the door.

She shouted out, her voice as big and deep as the voice of a man. So I went in and found her sitting in the dining room, reading a book. All around her were assembled boxes along with two trunks. The house was dismantled.

I stood at the door and nodded at her. "It looks like you're leaving, Aunt Lizzie," I said.

She looked sidewise up from the book at me. She did not answer for a moment. I could feel that she was casting about in her mind to find words that would be like rocks to throw at me.

"You come in to see it, didn't you?" she said. "You come in to gloat because you've broke up the home of a woman that loved you and slaved over you for years. That's the kind of a heart you got. You little snake! You're all poison and gall!"

I looked curiously at her. Suddenly I realized that she was all bad. There never had been any good in her. I had been feeling a bit of pity for Aunt Lizzie after the captain so thoroughly dressed her down. But I got over that as I stood in the room with her now. However, I made myself say that I was sorry and that I had not wished to break up her home and hardly saw how I had done it. In fact, it made me feel rather blue when I saw the old place dismantled; I had been there so long I had a fondness for the shack and everything in it. Besides, after the captain's house, this cottage seemed weak, flimsy, destined for wreckage. Aunt Lizzie sat there like a bird on a desert island.

"You don't see how you're to blame, don't you?" she said. "Here! Fetch me the coffee out of the kitchen. I put the pot back on the stove to heat up a little. You don't see, you little, ungrateful rat! Well, one day you'll know what you've done to me."

I was actually afraid to step into the same room with her, but I managed to squeeze past her to the kitchen and there I got the coffee pot off the stove and put the thing beside her on the table. Then I went to the far end of the table and sat down on a box that was handy there.

"Shut the door," said Aunt Lizzie.

"I guess I'd better leave it open," I said. "I might have to scoot any minute."

She smiled at me, not pleasantly, but with a sour understanding. "If I could do it, I'd flay you alive . . . I'd do it with a whip," she said. "After what you've done to me."

"Well," I told her, "you've left your marks on me plenty."

"Aye," she said. "And that's some satisfaction. I wish that I'd left ten times as many. And lemme tell you something."

"I expected I'd have something told me," I said, "when I came in here tonight. Go on and say anything you want to."

"I'll tell you, then," she said, "that the minute that you got out of your baby years I begun to hate you, and I've never stopped ever since."

"What made you, Aunt Lizzie?" I asked her. "I don't pretend that I ever was much good. I never was very bright or very strong, either. But have I been a lot worse than most other boys?"

"You had the look of your dad," she said, "when you were little. What made you change and get the look of the fool that was your mother when you were older?"

"You oughtn't to call her a fool," I said, getting hot in the face.

"I call her what she was. Her and her stuck-up ways, and her silly, affected laugh, and her always languishing around . . . she made me sick, she always made me sick," Aunt Lizzie hissed. "And she wasn't his kind. If it hadn't been for her, he'd be alive this day. But he had to fix her up in silks and satins. She drove him to make money, and he went to make it where he had to pay down his blood for it. It was her fault. It was all her fault. And when you begun to take her turn in the face, how could I help but loathe you? I dunno how I've stuck it out these many years, living with you."

She said these things slowly, with a look as though she re-tasted the bitterness that had passed through her heart in all these years. I could see, then, that she had suffered, and once again I felt an odd pity for her.

"Aunt Lizzie," I said, "you weren't always as hard as this and as mean about things. I'll bet you were jolly and good-natured one time."

"Good-natured?" she cried out at me. "There was a time when I was sunshine all day long, and if I could've had him that . . ." She stopped herself short and took a long swallow of that scalding-hot coffee.

"Who was it?" I said. "What man?"

"Shut your impertinent mouth," said my aunt. "I don't want no more of your tongue. You shut up. I've said enough and too much, but tell me how you find it, living up there in the captain's house, with that smart fellow Grey to wait on you, hand and foot?"

"Well," I said, "it feels pretty strange. I don't know what to make of it, hardly, it's so big and everything. The captain's mighty kind to me."

"He's got a reason for it," she said.

"What reason could he have?"

She banged on the table with her fist and shouted at me: "D'you think that he'd waste time on a brat like you without he had some good reason?"

I would not attempt to argue with her. I merely said that I found him kind and thought that it was right out of his own heart and for no better reason.

"Because you've been play-acting the little hero, ain't it?" said Aunt Lizzie. "Because you've been stealing watermelons and visiting ghosts. I guess that's why he's taken you in, maybe. But a sneak and a worthless thing you always was, and that's what you always will be. Get out of here, and take your fool face along with you. The sight of it gives me a sour stomach."

"I'm going, Aunt Lizzie," I told her, getting up from the box. "I'm going farther than the captain's house before long, too. You don't need to envy me a whole lot. It'll be a good many months after tomorrow morning before I ever see his place again."

"What might you mean by that?" she asked me, scowling with curiosity.

I was willing to gratify her just a little. "I'm going on a long, long trip, Aunt Lizzie," I said.

"Where to?"

"To Chalmer's Creek."

She half rose from her chair, and then slumped back heavily into it. "What for? To Chalmer's Creek? That beats all," she said.

"Yes, that's where I'm going. I'm starting tomorrow."

"With the captain?" she asked, agape.

"No, I'm going with the Swede, John."

She shook her head. "I never heard anything like it!" she exclaimed. "And what might you aim to do out there in Chalmer's Creek?"

"I'm going to clear my father's name," I told her. A rather self-conscious pride stiffened my back. "I'm going to give him as good a name as any man can have."

Aunt Lizzie watched me with gradually narrowing eyes into which came a look of extreme fox-like cunning. "And how would you be going about that, Donald, my dear?" she asked.

I was suddenly sorry that I had told her even so much as this. I felt like a chattering fool. Who could tell how far the gossip might be spread by her and how it might interfere with my plans?

"I guess that's all there is to tell," I said.

"You're going to make secrets out of it, are you?" said Aunt Lizzie.

"There's not much more than that to tell."

"Then get out of here," she ordered. "I've had altogether too much of you already."

I went to the door and looked back at her. "Well, it may be for a long time," I said. "Good-bye, Aunt Lizzie. I guess that I ought to feel a pretty big grudge against you, but I can't. I wish that you may have happiness." I felt it, honestly, at that moment, for my heart was softened toward her.

She broke out into a wild passion. "Bah, you lying snake!" she shouted. "That's the look of the mother that was before you . . . that's the very look and the lying sound of her. I hope you have fire and brimstone waiting for you to wade through."

I hurried out into the darkness, pretty badly shaken. But Aunt Lizzie's wish was to work out.

CHAPTER 21

On my way back to the captain's house that night, I began to wish that I had not spoken so freely to Aunt Lizzie, not that I could foresee what was to happen as the sure result of that foolish interview, but because a vague premonition troubled me and wrung me like a conscience. That night a good sleep was like a wall that separated me from my life before, and, when the Swede rapped at my door the following morning, although it was only the chilly, brain-killing gray of the dawn, I was up in a flash and dressed and down the stairs.

He met me without a smile. He merely looked me over from head to foot, with the air of one who wishes to find fault. Then we went out to the stable and quickly saddled the horses.

John had a rangy gelding as big as a mountain and with enough quality, also, to make it fast. I had Cherry, of course. In addition, the Swede had received permission from the captain to get a pair of second-string mounts. We had so far to go and the chances of mishaps were so many, that it was considered foolish to trust to only one horse apiece. So John had gone out the day before and got us a pair of horses to his own taste.

I am sure that they would have been to the taste of no other human in the world. Not even the hardiest Indian brave in those days could have desired one of those brutes. They were not like horses. Their natures were half bulldog and half wildcat. Each of them had a snaky look about the head and eyes. I never have seen such demons. They seemed continually to be smiling at the human fools who were trying to master them.

Well, John had bought them without trying them. The trying started that morning, for he insisted that we should put our worst foot forward in making the start, and so the mustangs were saddled and Cherry and the rangy gelding were kept for reserve. The mustang assigned to me by John was a dirty gray, one of those spotted grays with yellow stains working into the hair so that the brutes continually look ungroomed. It was called Scatter-Gun, or Scatter, for short. Once you saw it buck, you could understand how it got its name. It let me climb on its back that morning and settle myself in the saddle. It even turned its head and seemed to study with scrupulous satisfaction the moment when both of my feet were well settled in the stirrups. Then it exploded.

It exploded, and I was like a charge of small shot flying in all directions. It seemed to knock me apart. I came down in sections, as it were, under the lowest rail of the corral fence, and, as my brain cleared, I saw Scatter-Gun standing in the middle of the corral with its ears popped forward and its eyes smiling. It was a happy-looking demon of a horse.

The thumping of hoofs, the squeaking of leather, got my attention switched around until I could see what was happening to the Swede. He had for himself a paint horse with a slab of pink covering most of its left side. He called the animal Pinkie, and Pinkie was now showing that Scatter-Gun's talents would not be lonely during the trip. No, Pinkie would have been good company for the best-trained pitching bronco that ever made sore hacks and heads in a rodeo.

Pinkie was everlastingly lambasting the ground and sticking its head up to the eyes in the blue water of the sky. When it started up, it soared, and, when it got up far enough, it folded its wings and came down and tried to stick a hoof clear through to China. You never saw a horse whang the ground the way Pinkie was doing. And the whip-snap jars of its landings jerked the head of John, the Swede, from side to side, or snapped it forward so hard that I used to be afraid that his chin would break his breastbone.

But John's face was what amazed me. You've heard of the martyrs who burst into song as they found the red flames rising around them. That was what John's face made me think of. He was getting a terrific hammering, but he looked as though he liked it, in a mighty grim sort of way. His teeth were set, but his mouth was grinning. Pinkie, like a bulldog, was sticking to its work, and the Swede was sticking to his. His quirt rose and fell regularly. He was fairly cutting the stomach out of Pinkie, and that high-powered mustang began to grunt and wince a little under the blows. The twentieth lick on the same spot will dent even a mustang's conscience, and Pinkie was beginning to get pretty tender.

It began to deal from the top and bottom of the deck at the same time. That is to say: along with its straight bucking, it threw in little asides of its own that were worth the price of admission all by themselves. It tipped itself over backward, three times in a row, and the second time almost did for the Swede, whose foot stuck a fraction of a second in the stirrup. But every time John cleared himself, and every time, as the gelding got up, it found itself packing the Swede once more. Then Pinkie tried to scrape its rider off against the fence, then to rake him away against the lower bough of a tree that stood in the corral. There was a cloud of dust that rose from the ground like the smoke of a bonfire, and through that smoke I thought that I saw the Swede glorified. Certainly he was in my eyes, because he stuck to his job like a hero. Those big, powerful legs of his were cutting the bronco in two. He no longer looked clumsy, as he did when he was walking about on his own two legs. He looked rather like a big cat, clawing that mustang to death.

For the very first time it seemed to me that I saw the Swede at home.

Well, presently Pinkie quit, and quit cold. It stopped bucking with a jar, and remained stopped. It stood off in a corner, with its legs shaking under it, and its head down, and a furious look of satisfaction was in the eye of John.

He said as he got out of the saddle: "That's the first good time I've had in five year. Now you, Don, you get up and do the same by the gray, will you?"

It was a command, not an invitation. I had had quite enough of that pony, and I said so. I said that my legs were not long enough to go around it and keep hold. But the Swede only laughed. Then he raised his hand and pointed a finger at me like a gun.

"Climb onto that hoss!" he stated.

Well, I climbed. I saw what he meant. Insubordination at the very beginning would simply be the end of the trail, so far as I was concerned. I got well into that saddle and both my feet lodged in the stirrups, when the bronco exploded again. It popped me out of that saddle the way a small boy pops wet watermelon seeds out of his fingers. This time it hung me over a branch of the tree, and I had to climb down. I was frightened to death. Scatter-Gun began to look as high as a mountain and as deep as a sea to me. It seemed to me that a boy could fall any given distance from that saddle before hitting the turf.

I looked hopefully, pitifully at the Swede. He merely grinned and pointed at the horse again. "When he starts to buck, why don't you dodge him?" asked the Swede.

I knew that he had in mind the way I had made a fool of him not so many days before.

He had his revenge that morning. He said he would keep me at it until I could stick in that saddle, but he broke his word. John was terribly torn between two emotions. In the first place, it was heaven to him to see me getting such terrible punishment, and terrible was the right word for what I received. In the second place, however, it was torture for him to see a bucking horse win, and eventually that second emotion mastered him. I had been bucked off and thrown over the fence when the Swede, with a wild sort of a howl, rushed in and jumped onto the saddle on Scatter's back.

He jumped off again, I'm almost glad to say, and

Scatter supplied the up and outward power, I can tell you. Three times the Swede climbed up that ladder and fell off the top, as you might say. I began to laugh, but I stopped because it hurt me too much when I laughed. It hurt me to stir a finger. I was bastinadoed from head to foot, a great mass of blue and purple bruises. Besides, it was hard to laugh at the Swede once he got his grip on Scatter-Gun's sides. After that, it was all over with the gray. Not immediately. It was a tremendous battle to the finish, but the Swede won.

As I watched him and that spinning horse inside the dust column of their own raising, I began to see that I had underestimated the Swede. I had seen him working on the ground, but the back of a horse was the right place for him. It was a throne. It made a king of him. In half an hour he had so changed the mind of Scatter-Gun that even I could remain in the saddle.

I'll never forget the face of the Swede as he got off the back of that thoroughly subdued mustang and threw me the reins. The bucking had been so frightfully hard, a streak of blood was running down, pale and thin, from each nostril of the Swede. More blood—I never had seen such a thing before—was oozing from one of his ears.

I knew that the Swede was pretty sick, inside and all over. I knew it, but I saw that he kept on smiling as though he despised the small thing he had just accomplished. Suddenly I began to admire the Swede; at the same time, my fear of him was multiplied by ten. If John could break the spirit of a mustang, could he not break the spirit of a thirteen-year-old boy?

Well, when we were all ready to go, we went in to say good-bye to the captain. I was still a little dizzy—drunk from the hammering that I had received—when I stood before him, holding out my hand, forgetful that he would not give me that greeting. When I got back my wits and dropped my hand, turning red in the face, the captain said: "You're walking out into a hot fire, Don. When it begins to burn you, remember that you chose this particular kind of flame. If you stick to your trail, I want no other proof that you're the lad I've been looking for. Whatever you do, keep your hands clean and your tongue straight, and never show an angry man your back."

These words did not mean a great deal to me at the time, but afterward I recalled them, and they have rung in my mind ever since. I haven't lived up to them. I don't suppose that many men could follow those few simple injunctions that constituted his code.

Ten minutes later we were riding across the hills. John was not taking the road, but was saving time by cutting across country. When we climbed to the first height, I turned in the saddle and looked back fondly, sadly at Merridan. I saw the windows blink with the rising sun. I saw the captain's house among its cool, shadowy trees. Then the hill rose up behind me, the picture was gone, and I was alone under a hot sky with John, the Swede.

CHAPTER 22

Sometimes it seems to me that I should write down every detail of that long journey. The very length of it was enough to prove my folly in starting on a horse, because, by the time we arrived in Chalmer's Creek, we had traversed no less than 1,450 or 1,500 miles! That distance could have been cut by fifty percent, almost, but John, the Swede, chose to take the longest way around in every instance.

He could have taken innumerable short cuts across the hills and the mountain trails, but he preferred to wind his way through the twisting, interminable desert valleys, where the sun was gathered as water gathers in a flume. We averaged on that march only twenty miles a day. This may sound like a small number, considering that we had two mounts apiece and that each of us had at least one horse of extraordinary quality. At any rate, we were seventy-five days upon that trail, and, except for a few brief halts to recuperate, we were at work, hard, every day the journey lasted.

Now, when I look back upon that trip, it does not seem to me like a mere two months and a half. It appears more like a whole lifetime, spent not in this world, but in a sort of fiery inferno that must have been in some planet nearer to the sun. Excess of torment defeats its own end, and the Swede successfully tortured me so beyond endurance that my mind refused to retain and record the details of the suffering.

Yet, during that entire time, he never raised his hand against me. His way was more subtle. He indulged in no sudden outbursts of temper, but, for the time when I had teased him, he exacted full payment. Truly, as the captain had suspected, I had started upon that trip a mere boy, and at the finish of it I was a hardened man, in more ways than one.

I had better begin by describing my daily program, which went, as a rule, somewhat as follows.

First of all, I wakened at the first trace of the dawn. If I did not, I could be sure that I would be punished for the late sleeping by having all my duties uselessly doubled for several days. My horror of sleeping past the appointed time became so great that to the present time I waken, at least for a moment, when the dark of the night breaks a little and the day begins to show itself.

After wakening, I got the horses together. They were hobbled during the night, but, except Cherry, they were likely to work to a distance from the camp in spite of their hobbles, for desert forage is, of course, hard to come at and they had to cover some distance in order to get enough food. Cherry, however, grazed close to the camp and yet she remained in better condition than any of the others owing, I suppose, to her marvelous organization of body. She could have lived, I think, wherever there was enough herbage to support a goat.

After I had jogged across the open, got the horses and rounded them back to the camp, so that they would be handy for the commencement of the day's march, I saddled and bridled the two that were to be used for the day. Then I got firewood together and cooked breakfast. Breakfast was always meat that had been shot the day before, under circumstances which I shall describe a little later.

This meat was cooked by roasting it on splinters of wood or twigs before the fire, and the roasting was a process requiring the greatest delicacy, because John, the Swede, soon developed the taste of a connoisseur in the matter of his roasted flesh. If it were cooked dry, or singed, or underdone, or of any color other than a most delicate pink, he threw the food on the ground and refused to touch it. Three times, he made marches a whole day in length without tasting food simply because I had been unable to cook to his taste.

But you must not imagine that he was the chief sufferer on such occasions. No! For days and days afterwards, he tormented me with infinite skill and cunning.

During those early morning preparations for the march, he lolled in his blankets, but when the meat was cooked, he condescended to sit up and taste it, critically, rolling one eye up toward the sky while he mouthed the first few morsels. His big face swollen and red with sleep, he looked oddly comic while he went through this process, but I learned to wait for a silent verdict with almost trembling fear.

After he had eaten breakfast, I hurried to make up the packs and put them on the horses. If we were riding Cherry and the half-bred gelding, Judge, the matter was quickly done and we were soon on the march. But if we were to try mustangs for the day, I had a fiendish task before me.

For then I had to back each of those little demons, Scatter-Gun and Pinkie, in turn, and "take out his kinks," as the Swede called it. In the old days, every mustang was likely to have some of those kinks in his system in the morning, and it required a good clinch to stick in the saddle while the pony was un-limbering. Pinkie and Scatter-Gun were extraordinarily proficient in all of the arts. They had been mastered by the Swede in the beginning and so thoroughly beaten by him that neither of them ever so much as blinked at him throughout the rest of the journey, but they heartily despised me, and, for more than thirty days, I began each morning with a hideous session of horse-breaking.

No, it was not horse-breaking. It was boy-breaking. Scatter-Gun was the main demon, and I would be hurled out of the saddle again and again. There was only one advantage—we were most of the time in reasonably soft desert sand. Otherwise I would have broken my neck a thousand times. Every day I received that frightful beating. Not until the Swede had filled his eye with the show and consented to mount Pinkie, could I keep my seat in the saddle. As soon as he was up, Scatter-Gun gave up his antics and went along quietly enough beside his friend.

Sometimes the Swede would elect to keep me at it for an hour, putting back his head with that broad grin of joy as if he were tasting pleasure to the core. He never broke into laughter, no matter how brutal. There was simply that grin of varying dimensions, which never wore off his face. At last he would con-descend to mount Pinkie and end my torture.

Once, on the seventh or eighth morning, he de-layed so long that after getting on the back of Scatter-Gun and joining the Swede, I fainted before we had ridden a mile. I was so badly knocked out that I could not stand until noon of that day, and, while I lay prostrate, the brute allowed me to live or die, unaided by him. He simply sat on a rock under the broad shade of his sombrero and quietly smoked cigarettes.

When the march was well under way, I could not relax for a moment. I had to be the hunter for the party. The Swede was a beautiful shot with a rifle; in fact, he was a master hunter in every respect. Each day he gave me some new lesson out of a book that seemed to have no ending, for he never repeated those lessons and I soon learned to get every one by heart. I knew that he never would answer questions. Bluntly, sourly he would, for instance, point out a trail and tell me how to read its age by the way the grass was springing, or by the way the sand was still trickling from the edges of the imprint into the bot-tom of the depression.

He taught me the signs of the various beasts, and he gave me lessons, invaluable ones, in calculating range and in making allowance for windage and other details of fine marksmanship. But he never gave me one to equal what the captain had said—that in shooting, one should imagine the target to be a man capable of shooting back, and send the first bullet home to avoid death by the answering fire.

After the daily lesson, the Swede would point out the object toward which he was to ride that day, and I would go out to hunt for game. He was like the master huntsman, and I the hunting dog, scouring to this side and to that like a hungry beast searching for game.

Many a day, I failed to find it. On those days, we pulled up our belts a notch or two, for the Swede never fired a shot at a single head of game during the entire trip. He preferred to give me exhibitions of fancy shooting, at rocks and saplings, during the day's march. But I had to be the hunter.

I used to shake with fear and hunger and despair when I sighted anything, even a ground squirrel sitting up like a little peg beside its burrow. But after a few days I learned that tremors spoil the shooting and dim the eyes. When I got near a target, I learned how to freeze myself to a stone. Rabbits, squirrels, and birds made up the greater portion of our food, but I got two antelope and a deer during the course of the entire march. That meat, if the Swede would have stopped to jerk it, would have been enough to keep our larder comfortably filled, but he refused to make a halt, and the meat lasted only so long as it was fresh. Every day, I had to start out again on that precarious business of finding life where there was almost none to be found.

Perhaps my luck was very bad; perhaps my skill was lacking, in part, even with all of the Swede's lessons, but usually it was not until late in the day that I succeeded in getting any sort of a bag. The first hours of every hunt were almost certain to be a prolonged agony for me. I don't know how to give this fact its right importance. I can only say that even the bucking of the horses in the morning and the physical suffering it entailed was nothing compared to the mental hazard of the daily hunt. To the end, the strain hardly lessened, except, perhaps, in the final fortnight, when I had become a pretty fair hunter and a good deal more than a fair shot. One learns marksmanship when it is practically a matter of life and death.

Of course, you will wonder why I persisted, why I did not turn back under the torments that the Swede inflicted. It was because I had what seemed to be a great purpose, and, almost as potent an influence, I dreaded, nearly as a man dreads death, to go back and face the cynical eye of the captain and tell him that I had given up. Even the thousand bruises that I had received in my falls from horseback would seem a poor excuse. So it was the memory of my poor father and the thought of the captain's face that drove me along with whips.

I learned to lock my jaws and to endure as very few boys of my age have had to endure. Then I had my gradually achieved triumphs, too. The larder was fairly well filled, and I did learn to master both of those cunning demons, the mustangs.

In part, the schooling of those falls taught me to keep balance and maintain a leg grip. All day long, I used to practice holding as hard as I could with my knees so that I would have more strength for the morning duels. Then, finally, I began to study calmly the tricks of each of the brutes. More than once, as I sailed into the air, I told myself that at last I understood that trick and that it never could be used against me again. By degrees, I did master their cunning in great part. But the thing was very much like learning a foreign language, a long process of blunderings, haltings, and failures until one day the words begin to flow almost without a conscious effort. So it happened, when we were about thirty days out, on that morning I sat the saddle in spite of Pinkie's best and had a sudden feeling of glory and of triumph that he could not throw me, do what he would. So I used the quirt on him until he had bucked, jumped, and twisted himself in pain and had to surrender. After that, I jumped down and went for the other mustang, my own mount, and I shall never forget the chagrin and amazement on the face of the Swede as he saw me master Scatter-Gun in turn, and make a good job of it.

Well, I had learned to ride—at a pretty grim price. But I had taken the main bludgeon out of the hands of the Swede.

CHAPTER 23

More than the memory of my father or the captain, however, Cherry kept me on the trail. She was my comfort. She had an honest heart and gentle nature. From the first, she seemed to love me almost as I loved her. Perhaps she felt my weakness; at any rate, she never so much as sidestepped when I was in the saddle. And I used to think that at the bitter end of the day, when my brain spun with the force of the sun that had been beating on my head during the long hunt, and my legs shook with fatigue—I used to think at such times that she went on with a more conscious softness of gait, making the way easier for me.

At night, when she had finished grazing, she used to come and lie down beside me, like a dog. When I wakened in the morning, the first thing that I saw was sure to be her delicate, lifted head, and her eyes, in the dawn, like two glimmering, beautiful stars. It took away half the agony of struggling into my clothes and beginning the day's labor.

I think that the silence of the Swede would have driven me mad, except that I had Cherry. After the morning hunting and shooting lesson, he often spoke not a single word during the rest of the day, giving his accursed short orders with mere gestures. But I always had Cherry. I used to chatter to her, and she never failed to lift her ears and turn her head a little, as though she were understanding. I used to teach her tricks, too, foolish things such as hunting in my pockets, and we worked up a game of hide-and-seek that used to amuse us both when, at the end of the hard day's work, there were a few minutes to spare before bedtime. She was never so hungry for grazing that she would fail to play the game with all her heart. While she grazed, I would slip away behind her back among the rocks, and, when I felt that I was securely hidden, I would whistle.

With the whistle Cherry would come bounding among the rocks like a deer. Once she got wind of me, she ran me down in no time. Twice I almost fooled her, but never quite. Once I lay out on the bough of a big tree—we were passing through some wooded hills—and she went back and forth beneath me. She became so anxious and worried at being unable to locate my scent, that finally she stopped and stamped and whinnied, exactly like an irritated man exclaiming because he cannot find what he wants. I hugged myself and almost choked with laughter, but the very next moment she had found me and was rearing and nipping softly at me. I slid off onto her back and laughed all the way back to the camp, laughed at her and loved her.

Another time, I cunningly buried myself in the sand, leaving only my face above ground, breathing through some branches of a small bush. That day she spent a whole half hour, wandering back and forth and even nosing into the bush that covered my face. But at last she found me. I don't know what guided her, but presently there she was, daintily, carefully pawing away the sand that covered me. When she made sure that it was I, indeed, she went off kicking her heels into the air and frolicked around me in a circle, like a colt.

Yes, without Cherry I should have gone almost mad; I never could have endured, certainly, the long, the endless agony of the first month of that trail.

We had been almost two months out before I realized another thing—much as the Swede had tormented me, I was tormenting him almost as much because of the devotion that the mare showed to me. I learned this rather by accident. I had come back with only one rabbit to show for my day's hunt, to the place that he had appointed beforehand for the evening stop. As I rounded over the shoulder of a hill just above the hollow, I saw the Swede trying to play hide-and-seek with Cherry. It was ridiculous. He was only half hiding himself behind a rock not big enough to cover all of his great bulk, but Cherry would not have anything to do with him. She would not be lured into the game. When he saw that he had failed, the Swede stood up, cursed loudly, and shook his fist at her. I guessed, then, that the loneliness of the long march was telling upon him, also. Only, he had no companion. Even Judge was not the play fellow, the companion that Cherry was.

The next morning, when I was saddling, he said abruptly to me: "Put my saddle on Cherry. I'm tired of the Judge and Pinkie. I'm gonna try the mare."

I was turned to rock, not by fear, but by hot rage. I burned up to the eyes. I saw John, the Swede, through a red mist, literally. And then I walked up to him, found him through that mist, and looked him in the eye. "John," I said, "if you ever try to ride her, if you ever touch her, I'll kill you!"

He looked at me with a face that was white and twisting with a jealous rage, his lips moved. I could almost feel the turnings of his mind as he strove to call this rebellion a refusal to obey. But he could not. The mare was mine, and his own horse was not lamed. Right was on my side and he merely turned on his heel and walked away. From that moment, he wanted me dead, I think.

Still panting, still misty in the eyes, I felt that my right hand was aching, and suddenly I discovered that the fingers were locked with all of my might about the handle of the Colt Special. Well, that discovery sobered me with a sudden stroke. I had felt that I wanted to fly at John's throat, but I realized in that unpleasant moment that it would have been a bullet that I should have sent at that target.

I wonder if John realized the same thing? If so, why didn't he knock me flat? Or was he the least bit unsure about the speed of his fist compared with that flashy draw of the revolver that he himself had taught me with some pains, and which I practiced all the day long? I was somewhere between pride in myself and fear of something that was new in my nature. My temper had always been sufficiently hot. It was more than that now.

I sat down on a stone that instant and almost forgot about the saddling that had to be done. I understood, in that flash, that my father might have been guilty of the crime of which he was accused. Even against a brother, the white-hot fury I had felt toward John that morning might have flamed up and mastered me completely. I sweated, I turned cold, I shook like a man with chills and fever. And a very sober boy was I when I got the saddles on the horses that morning.

Perhaps it was this that aroused me sufficiently to let me see another thing that day. In the middle of my hunting, which all that day was a total blank, I came to a stream. Leaning at the verge of a small pool it formed, I saw my own face and started at the sight of it. I had last consciously seen myself a mere round-faced boy, but now the roundness was thumbed away from my cheeks, my eyes were pushed back farther into my head, and the flesh was worked back about the base of my nostrils, making my nose seem much larger. My lips were tight and straight-set, my chin stood out in a harsh ridge, and on the whole I looked less like a boy than like a young criminal. Certainly my boyhood had been left behind me somewhere on the desert. The torments of the Swede had killed one self for me, and it was another being that he was handling now.

I remember, after I had drunk, that I stood up and sleeked the neck of the mare, for I was riding her that day as a matter of course. I remember also that I said to her: "Cherry, maybe I'm going to be a bad one."

I recall this because of what happened then. She had just finished drinking on her own account, and, as she lifted her dripping muzzle, she shook her head a little, looking around at me. The gesture was so humanely pat that I broke into a roar of laughter.

"All right, Cherry," I said to her. "You believe in me as hard as you can, because maybe I'll need a lot of your faith and trust."

We were about ten days from our destination now, and I think that the Swede might have lingered on for a whole month more. But he began to be so punished by jealousy, as he saw me cutting up with Cherry at every halt, I think he preferred to push on to the mining camp, even though, the moment he came in sight of it, he was not the master—the authority, by the captain's word, would then be transferred to me.

At any rate, we now pushed straight ahead by longer marches. We left the desert, we climbed over a good range of hills, and, ten days from the moment when I quarreled with him about Cherry, we crossed a ridge and looked down into Chalmer's Creek.

It was a thing worth the seeing, I can tell you. The old town is almost forgotten now. There are still some of the old-timers who remember the days of the two great strikes. It has appeared here and there in books dealing with Western gold mining, but on the whole such places as Chalmer's Creek are forgotten. They have to make way for the great bonanzas that astonish the minds of men from time to time.

However, when I saw it, six miles of the creek were being worked. There was a ragged string of six miles of tents and shacks strung up and down, the string gathering into a ragged bunch of buildings in the center, the town of Chalmer's Creek itself. Early as it was in the morning, the clinking of the singlejacks and doublejacks had commenced against the drill heads. As the wind blew across the ravine, it lifted to my ears a faint moan of distant voices or, at least, I thought I heard that sound and the sorrow in it. There was to be more than sorrow for me in Chalmer's Creek. And I was a lucky boy that I could not see too deeply into what was to come.

But while we sat in the saddle and looked down

upon the mining town, the Swede stretched out his arm. "There you are," he said. "Go right down and make yourself at home, kid. I'm gonna start back."

I looked at him, for a moment, with a start. I would not really be sorry to lose him except for one thing. I could fend for myself, I thought, but I remembered what the captain had said about Cherry, and I realized that he was probably right. I could not keep such an animal for my own in a wild lot of ruffians, such as those who probably made two-thirds of the camp here.

"You're going to turn back?" I echoed after him.

He grinned at me. His grin was a snarl.

"You want old John, now?" he demanded. "You'd beg him to stay with you now, wouldn't you?"

I shook my head. "I don't have to beg you, John," I said. I actually felt older than that big fellow. I almost pitied him.

"You'll stay, anyway," I said.

"I'm blamed if I will," he said. "I'm going back . . . on my own trail and about my own business."

I sneered at him. "You'll stay here . . . you'll take my orders from now on," I told him. "Or you'll have the captain to account to. Do you want that?"

He quailed under my eye. He looked away, and I knew that he was seeing the captain's face in his mind's eye.

The sweetness of that moment almost repaid me for the torments of the long march.

CHAPTER 24

It was very true that I knew a great deal about the captain's overmastering will, and yet it surprised me enormously to see how, from such a distance, he overcame and subdued John, the Swede. After all, the United States is the land of freedom for the individual, but the big Swede was little better than a slave under the surveillance of his master.

Sullenly he put Judge in motion, and we went down the trail that offered the nearest way to the town. He said not a word and I did not speak again. Seeing his broad back before me, I was almost ashamed that the captain had put me in command of a grown man. But then I remembered what I had seen in taking a swim in a brook the day before. My body was still blotched and stained with pale green and yellow discolorations from the bruises that I had suffered in being flung from the horses during the first month of the trip. Six weeks had passed during which I had never lost my seat, but so deep were some of those bruises that even four and five months later there were still traces of them. I had been bastinadoed during every morning of that first month's ride.

When I thought of that circumstance and of the artful and continued malignance of the Swede, how he had used me as a servant rather than as a companion, I was filled with an unspeakable bitterness and wanted nothing so much as to humiliate him utterly. So I looked at those vast shoulders of his with a sneer and promised myself a perfect and an unforgettable revenge.

When we got down to the hollow of the valley, he dismounted to rearrange something about his pack, and I went on past him with Cherry, and Scatter-Gun on the lead. I half suspected that I would never see the Swede again, but that he would start away across country rather than wait to see how I would work out my malice against him. So I rode into an odd adventure and a dangerous one.

I came up the long and winding road toward Chalmer's Creek, the town, and a rattling of hoofs came clattering up behind me. There was too much noise to make me think of John's having hurried to overtake me. No, he would be well in the rear and without any purpose in coming up with me at all, I had decided. So I looked back and saw a party of half a dozen, rushing their horses along at a fast gallop.

As they came nearer, I pulled Cherry over to the side of the wagon road to give them room to go by, for they made a picturesque outfit. All of them were fairly young. All of them looked big. They wore the wide-brimmed Mexican sombreros. They were equipped with flaring chaps. All of them sat straight in the saddle and looked as though they hardly cared if their ponies jumped into destruction itself at the next stride. There was a fluttering of bright bandannas from around their necks; I heard their shouting and the chiming of many bells, from bridles and spurs and even from stirrups.

They came down about me in a cloud of dust and of chattering noises. I saw the flashing bodies of big, sleek horses. No mustangs in that lot. At least, if it were built upon a mustang base, then the pure thoroughbred blood had been crossed and re-crossed upon the original until there was little or no trace of the foundation stock. They stepped like princes, those horses, as though they were proud of running and yet prouder of the riders who bestrode them. They came about me like a volley from a strange world. I was full of fear and of admiration.

They shot past. Then a tingling cry broke from one of them, and he reined up his horse. He pulled back so hard against the reins that the horse squatted, as though going downhill. In twice its length, from a racing gallop, that horse was halted. Its rider turned it around with a rein so powerful that the horse reared and came down with forehoofs striking at the air. I saw the fear-reddened eyes of that gelding, and the blood-stained froth about its bit told of the Spanish curb and the relentless hand that used it.

I was frightened more than ever by the sight of this, for cruelty makes the most of us tremble first, and only afterwards we feel anger. Then my fear was followed by a feeling of bewilderment that a horse so beautiful should be so rudely treated, for it was a glorious specimen with the legs and the look of speed, standing over plenty of ground with a considerable sunlight between its girth and the road.

Next, I forgot the horse altogether and considered only the rider.

I should like to paint that picture, but even paint would have to leave the action out. I could paint his youth and his pride, his strength and the autocratic way he had about him. I could paint the depth of his chest, and the leanness of his flanks, too, and the suggestion of sinewy strength that fairly looked out of him. But I never could give the right gleam to his blue eyes, or the way his blond hair flickered and flashed as the wind struck it. I never could give that expression of his, which was always varying between a smile and a sneer. But, young as he was, the instant that I saw him, I put him down, with the captain, as a man of extraordinary force of mind and will. I was to meet one other man worthy of a place in that category in this same town of Chalmer's Creek.

"Look here, boys!" called out the big young man. "Here's the very pony for Chiquita. Come and take a look at it."

They had wheeled behind him, as young hawks might follow the leader. As a matter of fact, they were older than he, most of them. One fellow was nearly of middle age. But it was plain that each subordinated himself to this youngster, who could hardly have been more than twenty-two or so.

They came swarming back. The rising breeze caught up the dust their horses raised and knocked it away.

"It's a neat little trick," the leader said again. "What would Chiquita say to it?"

"Chiquita would pretty near sell her soul for it," said one of the others. "It's coming onto three months since she lost the bay mare. And she still ain't found a hoss to fill her eye. Better get it, Stingo."

I'll never forget how that name went home in my mind. "Stingo!" There was a sort of careless slang connotation about the nickname. And he looked the part. There would be sting in this fellow, right enough.

"What do you want for that mare, son?" asked Stingo. He pulled out a thick wallet and tapped it on the pommel of his saddle.

"She's not for sale," I said.

"Come along," said Stingo, smiling at me, with a brilliant flashing of white teeth that changed his looks wonderfully. "Come along and name a price. You've got a second horse to ride. And that mare is a neat trick. I'll pay you a couple of hundred for her."

I smiled in turn. I remembered the captain's price for her, and I knew that he did not think he had spent a penny too much for the mare.

"She cost a whale of a lot more than that," I informed him.

"Oh, four hundred, five hundred, then," said Stingo.

I shook my head again. "I'm not selling her," I said. "She's not for sale."

"Everything's for sale," said Stingo. "Look here. Boost the price. Eight hundred. What do you say?"

I remained unimpressed.

"A thousand, then, fifteen hundred, say," said Stingo.

"Look out, Stingo," said one of his friends. "Don't you go and make such a fool of yourself, even for Chiquita."

"Leave me alone," he snapped over his shoulder. "Fifteen hundred for the mare, boy. Jump down and peel off your saddle."

It was a good, round price. Yet, I suppose that, if he had showed to me a barrel filled with rubies, emeralds, and diamonds, I still would have shaken my head. Cherry meant more to me than money or jewels.

"I wouldn't be selling, sir," I said.

"She belongs to you, does she?" he asked me with a frown.

"Yes."

"Well, what's she good for? She's not much on size."

"She's a good one, though," I said.

"How good?" he snapped impatiently. "I've got to have her. I have a use for her. If she's good, try a race against this brown gelding I'm riding. He's not worth a penny more than five or six hundred. But I'll tell you what. I'll give you a good handicap, and show you that he's better stuff than your mare. What do you say, son? We'll have the race, and, if the gelding beats her, I'll buy her from you anyway . . . at a thousand, say. Is that fair?"

Some of his men swallowed smiles. I could guess from their expression, as well as the legs of that gelding, that the brown was known for a very fair turn of speed. But this appeal had touched my pride to the quick. Of course, I could tell that Cherry appealed to them simply as a pretty pony for a boy or a woman to ride. Dusty as she was, with her quiet, modest way, she did not show off her points. But many a dull-mannered racer has won the large stakes.

The swallowed smiles of the others fairly made me burn. I patted the shoulder of the mare and she lifted her kind head and glanced back at me, as much as to ask a question. Then I saw those long, reaching legs of the other's horse and recognized the sloping shoulders and the powerful, sleek quarters of a speed burner. Yet, as I said, I had faith in Cherry.

Then pride mastered me, choked me. I felt my eyes start, and with a rush of blood to my head I exclaimed: "I'll tell you what, Stingo, if that's your name. I'll race you the mare against a thousand dollars. And a thousand is what was paid for her, and two thousand is nearer to what she's worth."

"Come, come," said Stingo, grinning again, and delighted. "You mean to say there's two thousand dollars' worth in that little trick?"

"There's more of her than she looks," I said, "if you got an eye for a horse."

Stingo shrugged his shoulders. "You name the course, son," he said, "and how much handicap you want." He looked up and down the road, as though measuring distances. But I had no eye for the road, at all. The shining, trembling flanks of that brown gelding looked a little soft to me, as though the big brown were just off a green pasture. But I knew that the mare was hard as iron from the long marches she had made. She was cat-footed—goat-footed—whatever you choose to call it, as well. So I pointed across a mile of rough country to a low hilltop. Every inch of the way was studded with rocks like teeth, and the ground was formed in rough ripples.

"I don't want a handicap," I said. "I'll run you around that knot of trees on the hilltop, and back here. We'll start even."

CHAPTER 25

The moment I had spoken, of course, I regretted what I had said. I felt as though I had imperiled, willingly, my soul, and I was sick at heart.

Stingo, I must stay, hesitated a little. He said to me, kindly: "You're taking a long chance, kid. I tell you beforehand that this nag can move."

"He wants it," said one of the men. "The other hoss is good enough for a brat like him, anyway. And he needs a lesson in manners. This'll take him down a peg or two."

Nevertheless, Stingo persisted: "It's not too late to back out, son."

I wanted to back out, badly enough. But I got down and set about lightening the mare by taking off the pack. Then I unsaddled her and took off one blanket, rubbed down her back, and re-saddled her, giving the cinching a good, strong pull. After that, I hopped into the saddle again.

The men had been standing around watching me at this work. And they laughed and made comments to one another. They suggested that I cut off her tail, because then she'd have less to pull through the wind.

I let them talk. Stingo, on the other hand, said not a word. Neither did he sneer at me nor make any preparations to lighten his own horse, although, as a friend, I would have advised him to. His gelding might be as fast as the wind for all I knew. But two miles across rough going requires more than a mere flash of early speed. It takes stamina and bottom.

Already I started with a big handicap, although not in distance. The saddle on the mare was light. The pack was stripped away. And I myself must have weighed a full sixty pounds less than Stingo. However, these factors didn't appear to bother him. He was as confident as the rising of the sun.

Now I gathered the mare on the reins. Stingo, sitting easily in place, looked across at me. "She doesn't need a bit?" he said.

I shook my head. I was too tremulous with excitement to answer more directly.

The oldest of the lot of men now took a position in front of us and a little to one side. We were to start when he dropped a bandanna from his hand. Yet I looked not at the bandanna but at the horse he was riding. It was one of those picture horses, a pale chestnut stallion of a washy color, to be sure, but with the look of a perfect machine. I could thank heaven that my rival was not on that stallion. I could thank heaven and my luck, because in the first blindness I might have accepted even such a dare as this. This was the pure quill—a thoroughbred made of steel wires and ivory.

Then the bandanna fluttered, and I sent the mare away.

Yes, I fairly threw her off the mark. She was such a sensitive alert creature that she had gathered well before that something was toward, and, the moment I called on her, she nearly jumped out from under me. We went the first 100 yards like the wind. Then, over my shoulder, I saw the tall brown gelding stretching out, with Stingo jockeying it along with perfect horsemanship. For one instant I kept the mare at her pace. And I saw that the gelding did not gain, and knew that the race was mine.

Why, if that leggy brown gelding, when fully put to it, could not gain at the very beginning of a two-mile race, how could it expect to win in the end, over all that rough going? I could have shouted with joy. Then, with the emotions of a cat playing with a mouse, I decided to have my game with big Stingo and his brown gelding.

With a firm, steady pull, speaking softly at her ear, I took off some of the stress of effort with which Cherry was running. At once, her head came up a trifle and her gallop became more of an easy swing.

With this, the brown gelding came up to us, over-hauling us slowly. As it went by, I saw the face of Stingo, grimly set. Not until he was a length away, did he glance over his shoulder, and then I could see a look of surprise and of pleasure commingled.

Well, I chased the mare along behind him.

Half a mile out, the gelding was about three lengths ahead and there I kept it, plugging the mare in that position constantly. If the brown slackened a trifle, we were up to his quarters in no time, and Stingo had to freshen the pace again. So we went until we hit the hill that was crowned with the trees that were our goal.

The gelding, with his reaching stride, ate up the

first half of the slope, then he staggered. Cherry drifted smoothly up beside him, and I saw the fanning out of the gelding's red nostrils. But he went on. He was dead game, in spite of his long legs. However, I pushed him mercilessly up that slope. Cherry, compact as a cat, minded hills not at all. And she was fresh from a long schooling through all sorts of rough going. When the gelding rounded the group of trees at the top of the hills, he was a tired runner, I can tell you.

I gave him no peace. We went down the slope again with a rush, and I let the brown gain a pair of lengths on us. But Cherry was fresh as a swallow in the air. I had to bite my lip to keep from laughing, and gradually I worked my way up toward the leader. At any time I could have made my move. Cherry was ready on the reins, ready as a trigger cocked. But I waited until we were a quarter of a mile from the finish. Then the gelding began to labor. Its head started bobbing. Keeping the mare at the same unaltered pace, gradually, we crawled up and went by. It was a cruel thing to do. I could have let her out, and in ten seconds Stingo could have seen that the race was hopelessly lost and that Cherry was simply loaded with gunpowder.

Instead of that, I chose to steal the race from under his nose. I pretended to be urging Cherry on with heel and hand. But all the while I was steadying and sobering her with my voice. She actually ran with one ear cocked forward and another canted back to listen to me. And so we floated past Stingo.

I saw, rather than heard him curse. I saw his quirt flash in the air like a thin-bladed sword. I saw a red spot leap out cruelly upon the tender flank of the brown gelding. But that good horse had done its best. It could not match my small racer. How quietly and smoothly she pulled away, inch by inch. But I worked the thing so carefully that we were a scant length ahead at the finish, and Stingo kept to the whip all the way.

Those friends of Stingo yelled like maniacs.

One would have thought, to see them, that they all had bet their money upon my chances. But the point was that it gave them a chance to chuckle at the expense of Stingo, and I dare say that everyone likes to point his finger now and then at the man higher up.

I did not want them to suspect how far from blown the mare was, so I jumped down and began to lead her up and down, pretending to work her back gradually into her normal breathing. But there was no need. She was covered with a good sweat, of course, but her breath came as softly and easily as though she were asleep, and it seemed to me as though her eyes twinkled kindly on me, in sympathy with the game that I had played and won.

Stingo acted very well about the thing. He came over and counted into my hand fifty twenty-dollar gold pieces. It seemed to me a ton of wealth. "I didn't think she could do it," he said. "I didn't think that any little rat could possibly have so much in her."

"She's not a rat," I said. "She's all of fifteen hands."

"The mischief she is!" Stingo exclaimed. "I wouldn't put her within an inch of that. But she's made. I can see that. I didn't give her a full look before."

"I dunno," I said, "that I would want to take this money, Mister Stingo. You see, I guess it's not very good for me to begin gambling and things like that."

Stingo backed up half a step. He looked at me with a curiously bright eye. "What are you afraid of?" he asked. "What's the matter with you, son? Are you afraid that I'll want to run one of the other horses against your little mare and try to win my money back? Is that why you don't want to take it?"

I flushed at the insinuation. "It's only the gambling part," I said quietly.

He snapped his fingers. "Come, my lad," he said. "Do you take me for a fool? Gambling, your foot! You know that you're glad of the coin."

"I tell you," I exclaimed, blushing more hotly than ever, "it was only the gambling end that bothered me! I don't know that I've got a right. It wasn't the fear of the horses. I wouldn't be afraid of another race."

"You'd be glad, I suppose," said Stingo, "to match the mare against that stallion, wouldn't you? That chestnut, yonder?"

"I wouldn't care who I matched her against," I said.

Then, with a thunderclap of recollection, I recalled that stallion as it had stood there in the flash of the sunlight, a thing of gold, a thing hardly lacking wings, in my imagination, so fleet did it look to me.

He had turned away. Now he halted sharply. "I don't want you to make a fool of yourself, youngster," he said. "And I don't want to take advantage of you. But do you want to match that mare and the thousand against that stallion and another thousand?"

Hastily I retreated as far as I could. "Not the mare," I said. "But I'll try you for the thousand dollars."

How easy it was to speak of the thousand, so heavy in my hand. How frightful it would have been to wager the mare herself. No, I had taken that risk once, and I never would take it again. But, ah, if I had not run that unlucky race against the stallion, how many a difficulty I would have escaped.

Well, I could hardly tell that then. It seemed as though a current of fate were carrying me along, now, as it had carried me so often in the past.

In five minutes I was facing the start, and near me sat Stingo, no longer upon the brown gelding, but on this lordly chestnut king of stallions.

I may honestly say that at that moment I cared not a whit for the $1,000 that I had given to the stake holder. I cared only for the honor of the good mare. I did not dare to hope that she would win, but, as I patted her neck, I prayed that she might come in close enough to the leader to keep from mockery.

CHAPTER 26

I was prepared to find in the stallion quite another turn of speed. But I cannot say that I was at all prepared for what actually showed.

In fifty yards, I think he put us ten yards behind. In fifty yards that long-bounding stag of a horse dropped us four lengths to the rear. It seemed to me as though Stingo were riding a great ship before a full gale, and I was in a toy boat bobbing in the wake of the greater vessel. My heart fell to the ground like a stone.

I had worshiped Cherry, and some of my worship left me at that moment. I saw that she was crushed, ruined, destroyed in this competition. For a moment, I almost hated her, because she would involve me in her own shame.

Then I saw her eager, lovely head stretched out and the brave pricking of her ears, and she seemed so small, so delicate against the overmastering stride of the stallion that my heart rushed out to her—there were tears in my eyes. Yes! There were tears on my cheeks. I could not see. And she went on by herself, neatly, daintily swerving among the rocks of the course, dipping through the hollows, winging across the rises.

My wits cleared, and my eyes cleared, also, when we were somewhere near the bottom of the midway hill. Then I looked, and well up the slope I saw the lofty stallion striding, his scanty tail streaming behind him straight out in the wind. I admired that horse with a sort of distant worship, then, and I put the mare at the hill at a good round pace, pitching my weight so as to free her climbing muscles the better.

We went up rapidly. I was so intent upon her running that I paid little heed to the stallion ahead of me, but, near the top, I stared and saw to my total bewilderment that we had gained enormously upon the long-legged horse. Yes, we actually were close behind them and now I saw big Stingo jerk his head about and give us a startled glare. What a hope leaped up into my throat!

We gained the top of the hill, we swung around the level of the platform on top of the crest. Then down the return slope we shot. Alas for Cherry! That upward slope had checked the big stallion like a wall. But the distance that he lost in going up the slant, he regained again in sweeping down the same path. That descent added quantities to each of his flinging strides, and Cherry was anchored, drifting far behind. But with all her might, down she came and shot out onto the level.

How far behind? I cannot say. I only know that the distance seemed to me in my agony an infinite thing. I thought of the stallion being pulled up at the finish while poor we were bobbing foolishly down the course. I could foretaste the laughter of the waiting spectators. Then I called to Cherry. I let my pain and my dread get into my voice. A shudder went through her and she leaped ahead. Her ears flattened along her head. Her mane whipped into my face as I crouched low. I knew that she was running with every item of her strength.

I gave her a good pull, to steady and balance her. I felt her sink a little, as the lengthening stride brought her closer to the ground. She flew like an arrow. I exulted in her. Suddenly I felt that the spectators could laugh, but let them laugh if they would; I knew that she was a glorious mare. And if the course were four miles, who could tell? Perhaps they would not laugh, after all. Half a mile from the finish, the stallion seemed running at full speed, full effort, and yet was not gaining on the mare.

I scanned the distance between us repeatedly. No, Cherry was not being dropped behind any longer. She actually was holding her own. There would be no disgrace here, unless suddenly her strength failed her. I remembered what her breeder had said. Her strength would not fail until her heart broke. And a wonder came over me. Clearly she knew exactly what was expected of her. Although I did not call out to her and did not strike her with heel or hand, yet I could feel the fresh efforts and the fresh impulses of her struggles to get forward, exactly as though she were working under the repeated slashings of a whip. Oh, gallant Cherry! Man or beast could not rival you!

I saw big Stingo look back, and his face was dark and stained. Why should he look so dark? Why should he appear so desperate, when the race was so easily his? For the finish was not far ahead and the distance between us was still appalling. Then I noticed what I had not noticed before. That the head of the chestnut stallion was coming up and bobbing a little, like a cork in water, just as the gelding's had done before him.

Was it, then, possible that some ghost of a chance remained? I felt an ache and a strain in my throat. My eyes went half blind. A screeching voice, like the scream of a hawk, rang in my ears and blew over my shoulder. It was my own voice, I knew suddenly. I was yelling like a madman as I leaned above the head of the glorious little mare, and Cherry went on, furiously. A bit of foam flew back through the air. It had traveled from the gaping mouth of the hard-ridden stallion. Clots of turf, cut out by his pounding hoofs, shot into the air and hung there like small birds seen in the distance on a spring morning, above the plowed lands.

Again big Stingo looked back, and I saw his lips move. I saw the whip rise in his hand; I saw it flash downward with a speed that made it disappear to a shimmer in the mid-air. Now there was a plain reason.

It was plain, also, to the five men who waited at the finish. Yes, I could see, even from the distance, the straining forward of these men. I could hear their shouting.

The chestnut answered that whip stroke, and the next and the next. He pulled away for a frantic instant and threw us well behind again, but he gave something out of his last store of strength in the mighty effort. He paid, now, for the way we had hunted him up the hill. He paid as the gelding had paid. Long legs were never meant on horses for hill climbing. He had lasted that stretch, but the elasticity was no longer in fetlocks and knees and iron-hard hocks. And we drove up, up.

I was silent, except for a murmur, and that murmur was at the ear of Cherry. I knew she heard, although my appealing could not wring from her more than her gallant soul and body already were pouring forth.

We put her nose on the hip of the stallion. The finish was close ahead, a wavering line dug into the ground with the heel of a cowpuncher. Men stood on either side of the finish line. Two of them were squatting down, as though to take a better sight of the close finish promised.

But the close finish did not develop.

The fine chestnut had covered his ground in grand time. If that unlucky hill had not been there to sap his speed. But the hill was there, and now he paid all in a lump for the effort that it had cost him, when Cherry chased him so vigorously to the top. His head went up. I saw him stumble. And the next instant Cherry and I shot all alone across the finish. The stallion had stopped to a walk almost as it reached the line.

There was need to walk Cherry up and down this time. Her knees were trembling, her eyes were dull, and the sound of her breathing frightened me. I got the saddle off and the second blanket on her. I was sick with fear that I might have ruined her by such a call upon her nerve force.

However, in a few minutes she was much better. Even when she was at her weariest, she followed me quickly and willingly. Then I offered her a bit of grass I pulled up at the roadside, and, when she nibbled at it, I knew that she would be all right.

Stingo and his friends came up to me.

"She was only packing a feather," said one of the men. "And the kid's a little crook. You can see that. He was only playing with the brown."

Stingo paid no heed to them. He came up to me. Behind him, I could see one of the men working over the chestnut stallion and rubbing him down.

"Here's two thousand that belongs to you," said Stingo, "and you're welcome, son. Only . . . I'll tell you this . . . the next time you play horse-sharper, you're likely to run into trouble. I thought you were what you looked, but you're a professional jockey."

"I'm not," I contradicted. "I never—"

"You never rode a race in your life, before, I suppose?" said Stingo.

"No, sir," I said, "except around the village back home when the boys—"

"What's the name of the village you come from?" asked Stingo. "New York?"

I saw what he meant. He thought I was a crook who had come out West with a ringer to clean up money, betting in the mining camps. I knew that such things had happened before. I would have asked him if he thought a boy of my age would have dared do such a thing, but I no longer looked thirteen. The sun-blackening I had received, and the lean look of my face made me, I suppose, look a good sixteen or seventeen, undersized and just like a jockey. My face was pinched, just as dieting would pinch it and sweatings out.

So I could not say anything back to Stingo, and he rode off with his friends, while I remained behind slowly saddling the mare again and feeling guilty, I knew not why. I had played with the brown gelding, to be sure. But that was a pardonable device, considering the rather overmastering pride of big Stingo.

Well, I saddled and started up the road, and at the very next turn two masked men rode out of a nest of poplars. One of them had a naked Colt in his hand.

"Just pull up, kid," said one of the pair. "Just pull up and tell us where you stole that hoss, will you?"

CHAPTER 27

All of my experience in hunting and in the use of the revolver during the trip with John, the Swede, was pretty fresh in my mind, and, when I heard them speak of the mare and saw in a flash that they intended to take her from me, I actually got a hand as far as the butt of my Colt Special. But there my hand stayed.

I saw one of them jerk up his own gun a trifle to squint for a surer aim, and at the same time the other, who was covering me just as carefully, said: "No funny business, kid! You get man rations, out here!"

I understood that. As a boy, I would have expected a little more gentleness. But they would treat me exactly as they would have treated a grown victim. Well, I had to endure it. I could guess, without much difficulty, that this present pair had seen the running of Cherry, and, therefore, they wanted to have her.

So I fought with myself for a second or so, and

then I followed orders. They had me helplessly in
their hands. I dismounted and backed away, with
my hands above my head.

They fanned me. I mean, they went through my
clothes and took away the gun. One of them admired it and said that he had been looking for just
such an undersized beauty for years, and that he
had a more particular use for it than a bright, honest
lad like me ever could have. When they had me dis-
armed, I was helpless enough. Naturally my bare
hands were no good against the two of them. I
stood by, my hands now allowed down, my heart
breaking.

It seemed to me that all that was true, faithful,
and good in the world was to be found in my mare,
and she was about to be taken away from me. Then I
thought of the Swede, and with the bitterest hatred.
If he had been there, no two men could have pre-
vailed so readily against me. The captain should
hear of what John had done, deserting me and caus-
ing me to lose the mare. But I could not help feeling
a sort of odd, detached interest in the personalities
of the two robbers.

"Well, there she is, Dago," said one of them. "Just
what I told you. The kid ain't spoiled her any."

"You can take my other hoss on the lead," said the
one called Dago.

"I'll ride the mare back, Red."

"Oh, will you?" Red said very softly.

"I don't mind her being played out," said Dago.
"I'll take her along dead easy."

"Will you? But I'd rather ride her. I'm lighter than
you are."

"You're lighter in pounds, but you got a heavier
seat."

"I never heard that said before. My way of thinkin', you ride like a ton of bricks, Dago."

"You don't savvy a real rider," said Dago. "You don't quite understand the ways of a good 'puncher, Red. I'll ride the mare back. Till we got her safely returned to the gent that owns her."

"Who owns her?" I asked bitterly.

"You know, and we know," said Red. "But I'll ride her, Dago. My riding weight'll favor her a good deal, and she looks as though she's had her work cut out for her today."

They stared at one another for a moment. Dago said suddenly: "We'll roll for her, Red. That's the only right way to decide it."

"All right," said Red. "Here's the dice." He brought out a very small leather box and a set of five little dice. "Poker horses," he said.

"Yeah," said the other. "And aces wild."

"That's a go."

They folded a blanket neatly and laid it down on the grass beside the road. Cherry came over to me, hung her head over my shoulder, and looked on. Poor Cherry! I pitied her almost as I pitied myself. I remembered how the captain had warned me. And he had been right. Exactly as he had said, they had taken the mare away from me. I wondered if I might be able to throw myself into the saddle and sprint away. But no. There was something about the manner of these fellows that told me they would shoot straight, with rifles or revolvers, and they had both.

Red had to cast first. He threw a pair of fours and an ace and handed the box to Dago, to beat that throw at the first cast. The Dago rolled two aces and the two treys. So he won. He was so pleased and relieved that I heard him draw a long breath. Then he rolled in his turn and sent out two aces and a six. He handed over the box. He was standing, like Red in the first instance, on the good results of his first roll, but the best that Red could do was to produce three fives.

"All right," said Dago. "She's mine, I guess."

"How d'you get that way?" said Red. "Three nacherel beat three with a wild one in."

Dago chuckled. "You gonna ring in some laws and rules of your own?" he asked.

"Everybody knows that," said Red. "Three nacherel is better than three wild."

"Why, what's the use of having aces wild, then?" said Dago. "Even the kid could see that!"

"Could he?" snapped Red.

I sensed that serious trouble was in the air. The set of Red's shoulders and the forward thrust of his jaw told me that.

"I guess that Red is right," I said to encourage the fight that seemed in the offing.

"There you are!" said Red triumphantly. "I win this horse."

Dago said nothing for a moment, but his breast heaved with righteous indignation.

"You think you'll run it out like that?" he inquired with an ominous softness.

"Right is right," said Red.

"I'll see you blasted," answered Dago.

"You can't blast me!" Red barked. "You ain't man enough."

"I am, though," said Dago.

"You fat-faced fool," cried Red, "I'll take it out of your hide!"

"Back up till you've grooved twenty pounds," advised Dago. "I'm gonna ride the mare."

"Not till you've been salted," said Red.

"What d'you mean?"

"Anything you want me to mean."

"Why, you . . . ," Dago hissed.

Suddenly steel winked in his hand. I saw his draw. I failed to see the move that Red made, but it was the smaller man who fired first. Dago spun half around, his gun exploding high in the air. The revolver dropped from his hand into the deep dust at my feet; I stooped and whipped it up.

There was Dago, still staggering, grasping his right shoulder with his left hand.

He said in an intense whisper of hatred: "You've gone and ruined me, Red. I'll eat your heart one day. You've spoiled my gun arm."

"I wish I'd spoiled your head for you," said Red. "I'll teach you to be a bully, you great lump of nothing. You thought you'd kick me in the face, did you? Now we'll see who rides the mare!" He was shaking with exultation.

I raised the revolver I had picked from the dust. It was a great deal heavier than my own weapon, which I had been practicing with. But my grip was strong enough to draw a bead just over the heart of Red.

"Drop your gun, Red," I ordered. "And stick your hands up. I know who's going to ride the mare."

He froze in mid-air, so to speak. I saw his gun twitch in his hand as the thought of trying a snap shot passed through his mind. But as his hand twitched, my forefinger curled hard over the trigger of the revolver. If it had been as easy in action as the Colt with which I was familiar, Red would have died that instant. But the trigger gave only a little and resisted.

However, Red seemed to see something in my

face as compelling as the muzzle of the gun that was turned on him. He dropped his Colt and slowly dragged his hands upward, as though resisting weights were attached to them.

Dago uttered a savage growl of satisfaction when he saw the tables turned. "Drill him, kid!" he shouted at me. "Don't you trust the dirty little red-headed sneak. Plant him between the eyes."

I wouldn't do that, of course, but I made Red turn his back to me and keep his hands in the air. Then I stepped to where my own revolver lay beside the road. With this in my grip, I felt twice the man that I had been before. I backed up to the head of Cherry.

It was not easy—what remained for me to do. I had to jump into that saddle, and, while I was doing this, Red might turn and snatch a weapon from the road and shoot me into kingdom come. However, the thing had to be attempted. I made a bound, and I landed on her back, and, while I was in the air, I saw Red turn in a flash and reach for his fallen Colt.

A voice cut in from the blue of the sky, as it seemed.

"Drop that gun, Red!"

There I was, settled in the saddle, and Red, half bent over, gun in hand, about to straighten and shoot at me, but the voice had halted him and turned him to stone.

A very good thing for Red that he halted as he did. For yonder, outlined on top of the next hummock as he sat on his horse, Judge, was John, the Swede, a rifle glued against his shoulder while he drew a calm and perfect bead upon Red.

He might have been there for whole minutes, for all the three of us knew. We had had enough to center our attention on ourselves, in the moment preceding.

Red dropped the gun a second time and slowly straightened. "It looks like I've lost the game," he declared.

"Climb on your hosses," said the Swede. "You're gonna take a trip on up to the town, you pair of crooks, that try to jump on a kid. You're gonna take a little rest in the jail up there. It'll do you good and give you a shady rest."

I looked at John with amazement, with admiration, with a sudden and astonishing affection.

He paid no attention to me, but continued: "Even the kids, in our part of the world, they can handle a coupla dozen cheap thugs like you two. You oughta start in all over again and get a better field to work in. You oughta begin on babies in the cradle. You ain't got man-size yet."

That pair of rascals did not answer. They got obediently into their saddles. The shoulder of Dago was running crimson blood as they faced their horses up the road and silently went on before us toward Chalmer's Creek.

CHAPTER 28

"That was pretty good, John. I never will see any-body that'll look so good to me," I said to him as we went up the road. He answered me not a word, but kept his sullen, gloomy face set straight before him. Plainly he hated me as much as ever, and I wondered what had been in his mind. He must have seen all that had happened, keeping well hidden among the rocks. He had lain there with his deadly rifle in readiness to take my part and fulfill his duty to the captain, but there was no affection for me to dictate his attitude.

I wondered if he had not actually wished to see things reduced for me to the last extremity. Then he could intervene and turn the scale in my favor. Because I had come out of the thing fairly well on my own behalf, he was less pleased than ever with me.

I decided that this must be the case. But I had something to do, now, other than to wonder at the behavior of my strange companion. For now we reached the outer extremity of Chalmer's Creek, and the next moment we entered on the winding length of its main street.

It was the right sort of entrance into that wild town. The two of us kept the guilty couple before us, while the blood still ran down the arm and the shoulder of poor Dago to show the world that he had been badly hurt in a fight. They still had their masks on, also. I expected that everyone would turn out to see the sight and that we would be surrounded by an admiring crowd at once. I was set to enjoy the scene, to take a proud part in it, as the boy hero of the adventure.

Instead, we hardly made a ripple in the calm life of the town. When they saw us go by, some of the people gave us merely a passing glance. Others turned around and laughed loudly at the spectacle. There was neither curiosity nor excitement. Suddenly I realized that Chalmer's Creek saw stranger sights than this every week of its existence. Every day, perhaps.

Well, we got the two to the jail, where a deputy sheriff came out in his shirt sleeves, yawning. He carried a riot gun over the bend of his left arm. He was still yawning while he talked to us.

"Get off those masks, boys, and let's have a look at your pretty faces. They think that they're in Turkey. They think that they belong to some damn' harem. We'll write to the sultan and tell him where we picked you up. Don't you worry none, beauties. We'll take pretty good care of you here."

They took off their masks. Dago was a swarthy fellow, young and good-looking. Red was one of those pale, freckled men whose skin is forever blistering and peeling across the nose and the back of the neck. He looked half cooked by the heat of the sun.

"Why, it's Dago and old Red," said the deputy sheriff. "Whacha you been doing, boys? You ain't from a harem, after all, like I thought you was. You just been savin' your complexions from the sun, I guess. Step right in here into the shade, will you? Come along, you two gents, and tell us what you saved these boys from doin'."

We went into the jail. A doctor was called to bandage Dago's hurt, and the Swede and I made depositions. The deputy scrawled out what we said in answer to his questions, and we signed the paper. At least, I signed it, but John had to make his mark. It infuriated him to make that mark. He sweated and turned crimson.

But the deputy merely said: "Not hanging around a school, you been and saved yourself a pile of time, big boy. I wished that I hadn't wasted a couple or ten years under schoolmarms. You two may be needed when the case comes up in court, if it ever gits that far. But maybe the boys'll flock in here some night and give this couple a necktie party. It saves a lot of time and trouble, when they do that, and we don't like to overwork the judge."

I felt sorry for Red and the Dago, when I heard this, but they seemed utterly unconcerned. Dago, while his arm was being dressed, showed not the slightest sign of pain, but talked cheerfully with the doctor. He was a known character.

"What was it for this time?" asked the doctor. "You're lucky that bullet didn't get into the bones of your shoulder, my boy."

"It was a hoss, again," Dago answered. "A little old chestnut mare was what done me up this time."

"How many horses do you need?" asked the doctor rather impatiently. "Haven't you a dozen or so already?"

"I only need the right hoss," said Dago. "And today I nearly got her. But my luck was out, and the kid, here, made a bright play. He got me and Red to knife one another. Red got in the first lick. Different luck, maybe, the next time we have it out."

Red, however, fastened his pale, steady eyes upon me with an animal hatred. He seemed to study me, so that years would be unable to mask me from his relentless pursuit.

"I should've shot the brain right out of your head," he told me. "But I took it easy with you, because you was a kid, and this is where pity lands me. You ain't heard the last of me, kid!"

I was glad to get out of that jail into the white glare of the sun. A dozen people were gathered around Cherry. One man was lifting up her near foreleg and making sure, I suppose, of the soundness of her hoofs. This made me black with fury, and I did a strange thing. To this day I can't account for it, except to remark that I had been for many, many days subjected to the tyranny of the big Swede, and that the strain of the two races, the wagering of my mare, the theft and the recapture of her must have rubbed my nerves thin. I jumped at that curious fellow and slapped him on the shoulder. When he straightened up, I told him to keep his hands off my horse or I'd fix his hands so they would never touch anything again, horse or human.

This man was short, broad, with a face that looked squashed together, as though a weight had been put on his head when he was a baby. He stared at me without winking until I had finished my tirade. Then he smiled a little, slowly, and, turning on his heel, he walked away through the crowd.

Some of them laughed.

"That kid needs bloodletting. He'll get a high

fever, one of these days," said a lanky cowpuncher, who was leaning against the side of the jail and rolling a cigarette.

I realized that I had made a great mistake in addressing the stranger as I had done. I blushed and wished myself 1,000 miles from Chalmer's Creek. Suddenly I ran after the man who had been examining Cherry. I touched his shoulder and he turned quickly. There was a faint, hard grin on his face. I did not need court testimony to tell me that this was a fighting man.

"You come to clean me up, youngster?" he said.

"I've come to tell you I played the fool," I told him. "I've come to tell you that I'm sorry."

His smile changed. His ugly face brightened. "You'll be all right, old son," he said. "Just give yourself time for the second thought. That's all I have to say."

I shook hands with him. He had the grip of a bear and the inside of his hand was horny and callous; a man with a hand like that, I felt, was sure to be an honest laborer. Then I asked him where I could find Judge Hugh Carrol, in Chalmer's Creek, if such a man were still there. He lifted his hand and pointed. Right across the street from the jail, painted across four second-story windows in a frame building, ran the legend:

HUGH CARROL, ATTORNEY-AT-LAW

So I thanked him and went back to big John. He was leaning an elbow against the saddle flap of Judge and waiting for me with his usual sour look.

"Now what, boss?" he said with a sneer as he used the term.

I glanced at him in anger. It seemed to me that enough had happened that day to induce him to treat me a little better than this. But the sourness in that man's nature went clear to the bone. I told him that I was crossing the street to try to speak to Judge Hugh Carrol, and that he was to stay there and watch the four horses.

He nodded, and I went through the crowd across the street, and up the stairs until I found myself outside the Carrol offices. The first door invited me to WALK IN, so I passed inside and found a young chap in a shiny black alpaca office coat, beating a typewriter and frowning over the phraseology of his work. He gave me only a glance and looked down again to finish his sentence.

I told him that I had come to see the judge, but, without glancing up, he said the judge was busy. How long would he be busy? Until he had finished his business!

This hired insolence made me see red. But I had just had a lesson that had to do with fiery tempers, so I went over to a corner table, picked up a pencil, and quickly wrote on a pad of paper that I found lying there:

> *Dear Judge Carrol:*
> *My father used to know you years ago in Chalmer's Creek. You may remember him. He was Hudson Grier. May I talk to you a little bit about him?*
>
> *Donald Grier*

I folded this up and gave it to the man at the typewriter and asked him if he would take it to the judge.

That overbearing puppy tucked my message under some papers and deliberately kept on typewriting for fifteen minutes before he got up, threw me a look of weary contempt, and disappeared through an inner door. He came back almost at once, with a startled look, and said that the judge would see me. Still, he kept his hand on the knob of the inner door for a moment and looked me up and down. "You're Hudson Grier's boy, are you?" he said.

"Yes," I responded.

"I didn't know," he said, by way of an apology. "I used to know your father. I used to see him. He spoke to me a couple of times while he was here." He grinned and nodded, as though this marvelous fact gave him a claim upon my special attention. Then he opened the door, and made me go before him into the office of the judge.

"Mister Donald Grier, Judge," he said, and closed the door with a soft *click* behind my back.

So there I stood in the middle of a biggish room, facing a huge desk behind which sat a huge, fat-faced man. There was a window on either side of him, behind, and through these windows the light glared into my eyes and left the judge somewhat in shadow. But his complexion was such a bright pink that one might say he shone by his own light. He rose out of the shadow as soon as I came in and stretched out a hand toward me.

"This is one of the happiest moments in my life, young man," he said.

CHAPTER 29

When I heard him speak in this hearty manner, I told myself that my long trip was going to be repaid by discoveries that would be worthwhile. I told myself that I must be on the verge of making these discoveries at once. Then I took the hand of the judge and half of my enthusiasm melted away. For the hand was soft, fat, moist, and my hard young fingers sunk deeply into the folded flesh.

He reached across the desk and laid both of those heavy hands upon my shoulders. He beamed upon me. "It's poor Hudson Grier in the flesh," he said. "Sit down, my son. Sit down, my poor boy. Sit down and tell me all about yourself."

I sat down. The warmth of his greeting went a long distance with me. After all, I reflected, men can hardly help it if they become fat. So I sat there and smiled back at the judge and felt a real affection for his kindly face.

He was very fat, indeed. His body bulged a bit on either side, where the arms of his chair constricted it. There were even two thick folds that ran across his forehead and gave him a look of rather ponderous and loose thought, if I may call it that. He had two vastly flowing secondary chins that ebbed down toward his chest. When he smiled, his cheeks moved back in waves. But he glowed with good health and his smile was both friendly and reassuring. I could imagine him as a defending, but never as a prosecuting attorney. Well, the longer I looked upon him, the more he seemed to brighten under my glance, like a harvest moon rising full through the horizon shadows.

"What brought you here, Donald? And where have you been these years? Many a time I've heard your father speak of the boy he left behind him. It was a sad thing to him to have you so far away. A very sad thing. There was a man of heart, though I don't suppose that I need to tell you this, my dear lad." He had a way of running along, in this manner, covering up his questions with answers of his own, and leading to other matters.

I was astonished that anyone should care so much about me, distant as I had been. "I've come out here about him, sir," I said.

"Ah, you've come out here, all the way to Chalmer's Creek," said the judge, "to see about your poor father, my lad? Well, well, well." It seemed to me that his glance shifted just a little way from me toward the door. He went on: "You will want to see the very claim he had, won't you? You've heard of the prosperity of it, of course. Ah, if he could have kept it for you, you would be a rich young lad today, my boy . . . a very rich young lad, indeed, but you understand how it is. The wealth we come upon in our early days, we allow it to slip away easily. We allow it to slip away from us and from our heirs. Although, of course, who would have dreamed that there was so much money in that strike? No, not a one, to be sure. And your poor father least of all."

I began to feel that a mist of words hung between me and him. I said, simply: "I don't care a whit about the claim, sir. I suppose that's in other hands."

"And you're very right," said the judge. "Of course, you're very right. In other hands it is, and you're not one of the babies and the weak wits who cry over spilled milk. The thing being gone, you can forget about it. I see that you are a lad of sense, Donald. I'm delighted with you. But what else should I expect, you being the son of such a father? What else should I expect?" He shook his head. He smiled upon me with more than fatherly affection, I might almost say.

"It's the other thing," I said, lowering my voice to keep it steady. "It's the other thing that I want to know about. I want to find out about the . . . the death of Will Grier."

"Ah, is that it?" said the judge. He blinked rapidly. Then he began to shake his head and his cheeks wobbled like half-set jelly. "Is that it?" he repeated. "Ah, but that's a painful subject, my dear lad. Would it not be better to leave that until you're much older? Yes, ever so much older. You had better wait. Such things come grimly upon young hearts and young minds. I wouldn't want you to be hurt, my dear boy. I would detest seeing you hurt, even at your own request."

I must say, that my hopes fell away, as I listened to him. Yet I had a stable faith in me that my father could never have killed his own brother. I said: "Judge Carrol, I suppose it's true . . . that he really killed Will Grier . . . that my father really killed him, I mean."

He merely sighed and closed his eyes. His vast forehead darkened and wrinkled with pain. At length he said: "Donald, I ask you to remember one thing. Your father was my dearest friend. He was the dearest friend of my youth. We were as one together. It was I who stuck by him to the end. I defended him. I brought the case to a superior court by appeal . . . I struggled to the last for his sake. May I say that my time, my strength, my poor wits, my money I poured out like water in his behalf. And if you ask me to speak of him today, you are asking me to recall a thousand miseries . . . even the miseries of our friendship, so unhappily cut off in its prime. No, no, Donald, do not ask me of him. Not today. Let it be another time."

I was overcome by the emotion with which he spoke. I trembled. I could not speak for a moment. Then I said gravely: "I'll only ask one thing, then. You were his friend. You defended him. Then you knew that he was not guilty?"

He pressed both of his great, fat hands against his face. "Ah, my son," he said at last, lessening the pressure, but still keeping the hands before him, "I know it is true that a lawyer takes an oath not to defend where he is convinced of guilt. But what could I do? My heart bled for my friend. I fought with all my might to save him, but every moment I knew that justice was against him, and that he was as guilty as a man can be."

He lowered his hands. I looked at him with horror and amazement, because upon his cheeks I saw real tears. Grown men could weep? It was a thing to see, but it was not to be believed.

When the judge had regained some control over himself, I was still shaking. He looked at me with a consoling smile and a shake of his head, as much as to say that it was a pity that such things should ever be.

At last I said: "Judge Carrol, you think my father was guilty. It's mighty hard for me to believe that. I've come all this way here to Chalmer's Creek to try to prove that he wasn't guilty. And I can't sort of gather in what you say, all at once. Will you tell me just the way that things happened?"

The judge sighed. One of his sighs was an amazing thing to watch, for it made him close his eyes and swell first his breast and then his cheeks. One sigh was not enough for him, because he would sigh and sigh, as though the soul of him were stifling and gasping for air.

"I can tell you, poor lad, if you must hear . . . and hear you must, I suppose. Better from me than from another. A dreadful thing. A thing not even to be thought on. Yet, after all, it was the second great crime, according to the Bible. Cain raised his hand against Abel his brother. In a fit of madness, I think. And so with your own father. So complete was the darkness of his mind that he himself, afterwards, could not remember that he fired the shot."

"But other people saw it done?" I said.

"Other people? Yes," said the judge. "That is to say, not actually saw it done with the actual eye, but with the eye of the mind it was extremely clear before everyone."

"Oh," I said, "but if no one actually saw and if he himself denied that . . ."

I was on fire with a great hope. The judge merely smiled gently down upon me.

"Ah, my poor lad," he said as he shook his head.

I sank back in my chair. I began to feel tired out, as though I couldn't stand another moment of this interview, but still I had to go on with it. I looked with fascination on the face of this man who knew what I must soon learn.

Then he said: "Shall I tell you from the beginning?"

I nodded. I could not speak.

But suddenly he said: "Why should I tell it all? Why should I give you all the details? Two brothers who have come to hate one another . . . well, that's a sad thing, but a true thing. It happens in this unlucky world of ours. And when one of them threatens the other's life, publicly, what is to be expected when the threatener is found dead at the mine of his brother?"

"Did Will Grier threaten my father's life?" I asked.

"Yes, yes! That was the way of it. Will was a wild, impulsive fellow. Perhaps he was not altogether sound in the brain. Your father had done a great deal for him, from time to time, and Will only became more and more annoying. He had a great weakness. He was too fond of whiskey. To satisfy his thirst, he would take anything that he found at hand and sell it, so that he'd have money to buy the accursed liquor. A dreadful example, my boy, and one which you may keep in mind. By the sad steps of others, we best learn where we may safely base our feet."

"And then?" I pushed. "My father . . . but if Will Grier had threatened him, publicly, then surely he went out to the mine and attacked my father, and it was only self-defense."

Judge Carrol sighed again. Again he smiled down

at me from the height of his great position, his greater wisdom. "Will Grier carried no weapons," he stated. "And he was shot through the brain. Yet one can understand the sudden passion rising in your poor father's brain, when he saw, standing before him, the man who had repeatedly stolen his property from him in order to turn it into poisonous whiskey. The very claim on which he was then working had been stripped of every tool by the madness of Will Grier, and poor Hudson had to come to me for help. I gladly supplied him."

"Ah," I said, "you were a friend to him. You were a real friend to him. You fought for him to the end."

He raised a fat, pudgy hand and pushed the suggestion away from him. "One always does what one can," he commented.

"But you know for sure that my father killed Will Grier?" I asked him.

He nodded. The solemnity of his emotion and of his conviction made him shut his eyes again, and I felt that a door had been shut in my face and that it never would be opened again.

CHAPTER 30

"You're mighty busy, sir," I said, "and, of course, I don't want to take up too much of your time, but..." I stopped speaking as Judge Carrol interposed an uplifted hand.

"Time? Time?" said the judge. "Is there such a thing as time to be mentioned when at last I find the boy of poor Hudson Grier sitting in my office, in the very office, the very chair in which your father sat before you? My time is yours, my thoughts, my best will," said the judge. "Ask me whatever you will."

"Only this," I said. "That there must have been somebody who saw the act."

He started. It was an odd thing to see his eyes open, so that he was looking at me as at a new creature. He did not seem pleased. "What makes you say that there must have been an eyewitness?" he asked. "Who told you that?"

"Why, sir," I said, "how could they have convicted my father and taken his life unless there were the testimony of an eyewitness?"

"All was law, my lad," said the judge, regaining his fluency at once. "All was the perfect process of law, though I fought with all my might to hold up the terrible machine in its progress toward destruction. Yes, I think I can assure you that I secured for your poor father justice, at least. Ah, it's a bitter thing to say, my boy. But the law asks a life for a life. And such it will have."

I shook my head solemnly.

"Why do you shake your head?" he demanded. "Do you doubt what I've just told you?"

"I was only thinking," I explained, "that, if my father was innocent, there are two lives owing, now."

"Come, come," said the judge, with asperity at last. "Are you still considering the possible innocence of your father?"

His tone crushed me, but also it roused a faint feeling of anger and of revolt against him.

"I wish that I could see the place where . . . where Will Grier was killed," I said.

"Merely an old claim up the valley from the town," said the judge. "It wouldn't interest you. Not in the slightest. And now, my lad, I want to take charge of your time here. Chalmer's Creek is not a proper or a safe town for a boy of your age . . . I will get you out of the place as soon as possible."

I broke in: "You don't understand, Judge Carrol. I've ridden nearly three months to get here. I can't turn around and go back. I've got to do something."

"You came here with whom?"

"With a Swede named John, who works for a friend of mine, a mighty wonderful man, Captain Slocum, of Merridan. Captain Slocum let me come on here. He wouldn't have let me come, if he hadn't thought that there was something I might accomplish here. Captain Slocum could hardly be wrong."

The judge spread his big, soft hands on the edge of the desk and smiled at me. "If a man at a distance, who knows nothing of an affair, can judge it as well as a person of some discretion on the spot . . . ," he began, and then broke off, to say with a smile: "I'm glad that you have a friend in this Captain Slocum. I hope that he's well off and well able to assist you through the world?"

"Oh," I said, "he's terribly rich. But the most important thing about him is that he's wonderful. There's nobody like him. But will you tell me, sir, where the claim is . . . the one where Will Grier was killed?"

He hesitated. "I don't like to do it," he stated. "I don't like to allow children to take such gloomy reflections into their minds. However, since you must know, the place is called the Second Chance. Because, do you see, it was the second time that your father worked at it when he first opened the vein. The second chance was the one that paid him . . . and it was while he was working at it that one evening . . . but enough of that. The mine has done quite well . . . it belongs to me at the present."

"Does it, sir?" I said, my mind occupied with other things.

"It was as a fee that your father insisted upon my taking it. I wanted no money. My service to him was a service of love. But he insisted. And if—"

A heavy blow fell upon the outer door of the offices. Then the inner door to the room in which we sat was jerked open by the clerk. He had a frightened face and exclaimed: "Sheriff Lane is here, sir, and old Tom Vickers!"

My friend, the judge, turned crimson. "The old fool," he said. "I wish they'd hang him. I'm tired of helping him."

In the doorway appeared the wavering figure of an elderly man with a weak, foolish face. He never could have been a person of any force, but liquor had melted away the last remains of willpower. He wore thin gray side whiskers. They were partly wet and partly dusty. It looked as though the man had been sleeping in the street.

Behind him came the sheriff. He was a sun-tanned lion of a man. He was roaring.

"I've picked up this guttersnipe for the last time, Carrol!" he declared. "The next time, I'm going to slam him into jail, and I'll slam him so hard that he'll remember it. You can trust that."

"No, Sheriff," said the other man. "You won't put me in. You'll never put me in." He leaned against the side of the door and began to laugh foolishly. His head was unsteady on his shoulders.

"Why won't I jail you?" roared the sheriff.

Vickers continued to laugh in that maudlin way. He pointed a wobbling finger at the judge. "Because the judge, he won't let you," he said.

The judge hurried me out, his heavy hand on my shoulder. "Pitiful case, human derelict, but we must not grudge our charity," said the judge. "Come back soon to talk to me. Come back soon, my dear boy." He took my hand in both of his. He pressed my skinny fingers. He smiled down upon me, and I went on down to the street feeling that the judge was one of the very kindest men in the world. I had a passionate desire to repay him, one day, for the sacrifices that he had made in behalf of my father. I was a sad comfort, too, to consider that my father had been able to make a friend of so good a man.

Now my journey to Chalmer's Creek did not appear quite so foolish. If nothing else, it had put me in touch with Judge Carrol.

I found the Swede with the horses, and nearby was that handsome young fellow, Stingo. A group of his followers was gathered nearby. Apparently he was always attended by satellites. I must say that he shone like a sun through that dingy crowd, what with his good looks and his gaudy clothes. He was telling how he had lost the two races, this day, and he laughed about the thing with the most perfect good nature.

"The kid's a regular jockey," he said, "and he's going to clean up a lot of loose money in this town, boys, unless you look out. Hello, here he is now!"

I walked through the crowd and stood in front of him. "I'm not a jockey," I said. "I told you so before. I give you my word, now."

He put a gloved hand on my shoulder. "It's all right, son," he said. "I don't grudge you the trimming you gave me and the stallion. That's all in the fall of the cards, and I understand how to take my lickings, I hope. No bad feeling on my part. You just came out here for your health, youngster. Isn't that it?"

I saw that there was no use trying to persuade him that I was not a professional, so I went off with John and the four horses.

"Where to?" said John.

I put the thing to him just as I saw it. "If we stay right in the town," I said, "we're going to have trouble, I'm afraid. They've got us spotted as a couple of gamblers. If we go outside of the town, somebody may decide to steal Cherry and do it. What d'you think is best?"

John shrugged his shoulders. His face had no expression in it whatever. "You're the boss, and I'm the servant now," he said.

He would offer no suggestion, no criticism, and I felt the burden of responsibility pretty keenly. However, I decided on camping outside of the town, and we struck out to find a good place. There was no difficulty about that. Down the side of the valley, a dozen little streams went tumbling and all poured into Chalmer's Creek. Along the twisting courses of those tributary brooks were a thousand places where wood and good water were to be had, and half an hour from the town we got what I wanted, a place that was well back into the hills, secluded, and with trees growing in a big grove up to the edge of the twisting brook. There we unsaddled.

"Now what?" said John.

"I've done the camp work for twelve weeks," I told him. "You can start that now. You chop some wood and make down some beds with young boughs. I'm going to get some information."

He started about his work without a word or a murmur, only giving me a dark side glance, while I shifted the saddle I had taken off the back of Cherry and put it on Scatter-Gun. That mean little bronco gave me an ugly five minutes, while he tried to pitch me into the air or scrape me off against one of the trees. Coming out of the desert, he seemed to feel his oats again, but I got him in hand and jogged off up the valley to find the Second Chance.

That was easily done. The first man I met was driving a pair of heavily loaded pack mules up the trail and he looked at me as though I were asking where the sun was to be found in the sky. When I told him that I was a stranger, he pointed to a gulch that stepped back from the main valley like a great axe-cleft among the rocks. I turned in at the mouth of this and found my way blocked by a man with a rifle, sitting on the stump of a felled tree.

"This is the end of the way, boy," he said. "This here is the Second Chance."

It seemed to me strange that he should speak in this manner. "That's where I want to go," I said.

"Yeah, a lot of people do," he said. "But this here is the end of the road."

"Judge Carrol told me that I could see the place," I said.

"Show me a note from him, then," said this guard. "I don't go by his word only. I wouldn't last here half a day, if I did."

I saw that I would have to contrive some maneuver to avoid this obstacle, and began to consult my wits.

CHAPTER 31

I looked about me. The gulch was narrow at the entrance; it widened toward the back. The lofty rock walls jumped up against the sky and at the foot of them stood a huge growth of trees. A good many of these had been cut down, for the work at the mine, I supposed, but still there was a considerable stand of trees. The place was a shadowy pocket in the side of the valley wall.

From behind the trees I could hear the clinking of the jacks on the drill heads. Someone began to shout and wrangle in a huge voice that died away, and the flying echoes died in their turn. The guard was now working off a corner from a cut of chewing tobacco.

"It sounds kind of busy," I said.

"It sounds busy and it is busy," said the guard.

"They take out a lot, I guess," I said.

"They take out a pretty fair lot," said the guard. "Your friend, the judge, I guess he told you how much."

"No, I didn't ask him."

"Well, they've cleared something around a half a million. That's what they've taken out."

The thing jarred on my mind. A half a million! But then I was glad. It showed that the law of compensation was at work, rewarding unselfish generosity, now and then, by a return of hard cash. Yet, it was a great deal of money. I could not help looking back, with some bitterness, to the poverty-stricken years through which I had grown. A tithe of that money would have made me comparatively rich.

"But the man that found the gold and made the strike, then failed and came back, tried again and finally opened up the good vein of it . . . he got no good out of it at all," said the guard.

I looked at that fellow with much attention. "No, I know he didn't," I said. "But then he didn't know how much it was worth."

"No, he didn't know, but he knew that it was good. Your friend, the judge, knew, too, I guess." He laughed in an ugly, sneering way.

"Look here," I said, "I wish you wouldn't say things against the judge."

"Why not, kid?" he said. "D'you like him a lot?"

"He was my father's best friend," I said. "Of course, I like him."

"He never was nobody's best friend," said the guard. "That's my way of looking at it. What did he ever do for your father, the old fat bluff?"

It was a terrible thing for me to hear the judge spoken of in this manner. "He fought to save my father's life in the law courts," I said. I felt my face grow hot, and then cold. "My father was Hudson Grier," I told him. I straightened myself; I would rather have faced a gun than look at anyone now that my identity was out. But the guard was not at all hostile.

"Maybe your father had a bad break," he said. "Anyway, he paid in full. There ain't any reason why you should blush because of him. The law had its way with him. So you're Grier's boy, are you?"

"Yes," I said, "and I wanted to see the place where . . . where Will Grier . . ."

"You come along with me," said the guard. "I'll show you. If you're Hudson Grier's boy, you got a right here, I guess."

He led me back among the trees. We came into a clearing. Just beyond a thin screen of trees, the hammers were raising a din and in the clearing there were some large boulders, scattered here and there. One of these was a great rack with a black surface as smoothly polished as though it had been glass.

"Right at the foot of that, Will Grier was found dead," said my companion.

I looked at the spot with awe. The shadow of a dead body was there in my mind's eye, the face up-turned and white, and the horrible stain of red.

"Now you've seen it," said the guard, "you better get along. It's against orders to let folks come in here."

"What's the matter?" I asked. "Is this a diamond mine, where somebody could pick up a million dollars in two fingers and get away with it? I didn't know that mines were guarded like this one."

"Neither did I," he said. "And why the judge does it, I dunno. There's a lot of things he does that nobody could explain very easy," he went on with a thoughtful nod.

He took me back to the entrance to that small gulch in which the mine was being worked. There he resumed his seat on the stump of a tree.

"And what about the things he does that can't be

explained?" I asked, mildly curious. Now that I was on the spot where the crime had been committed, I wanted to make the most of it, and draw out the guard.

"Nobody's simple," said the other, "when he's got as much money as the judge."

He began to yawn; I saw that he was tired of talking to me, and so I went off and climbed on Scatter-Gun and rode back toward the camp. On the way, I met the old fellow I had seen at the office of the judge, Tom Vickers. He was rigged out like a prospector, with a little burro trudging slowly before him, piled with his pack. By this time, the liquor was out of his system, it appeared; the dust had been brushed from his clothes, and, as he went along, he used a walking stick. He went gloomily, his head down. His walking attitude was a good deal like that of the burro before him. As he came up, I stopped and spoke to him.

"Hello, Mister Vickers," I said.

"Hello to yourself," he said. "Don't hog the trail. Move over and let the burro get by, will you?"

He was so testily ugly that I merely laughed. "You don't know me," I said.

"I'll live without knowin' you, I reckon," he said.

I laughed again. Apparently he was simply a worthless old reprobate. But he was so harmless and so foolish in appearance that he merely amused me.

"Well," I said, remembering the flask of brandy that we carried along with us in the pack as a medicine in case of cramps or a cold or some such trouble, "well, Mister Vickers, you're certainly missing something worthwhile. You're missing a drink of mighty good brandy that you could have if you came with me to my camp."

He rubbed his eyes with the back of his hand, the same gesture pushing back the hat he wore. Then he gave me a good long stare. "Who are you?" he asked.

"Why, I'm a boy, that's all," I said. "And I see that you look pretty thirsty."

"What kind of brandy is that?" he asked me. "No, I can't stop. I've given my word to get out of the valley quick, and get I've got to. There ain't any stopping for me. I'd catch it, if I stopped."

"It's mighty good old Hennessey brandy," I said. I knew it was good, because it came from the captain's stores.

"Hennessey? Hennessey?" he said. He licked his lips, and his watery eyes rolled. He was a contemptible and pitiable old man. I wondered at myself for having attempted to bribe him to come to the camp. But he interested me as a stray dog always interests a boy.

"It's real Hennessey," I said. "We'll spare you one drink."

"Where's your camp?" he asked. "I can't go, though. But where's your camp?"

"It's right up this gully, Mister Vickers," I told him.

He sighed. There was a flash in his dim eye. "Well," he said, "it would hearten me a lot for the trip out. It would make my march a good bit longer, I guess. How far up the gully?"

"Only a step."

"Well, then, hurry along, hurry along," he said, "and show me the way. Now, it seems to me that I'm beginnin' to remember you, son. What man's boy are you? There was a time when boys was raised to be like you, respectful to their elders. Them times is gone, mostly. Hurry on, now."

He babbled along as I went up the gully, and I took him straight to our camp. When John, the Swede, saw the tramp, he reached for his rifle and stood on guard like a soldier. I despised John for doing that. He could have seen that there was no danger in the old wretch I had brought in. Vickers spoke to him politely. The poor old vagabond actually tipped his hat when he saw the size and the sour look of John, with the rifle to finish off the picture. But John said not a word in reply. He just looked at Vickers as though the old man were a bloodthirsty wolf.

I got out the brandy flask and poured two fingers into the top of Vickers's canteen cap. He smelled the drink first. Then he rolled his eyes and gave a little, shaky laugh. Afterward, he tossed off the drink, holding the cup at his mouth for a long moment, while the liquor ran slowly down his throat.

It was so strong that, when he had swallowed it, he put out a hand and leaned against a sapling, made faces of pain, and coughed, then held his shaking, soiled old hand against the base of his throat. Tears stood in his eyes. They were tears of pleasure.

"That's the right stuff," he said. "That's the good old pure quill. A drink like that is worth ten bottles of the swill they sell for red-eye around this neck of the woods. There's only one thing better than a taste of that . . . two tastes is better." He laughed and looked greedily at the flask.

Well, I pitied him a good deal. I had to keep straightening my mouth to keep the sneer out of it, but still I was interested. "Judge Carrol is a great friend of yours, I've heard," I said. I wanted to make conversation in some way.

"Him?" cried the old chap, with a surprising violence. "Friend? He's no friend of mine. He's no friend of nobody! He's a ... a ..." He stopped short. He was panting with the violence of his emotion. This was the second time that I had heard the judge spoken of in a slighting fashion this afternoon. I felt that I ought not to put up with it, considering what the judge had meant to my father and the kind, warm reception that he had given to me.

So I said at once: "Look here, Mister Vickers, how many times has the judge kept you out of the hands of the sheriff?"

"D'you think it's because he loves me?" shouted Vickers, in a foolish rage. "No, no! He don't care anything for me. He hates me. But he's scared! He's scared! He's scared!"

CHAPTER 32

It was a shocking thing to hear the old fellow speak like that, making a movement with his open hand as though he had the judge in the hollow of it and were crushing him.

"You don't mean that," I said. "You don't mean that, Mister Vickers. I guess the judge is one of the finest men."

"Fine, is he? And I don't mean it, don't I?" said Vickers. "What else for should he keep me in money and food and drink and what a man needs? What else should he do that for, if he ain't afraid of me? But what he gives me, it ain't all that I should get, and he knows it and I know it. He knows that I know it, and one day I'm gonna have a reckoning with him, I can tell you. Boy, lemme have another look into that flask, will you?"

I don't know why I complied. I was horrified. I was disgusted. The man was more animal than human. Whatever had been decent about him was gone now, and I didn't believe a word that he said about the judge.

"Well," I said, "you tell that to the Marines. I know something about Judge Carrol. I know that he's a fine man, and I don't want to hear you talk about him any longer. But here's another drink for you."

He took the drink, begging with his eyes for more when I stopped pouring. Then he began to mutter, staring down at the brandy.

"You know something about him, do you?" he mumbled under his breath. "A precious lot that you know, you or any of the rest. But I know! And nary a lick of work will I do in my lifetime. Here's to you, my lad. Good health and good luck to you, always, because you got manners, and you was raised right, not like the unlicked cubs that the world is so filled with nowadays. Here's in your eye, and askin' your name to remember."

"My name is Donald Grier," I said.

He lowered the canteen top with a jerk. "Your name is what?" he said with a gasp.

"Donald Grier," I repeated. "My father was—"

"Hudson Grier!" cried Vickers.

"Yes," I said, "and . . ."

The canteen top dropped to the ground. The brandy spilled across the rocks, and, whirling about with a wailing cry, he fled away down the gully, his hands thrown out before him like a man running through the dark.

There was something frightful in that cry of his. Even the little down-headed burro was startled by it and went scampering like a dog ahead of its master down the trail. Vickers kept on yelling as he ran. Even after he was out of sight, I could hear his voice trailing faintly in the air for some moments.

"Jiminy," I said to John, the Swede. "What d'you make out of that?"

"*Delirium tremens* is all that I make of it," said John. "I've heard 'em before. He'll fall in a fit. That's what'll happen to him. He'll drop in the trail, and he'll have a fit, the old fool, and I hope that he does. I never seen a lower-looking kind of a man."

"If that's right," I said, "let's go after him and try to take some sort of care of him. I guess his mind isn't very good. What could have upset him so much, anyway?"

"Bad nerves and a bad conscience, maybe," said John. "I won't budge a step after him. Why, things like him, they oughta be chloroformed and put out of their lives, painless. They're no good. They're just a drain. Let him go, for all that I care."

I was of two minds about going after the old man. In the first place, I was extremely curious to find out why the mention of the name of Hudson Grier should have put Vickers in such a tremor. In the second place, I did not want to be alone with him in the night, particularly if he were in a frenzy from alcohol. There was something very odd about it, though. I never had heard a human voice such as the screeching sound that he made—nothing ever so curdled my blood. A ghost story at midnight was nothing compared with it.

The evening was now coming on. We built up a small fire and cooked some venison. Those hills must have been combed a thousand times by hunters, but there was never a hunter like the Swede. He had found a trail, and he had run it down in the brief time while I was away looking at the place where Will Grier had been found, a murdered man.

We toasted that venison, each man for himself. It

tasted so extremely good and I was so surprised that John had found it, that I looked at his sour face by the firelight with a sort of affection. I said to him at last: "Look here, John . . . I didn't really thank you this morning. There wasn't hardly a chance."

"Don't thank me," said John, who had finished eating and was beginning to load his pipe. "Don't thank me. There's no good of that. Thank the captain. There's never nothing that I ever wanted to do from liking you, and there never will be, I can tell you."

Well, I sat back and fitted my shoulders against a broad-faced rock, and gave my attention to something more than the Swede. If he had made but half an effort, I think that I should have forgiven and almost forgotten his subtle and long-continued brutalities during the march, but he was like a sullen, wild beast that never forgets.

I watched the gold of the firelight running up the jagged foreheads of the upper rocks and streaking the tree trunks. I watched it running and rippling over the brook and I thought that this was a very wild and beautiful place, but the loneliest in the world and that this was the saddest evening of my existence.

There was no doubt about it. What the judge had said had killed any vestige of hope that remained in my breast. I was fairly sick at heart, for I had to tell myself that my father had deserved the fate that he suffered. Yet all my instinct cried out against this violently.

I wanted to talk. I said: "Listen to me, John. Why do you hate me? What have I ever done to you?"

He stared at me like a dumb beast and made no reply.

So I got up and walked across the patch of the

firelight to get to Cherry. John lifted his head a little and watched me with what was half a sneer and half a scowl. That was too much for me. I turned on him and said: "You'd talk to her, if she'd pay any attention to you. I saw you try to do it. But she had better sense. She wouldn't waste time on you, you square-head!"

There was a good-sized rock beside him. He picked it up with literal murder in his eyes, but I stood there braced, defying him. I knew that he wouldn't throw that rock unless I ran, and I was right.

"You're a coward, too!" I taunted him.

He roared at me suddenly, rage making his articulation as thick as a drunkard's: "D'you think that it's you I fear?"

I knew it was not. It was his terror of the captain. Again I yearned with all my might to find out what the source of the captain's power might be. I gave it up, and, with a snap of my fingers, I turned suddenly away.

That same instant a rifle clanged close by. I saw the finger of red light dart from the muzzle and felt, rather than heard, the sound of the bullet tearing the air beside me. The explosion lifted me as if with its own force. I jumped like a wildcat and landed behind a rock, on my knees, shaking like a feather. The Colt Special was in my hand, and I didn't know how it got there. I had no memory of drawing the thing. But I said to myself: *They're after me. They're after me. I've got to fight back, or they'll murder me.*

Then I heard the jar and grating sound of the feet of a man who was running hard over the rocks and pebbles down the gully. I jumped up from my rock and looked. His head and shoulders loomed up for one instant in the darkness, and then he was gone.

"He meant murder! He meant to kill me, John!" I cried.

John did not answer.

I turned about and saw the big Swede lying in a crumpled heap beside the fire.

It was as though I heard the crash of the explosion again and the whir of the bullet. After a moment, I ran to him. When I called, he did not speak. I laid hold on his arm and shoulder. He was as heavy as lead and as limp as water. My own knees were wobbling so that at first I could do nothing, then I managed to roll him over on his back.

His face was like death. His mouth gaped open. His eyes were half open, too, and looked like the eyes of a fish. There was a frightful slash of red across his face.

"He's dead," I remember saying aloud, quietly and calmly. "John's dead."

Then I got on my knees and lifted the massive, loosely mounted head. I could see, then, what had happened. The bullet had cut through the side of his mouth and gone out at the base of the skull, behind. That same instant, as I told myself that the bullet had cut through his brain, I heard the sound of a faint bubbling. It was his breath choking with the blood that ran down his throat.

"Thank God. Thank God," I heard a voice say. Then I realized that it was my own voice that had spoken.

I struggled and managed to turn him halfway back onto his face again, so that the blood would flow outward. This exposed the gaping hole in the skull, a frightful thing to see. Some fragments of dead leaves and some pine needles stuck to the blood there.

For a moment I could do nothing, think of nothing. I told myself that the finest doctor in the world would possibly be of some help, possibly not. Then my wits came back to me. I got water and washed the skull wound. I turned the loose head a little and washed the mouth a little, too. He was breathing steadily. There was a dull groan in every breath; every fifth or sixth inhalation was a greater and longer groan than the others.

I listened to his heart. It bumped along slowly, I thought, but with a good deal of strength.

He's got no brain, I thought to myself. *He's a wooden head.* I laughed a little at this, and then stopped in horror, disgusted and despising myself because I had been able to be amused at such a time.

Now I made a bandage out of a clean shirt. I had heard that moss made a good pad to place over the mouth of an open wound. So I got a good quantity of that and bound it over the wound at the base of the skull. His groaning stopped, and I told myself that I had eased his pain.

But every moment my nerves were jumping. Every instant I expected another shot to ring out nearby and the death pang to strike through my own brain. Besides, I didn't know what else to do, so I jumped on Cherry's bare back and raced down the gully to get help.

CHAPTER 33

I say that I rushed down the valley on Cherry, but, before I had gone twenty jumps on her, I knew that I was doing the wrong thing. Instead, I turned the mare around and went straight back to the camp. There I found a ghastly specter striding. It was John, the Swede, with his arms cast out before him, his eyes a blank, and the blood upon his face. As I came up, he fell in a heap and lay still. I went to make sure that he was dead, but, when I touched him over the heart, I could feel a slow and faint pulsation.

He was alive, but dying. However, I could not wait there, doing nothing. I started to work like a madman. I cut down and trimmed—in a moment or so—two slender saplings, and fastened across these, from side to side, the Swede's own blanket. Next, I dragged this stretcher over beside John and rolled him onto it. His body was like leaden jelly under my hands. His breathing was a faint, horrible gurgling that I can hardly describe. The thought of it still sickens me.

Now that I had him on the stretcher, the worst part of the job remained. That was to lift up the stretcher and get it fastened to the stirrups. I finally managed that part, taking up the pole ends, one after the other. The last heave was the hardest and nearly broke my back.

Now I had John on a horse litter, of course, and I could start on toward the town. I had Cherry in front because she was as gentle and slow as a human could have been. I had Scatter-Gun behind, because he really was in some awe of me and trembled when I barked at him. The two horses belonging to the Swede I simply left behind me, together with all of the camp equipment. We had no time to pause for that, with every breath of the Swede sounding like his last.

That was a hideous journey, I can tell you. Every time one of the horses stepped short or long to avoid a stone in the way, every time there was a slip or a sign of a stumble, a groan came from John. Midway to the town, he sat bolt upright. I ran to push him back upon the stretcher, and I found him gasping and biting at the air like a dying wolf. I was so frightened that I dared not come near him. I felt that this must be the death struggle and that, if he laid his big hands upon me, he would crush the life out of me in an instant.

At last, he sank back with a sigh that I thought must be his final breath. But it was not. I got John alive into Chalmer's Creek. I expected to find the streets black and deserted, as the streets of Merridan were at this hour. Instead, they were almost more filled than they had been during the day. There were many lights shining, while noise and excitement split the air. I heard music from several places.

Just as I entered the head of the main street, there was a chattering of distant revolver shots, followed by a screeching that I can still find, with a tingle, in the roof of my brain. But that jolly, rough crowd paid no attention to the tragedy that was going on at the other end of the town. Their own end was enough to occupy them, I must admit.

As I got through the first two blocks, I saw two fistfights, a rough-and-tumble, and a Mexican drawing a knife. He would have used it, too, but someone brought down a clubbed rifle butt on his head, and the Mexican dropped into the dust of the street. He was not carried off to justice or a doctor. People simply walked on over him, stumbling, cursing the body they found under their feet.

I had intended to go straight for the judge and get his advice and help. But suddenly I remembered that I did not know where he lived—only where his offices were. So I asked where I could find Judge Carrol.

"In the infernal regions, rolling dice," said the tall fellow of whom I asked this.

I asked another.

"I've got a dying man here!" I shouted at them. "Will you tell me where I can find a doctor?"

A man stepped out of the little crowd that gathered around me, as water gathers above a rock that stop its flow for a little. This fellow said that he was a doctor, and he lifted the bandage. When he saw the hole at the back of John's head, he said: "This one is dead already. He ain't alive. He can't be, unless he's got jelly in his head instead of brains. You better take him to the cemetery. Don't waste your time hunting for a doctor." He did not even replace the bandage as he had found it, but walked on up the street.

The others laughed.

I've heard about the great heart of the Wild West. I've seen that great heart, too. I've tasted the fruits of it. But in Chalmer's Creek the gentler emotion got out of practice, as one might say.

Suddenly a voice called above me: "Is that the boy's father?"

I looked up. From a saddle, looking over the heads of the others, a girl was watching. She was a pretty, bright-eyed thing, all rigged up in a spangled and shining Mexican outfit.

"He's not my father," I told her. "He's just a murdered man. They shot at me, and they happened to hit him. He's not dead, and I can't find out where there's a doctor, or where Judge Carrol lives." I was outraged and desperate.

The girl took command. I never saw such a rude self-reliance and such a fearless way of handling men. She dropped her hold on the reins, and, reaching out, she pulled off the hats of two men and flung them into the street.

"Run get the judge," said the girl to one of them. "You . . . you take him to the doctor's."

These people picked up their hats with wonderful patience. The second one said: "What doctor, Chiquita?"

"Old Doc Cole is the best bet," said the girl. "He'll either kill you or cure you quick, and I guess this poor fellow needs something quick."

She jumped off the horse and stood beside the litter on which the wounded Swede was turning a little from side to side, with a continual moaning. He rolled his eyes, too, in a way that made one think of a beast tormented until it is mad.

"He's stung in the brain, all right," Chiquita said as calm as could be. "I don't know why he's alive even now, but there he is. Nothing but sawdust in that square head, I guess. Start on, boy, will you? Turn down the first lane to the right. Hey, Stingo!"

Stingo himself came bursting through the crowd. He seemed willing to trample down anyone who happened to be in his way. I never saw a rider have such a way in a crowd, and what a crowd that was. Every man was armed; every man was more or less quick on the draw and quick on the trigger. But that fellow Stingo overawed the lot of them. He came through them, parting them the way a plowshare parts the soft ground in the spring. He jumped down beside Chiquita and walked along with her, laughing and cheerful.

"Do something for him!" cried out Chiquita.

"I'm not a preacher," said Stingo. "And a preacher is the only one that can do him any good, now."

"There's no feeling in you . . . you're pretty hard, Stingo."

"I've got sense. I'm not a fool," said Stingo. "Don't be rough with me, Chiquita, except when we're alone, but don't try to make a slave out of me in public."

I admired him a lot, when I heard him say this. It was as though he protested against being upbraided before a crowd that in itself he despised. As he walked along, there was his chin in the air and his eyes on the search, he looked to me like a young prince of evil. The girl herself was a star. I never had seen anyone quite up to her. But, compared with

Stingo, she was nothing at all. She walked in a shadow, you might say.

Stingo picked her up by the elbows and lifted her into her saddle. "How does the pony do?" he asked her.

"Oh, it will step, and that's about all," said Chiquita, shrugging her shoulders. "If only you'd got that mare."

"Hai!" cried out Stingo. "This is the one here and now. This is the one, this is Cherry, and this is the boy." He turned on me. "Sit up in the light. I want to look at you," he said.

He picked me up by the nape of the neck and under one armpit, and actually lifted me to the croup of the girl's horse. I never saw such strength. John, the Swede, was a powerful fellow. But Stingo was an electric charge, as much of it as was wanted for any job that might be at hand. He raised me so easily, at arm's length, that my eyes popped. Withal, he seemed so light-footed that I had a feeling he could jump over a house, if he cared to try it. One could not help a feeling that there were wings on his heels.

When he had me there, where the lamplights flicked at me, Stingo said to Chiquita: "Look at this sawed-off little runt. You wouldn't take him for a professional jockey, would you? Ask him how old he is, Chiquita."

She turned around and asked me. "I'm thirteen," I said.

They both broke into a shout of laughter. I made no argument, because I could see that they were convinced and that everyone else was convinced that I was one of those undergrown lads who might easily be seventeen or eighteen and no larger than I was at that moment. The miseries and the privations of the long march across the desert with John, the Swede, had given me the starved look of the jockey in good training, too.

So I let the pair of them laugh, but now we came to the doctor's house, and Stingo rapped at the door.

We were alone. The crowd had not followed farther than the mouth of the lane, because there was nothing to excite curiosity in the sight of a wounded man. They were on view every day, more or less, in Chalmer's Creek.

A voice roared at us from inside the house: "I ain't at home! Get out of here! I'm away for a day and a night!"

Stingo kicked the door in with one stroke. Then he lifted the Swede out of the litter and carried him inside.

The doctor was approaching the door in his nightshirt, with a rifle under his arm and a lantern in the other hand. He came roaring with rage, threatening to blow the invaders to kingdom come, but, when he saw who it was, he merely growled out: "Oh, it's you, Stingo, is it? You worthless hound. Who's your murdered man this time? Lemme have a look at him. Why, he needs a funeral, and that's about all. No, wait a minute. I think he's got a chance. Who did this?"

"Who did it, boy?" Stingo asked me.

"I don't know," I told him. "But I think that old Vickers could make a pretty good guess about it."

CHAPTER 34

When I said this, they all looked at me. Chiquita said: "You mean Vickers, the old boy that hangs around Judge Carrol? He wouldn't shoot at a squirrel. He'd run if a raccoon looked hard at him. What makes you want to load the blame on him?"

There was a certain gleam in her eyes when she said this, and I saw that my accusation had angered her. To look at that girl, one would have thought that she was all softness and sweetness and coquetry after the warm Mexican nature. She had the look, but she was as cool as flint beneath the surface of the first five minutes. Now I heartily wished that I had not angered her.

The others were almost equally hostile. I said: "I mean that he was at the camp with me and John, this wounded man. When he heard that I was the son of Hudson Grier, he acted like a madman and ran away screaming. That's why I thought he might have had something to do with it. He was the only person who knew where we were camped."

"The son of Hudson Grier?" said the doctor. He came and flashed the lantern in my eyes. "The son of . . ." Suddenly he began making a clucking noise of surprise. "You have the look of him, after all. You have the look. How did this shooting happen? They aimed at you, you say?"

"I was standing up in the firelight. I made a quick turn, and the bullet whistled by me that instant. It knocked over John and the man who did the shooting ran away."

They all watched me for a moment. Then Chiquita said in that quick, sharp way of hers: "He's telling the truth. He's not lying. He didn't lie about the other thing, either, Stingo. He's not more than thirteen years old . . . and he's had troubles of his own."

I looked at her with gratitude. Then the attention shifted away from me to John. He had begun a horrible groaning again, and he was making choking sounds.

Well, I stayed on there with the doctor for two or three hours, helping him to work over John. Stingo remained, too, and Chiquita was the busiest of us all. There were times, particularly when the doctor put some sort of powder inside the mouth of John, that it needed all our hands to master him. He never quite regained his reason that night, but he bellowed like a bull and he fought like a bull. I shall never forget how Stingo took a grip on the hands of the Swede and mastered them, in spite of the frenzy of the wounded man. It was just about all that even Stingo could manage.

As soon as John quieted down and fell into a good sleep, I got out of the house and rode my mare back to the camp to pick up the horses and the other things that had been left behind.

Nothing had been disturbed, as it seemed to me. I made the pack and returned again through the night, with a feeling that ghosts were flying behind me along the trail. I returned to the doctor's house and found him still sitting up beside John. He had the shaded lantern on the table beside him so that no light would strike in the Swede's face; he looked worn out. As he sat there with his sleeves rolled up to the elbows, and a pair of glasses hanging on his knees, he looked like a tired laborer reading the paper at the end of the day. My heart went out to him, in a way.

He gave me only a grunt and a warning to be silent. So I dropped down on a rug near the bed of John and was instantly asleep. It seemed to me that I had barely stretched out, when the bright morning sun hit my eyes and got me to my feet.

The first thing I saw was John propped up a little in the bed on a mass of pillows, his eyes wide open, their expression clear and rational. He gave me such a smile as I never had thought could come on his face. Then he pointed to his throat to indicate that he was told not to try to speak and held out his hand to me. I took it gladly and he gave me a long pressure. We buried the hatchet in that single instant. After all, most of the forgiving was on my side, but boys generally don't hold malice very long.

Then the doctor showed me where there was a swimming hole in the brook behind the house. I went out there and took a plunge that filled me full of electric sparks of cold, and I was not through shivering until my second cup of coffee at his breakfast table. But the plunge and the food waked me up.

Dr. Cole said hardly a word to me. He had a brutal, seamed face and a dissipated look about the eyes. He looked rather like an ex-pugilist, a fellow who had stood a good many blows and returned them with interest, but, although he seemed to scowl, I felt a certain amount of kindness in him.

"I told John what you did for him," he said at last. "And now I'll tell you what you've got to do for yourself. Get out of Chalmer's Creek. That shot was fired to get you. The first shot missed. The second will plug you, surely. They don't miss twice. Not in Chalmer's Creek."

I couldn't go, and I told him so. He made no argument. His attitude was that of a man who speaks his mind once, and then lets the other fellow go his way. But he agreed that he would take care of John, and I paid him for two weeks in advance, which was ninety dollars, and very cheap, at that, considering what food prices were in the Creek.

When I stepped out into the street, afterward, I felt as though I were diving into the cold waters of the brook again, I got so much curious attention, and I could not tell what part of this was merely casual and what part might be from a stalking enemy. But it was plain that I was now known in Chalmer's Creek, what with the race against Stingo's two horses, the attack on me in the camp, and the fact that I was Hudson Grier's son. I regretted being known. I felt, now, that, when I came in, I should have interviewed only Judge Carrol, and maintained a certain privacy.

Well, it was too late now. I went down to the telegraph office. A side line was being built up from the railroad, and the telegraph was already there. So I wrote out on a blank:

Captain Slocum,
Slocum Hill, Merridan
  Shot by night at me wounds John through head,
but he will recover. Have seen Judge Carrol. He
thinks I am on wild-goose chase.

Donald Grier

I paid for the telegram, and, turning away from he desk, I saw a big woman standing in the doorway, almost blotting out the light. I was amazed, for t was Aunt Lizzie, as big as life. The surprise was all on my side, however, for she gave me a sour look and merely said: "Raising Cain here just the same as at home, eh? But they've got a short way with bad men and fools out here."

What an ugly, shrewish nature she had. I could not help blurting out: "What in the world could have brought you out here, Aunt Lizzie, and what are you . . . ?"

"Ask the postman," she said, and marched up to he counter without another glance or word addressed to me.

I went out into the sunlight, a little dazzled by this encounter, and a good deal worried, for I felt that her trip to Chalmer's Creek surely had something to do with me. I had told her, I could remember, that I was coming to this place. What with Aunt Lizzie, the odd behavior of old Vickers, and the shot that had been fired in the dark, I began to feel that forces were at work around me, and that I was in the middle of happenings, whose outcome I could only guess at what they might be.

I went to the office of the judge and had to wait more than an hour before I was admitted. The clerk was polite today and gave me a chair. He even looked as though he would have been glad to open a conversation with me, but dared not attempt it. I sat in the stiff-backed chair, and saw fully half a dozen clients come in after me and succeed in getting in the office of the judge before me. I was very angry and hurt before—at last—I was called.

However, he dismissed my troubles with a bland smile and a gesture. "One of my busy days, full of appointments," he said. "And now, my dear lad, tell me what in the world has been happening? What sort of rumors are these I have been hearing?"

"I've come to tell you about it," I said. "I was missed by a span, last night, or I wouldn't be here to tell you about it."

He raised his big, pink hand, and pointed a forefinger at me. "My dear boy," he said, "let me tell you one thing. You will be safer away from Chalmer's Creek. I know it . . . I feel it in my bones."

"Can you tell me," I said, "why anybody should have it in for me? What have I done?"

He shook his head solemnly. "People don't forget, readily," he said, "in this part of the world. Feuds are passed on from father to son. Remember that your father was a wild, brave, reckless fellow, fond of action, really loving a fight. He made friends. He made enemies, too. In this world it takes as many as a dozen friends to offset a single enemy. One enemy can shoot you through the back. I have enemies myself, Donald. Every honest man is sure to make them in the course of an honest life. And here in Chalmer's Creek, who can tell what hidden enemies you may have, unknown to you yourself? The bullet fired last night . . detestable murderers! . . . is the indubitable proof. I'll tell you what I am ready to do. At noon today, I intend to take you with me on the drive to the railroad. We ought to reach it before night. I want to see you on a train bound toward safety."

As he spoke so solemnly, my hair stood up on my head. I had to swallow once or twice before I could answer him. Then I said: "Well, sir, of course, you know a lot more about these things than I do. But I've another idea. I've an idea that I'm being shot at because I'm the son of Hudson Grier, and because people think that I may be out here to try to get at the truth of the killing of Will Grier. That's why I'm here. And people know it. I may be wrong, but I think that I could get something out of Vickers. I don't know just what."

He stared at me, struck dumb for an instant. "Vickers?" he exclaimed. "That old drunken fool? What in the world could he have to do . . . ?" He stopped. Amazement seemed to throttle him. He actually changed color.

"I don't know," I said. "But I'm going to find old Vickers, or else I'll bust trying. I've got to follow the only trails that seem to be open to me. Vickers is all I know. There's something about him. I don't know what."

The judge stood up. He was in a passion. "Are you young idiot enough," he roared at me, "to put your brains against mine?"

I trembled, but I said: "I've simply got to do the thing that seems right."

"Then," he said, "there's no use in wasting my time. And your danger be on your own head. I've given you the best advice from the bottom of my heart, and you've seen fit to trample on it."

CHAPTER 35

It was a frightful thing to me to be deprived of the support of the judge, his wisdom, and his affection. Somehow, it was impossible for me to excuse myself, to stand up against his denunciation. Before I knew it, I found myself down in the street, feeling very lonely and helpless in a cruel and stern world.

One thing was clear. I could depend upon no one. My hands were bare, as it were. Aside from the judge, everyone to whom I appealed for help might prove a secret enemy. I strolled out from the town to think things over, but every thought returned to one point—I had to find Vickers. There was the only trail for me to follow, and I had better pick it up as soon as possible.

I went back into Chalmer's Creek and started for the doctor's house to make my pack and to get Cherry. I longed to be with her, now that she was again my only friend and companion.

So I went along with my head down, kicking at the dust, hardly seeing where I was going, until I cut across, diagonally, from one corner of a crossing to the next, right on the main street of the town. I was out there in the middle. I remember everything, because of what happened in the next moment, printing the scene like a photograph on my mind.

A big freighter was in the middle of the next block, coming toward me, eight spans of mules lugging at their creaking harness, and the high-wheeled wagon lumbering behind them from chuckhole to chuckhole, with a great groaning of the wagon bed and the running gear. Dust went up in a cloud behind it. The driver walked midway on the right of the team with a long lashed whip curled around his neck. I remember how he uncoiled that whip and popped it at one of the mules, and how the whole team gave a lurch as it heard the pistol shot of the cracking.

Over on the boardwalk in front of the grocery store, there was an old Mexican peddling a big tray of things woven out of horsehair, bridles and such things, that would be likely to catch the eye. In the middle of the block behind me, a young fellow was trying out a new horse, and the horse was just humping its back and getting ready to pitch.

Otherwise, there was nothing close at hand in the street, when from the grocery store a tall man walked out, a man with a small head set on a long, sun-reddened neck, with a very loose bandanna girt about it. He wore two guns that hung extremely low on his thighs. I had heard that men who wished particularly to get a fast draw were apt to wear their guns in that manner. As a matter of fact, I never before had seen a man wearing two guns in a single belt. The contraption looked awkward and foolish, and very heavy.

As he came out, he shouted suddenly: "Blast you, Walker, I've got you now!"

At the same moment, from just behind me, another voice roared: "Clark, you sneak, I'm gonna send you where you'll get free board!"

The next instant, the two-gun man had both his weapons in his hands and fired straight—at me!

I saw the two muzzles jerk upward as the weapons exploded. My hat was knocked forcibly from my head. In my surprise, I stumbled backward and fell flat at the same time that I heard the rapid sound of two shouts fired from behind me, from where the second threat had been bawled.

I heard the bullets, mind you, tear the air just over me. I told myself that I was dead. I lay still as a corpse with fear. Then many voices shouted. People ran out into the street, and, getting back my senses, I heaved myself to one knee, and then stood up.

I found twenty men around me, a very excited lot. They were all shouting out at the same moment. I saw others mounting horses that had been tied to the rack in front of a nearby saloon. Men were calling out that Walker and Clark would have to be caught and given a vigilante trial, because of this thing.

"They've killed the kid," said one.

I looked at him in amazement. He was pointing to my head, and, when I raised my hand, it came away red and wet with blood.

I felt no pain, but suddenly I went sick and loose all over.

Somebody picked me up and ran with me into the saloon. I was stretched out on the bar before I could protest.

"I'm all right," I said. "I guess the bullet just

nicked me when it took my hat off." I could feel the sting of the thing for the first time now, and the surface feeling of that pain told me that there was no real harm done.

They wouldn't listen to me. They kept roaring out and shouting all at the same time, in a fury of excitement. One man got up on a chair and started a tremendous speech, calling on the good citizens to get together, now that the roughs had started in on child murder.

But another man pulled the speaker off the chair. "Don't be a fool," he said. "Clark and Walker have hated each other for six months. I know all about 'em. They couldn't help taking a crack at one another, and they might very well have been blind to the kid that was standing there between them!"

The argument grew hotter. Then someone washed off the side of my head and found that I had received only a scratch. So I was allowed to get to my feet again, and a bandanna was tied around my hurt.

It wasn't the wound that hurt me, now. It was fear that had me turned to ice inside. The judge was right. The doctor was right. I had to get out of that town as fast as I could!

I wanted to go that minute, in fact. As for Vickers—well, let Vickers take care of himself and his memories, whatever they might be. Life seemed mighty sweet to me just then. Cherry, the captain—I wanted to be with them, and to see Charley again and the old town of Merridan, that appeared to my imagination like a paradise.

But I couldn't get free from that crowd until the sheriff came in. They opened up a lane in front of him. And there he stood, fixing me with a cold eye.

"Tell me what you think," he said. "Did they shoot at one another, or did they shoot at you?"

I looked back at the sheriff and wondered what I should say.

"Well," I said, "one of the slugs nicked me. Did they nick each other any?"

The discussion was still going on in corners of the barroom up to that point. I must say that I had reversed my opinion about the indifference of these far Westerners to crime in the streets. They seemed all as hot as could be. Now, when they heard me answer, they fell silent.

The sheriff nodded.

"You're no fool, my boy," he said. "Still, old enemies like that might have forgot all about you being in between. Such things have happened a good many times before today. If the fools would keep their guns inside the leather, they'd surely save the lives of a lot of bystanders."

I thought for a moment. "Sheriff," I said, "did you ever have a snake point his head at you."

"Yes, son," he answered. "What of it?"

"Did you have any doubt that it was you he was pointing at?"

He grinned. The whole room suddenly roared with mirth. One or two men slapped me on the shoulders.

"The kid's all right," said one of them.

Well, I was not flattered. I had something else on my mind.

"If you're right, son," said the sheriff, "this is the meanest, blackest thing that ever happened in Chalmer's Creek, and, I'm afraid that we've had our share!"

"They missed me last night. They came closer today," I said. "That's all I know . . . that, and the fact that the tall fellow with the long, red neck was certainly aiming at me."

"You're sure, are you?"

"Well," I said, "I saw the light on top of the gun barrel shorten to one bright point."

"The kid knows what he's talking about," said one of the bystanders. "The thing's settled. It was a dirty trick planned between Walker and Clark."

"I wish I'd been on hand." The sheriff sighed. "That's just what I wish."

His heart was in his voice, too. He was a fighting man, that sheriff. More power to him and to his kind that fight on the right side.

"I'm going to have Clark and Walker," he told me. Then he added: "Now, Grier, what do you want to do with yourself?"

It was the first time, I think, that I ever had been called by my family name. It should have roused my manhood, but my manhood was gone, for the moment, at least. I said: "I want to go home!"

Suddenly they all shouted with laughter, every man in the room. Some of them laughed until tears came into their eyes. Others got over the spasm soon and tried to shut the others up.

"The poor kid has had enough, and no wonder," said one of them. "He's not the oldest man in the world, I guess."

The sheriff had only smiled a little at my answer. "Do you know why men are trying for your hide in this town?" he asked me.

"I don't know," I said. "Unless there are enemies of my father still around here."

The sheriff answered with an odd, solemn voice, so that the words seemed to boom heavily in my ear even at this distance of time. "Dead men have no enemies. And orphans, they have no enemies, either. Not among men. Among mangy wolves and hyenas, maybe, but not among men."

There was a brief, savage mutter from the others.

One man said: "Tom Perkins was one of the lads that lined out after Walker and Clark."

Another said: "Stingo was there, too."

The sheriff started. "Was Stingo along?" he said.

"Yes. I saw him on his gray."

"Then we'll get one of the pair, at least, living or dead," said the sheriff, with satisfaction in his voice.

"Dead, I'll bet ten to one," said another. "He lined out after Clark, and Clark won't lie down in a fight, not even to Stingo."

"And you want to go home?" repeated the sheriff to me.

"Well," I said, "I'm sort of getting a second wind. Chalmer's Creek maybe is not as hard as I thought. And I've got a job to do that I came a long way for."

"All right," said the sheriff. "You may want to stay, but I've got a mind of my own. You start for the railroad inside of half an hour and you travel till we've got you on board a train bound out."

CHAPTER 36

It was no shock to me to hear the sheriff say I must get out of town. I was glad he took that attitude. I only wanted to get out of the town safely, and to stay out. However, I was not destined to leave Chalmer's Creek so soon. The trouble was that the sheriff could not leave town himself, his hands were too full, and he could not hit upon just the man he wanted in order to send me safely to the railroad. Each day I was told that the next day would see me out of the town, and each day there was a postponement. This went on for a week.

In the meantime, I was given the safest lodging anyone could have asked for—the town jail.

The sheriff said that he could not think of a better place for me. So he fixed up a comfortable cell; that is, he put in a good cot, and he saw to it that I had the best of everything to eat. But he would not let me put a foot outside of the building. He said that Chalmer's Creek was about as hot and worked up over the two attempts upon my life as it could be. It chose to make the thing a matter for communal concern, and, if another person took a shot at me and was not apprehended, the crowd was very likely to lynch the sheriff himself. Even Stingo, it appeared, had failed to get either Walker or Clark. The two men in some clever way had disappeared.

That week in the jail was rather amusing in some respects. In the first place, there was no dull time on my hands. The judge came over twice a day, regularly, and every time he came he brought me something. It might be a bag of fruit, or candy, or a pocket knife, but there was always something in his pockets, so that I loved to see his fat, rosy face approaching down the aisle between the rows of cells. I told him I was sorry that I took him so often from his business, but he said that business must wait on friendship, and that he was ashamed he had lost his temper the other day.

Of course, I forgave him. I really began to love the judge. His one concern was to get me safely away from Chalmer's Creek. He told me, secretly, that he did not have a very high respect for the sheriff, and that he was beginning a private investigation of his own to discover the identity of my enemies.

The doctor also came in nearly every day to report John's progress. The Swede still could not speak, but he was making a wonderful recovery. Dr. Cole said that the bullet had luckily ranged below the brain. He only had heard of one other case like this.

Other people came in, also. Especially there was Stingo. The first time, he wanted to buy Cherry. I had an inspiration. I told him that I would like to lend Cherry to Chiquita while I was in the jail. I felt that if the girl had my mare, she would be safe from theft, because who would dare to steal anything from Stingo's lady? So Stingo thanked me, and the next day Chiquita herself came in with her eyes shining and talked to me about Cherry. It was a pretty sight to watch her. When I whistled, Cherry heard me, outside the jail, and whinnied in answer. She actually went up the jail steps and pawed at the door to get in to me.

I was so pleased that tears came to my eyes. The sheriff opened the door, and Cherry came down the dim aisle, stepping very daintily, and sniffing at the peculiar jail odor. It was a thing to see, I can tell you, when Cherry got to me and gave me a welcome. I was outside that cell in a jiffy and had my arms around her neck. I felt that I hadn't seen her for years.

This greeting made Chiquita a little more sober. She looked at me in a gloomy way, when she said good-bye.

"She's the only horse I've ever ridden," said Chiquita, and went off moping. I suppose her reasoning was that this was the finest animal she'd ever saddled, and that it was clear I would not give her up.

Stingo, Chiquita, the judge, and the doctor were not the only people I saw. There was the sheriff, of course, very crisp and business-like, but kind under it all. Most of all, there were the other prisoners. The second day, the sheriff brought in an outlaw from the western Jental Hills, and of course I saw a good deal of him.

This man had a reputation as a man-killer. Except Stingo, he was the first I had seen of that sort, but he was very different from Stingo, you can be sure. This fellow had put up a terrific fight. He had a bullet through his left shoulder and through his thigh, but he lay in his bunk in the jail and never complained.

They let me in to talk with him. I used to roll and light cigarettes for him. Sometimes I rearranged his bandages and moistened them during the heat of the afternoon.

Whatever I did, he thanked me for it in the softest voice you ever heard. He was small, not more than three or four inches over five feet. He had extremely slender hands and feet like a baby's, and his face was tired-looking and disillusioned. He wore a pair of drooping, pale mustaches, after the old fashion, and altogether he looked the gentlest, kindest, most timid soul in the world. Almost from the first I had glimpses of the man inside him.

He talked to me freely of his life. He gave me the picture of the dreamy little Louisiana town he had grown up in, and how he first came West, and how he went wrong. He told it as simply as could be, and how he had his first fight, and saw his first man die. Then he let me see the frozen winter hills he had ridden over to escape the law, and the blinding bright rocks of the desert where he wandered in the summer, like a half-starved coyote. I asked him if it were not a dreadful life, but, after a moment of thinking, he said that it was not, because it was free. He said that word thrice over, looking past me, at the horizon, and I was greatly impressed.

I spent hours with the outlaw from the hills, but I spent even more time with quite another sort of criminal who was brought in shortly after the man-killer. He was a safe blower, and he had succeeded in blowing the main vault of the Chalmer's Creek bank. He could have gotten away with everything, if it had been in securities, but this was gold dust and gold nuggets and, of course, the weight was frightful. That man, whose name was Jigger Thomp-

on, actually led in two mules and loaded them inside the bank with the loot, and then got away. But
he did not get far. They rode down on him. He tried
to fight them off, but a young chap got behind him
and actually caught him with a rope, like a colt.

Jigger Thompson always carried his head a little
to one side and a little down, and he was always
smiling, as though he had just heard some very
amusing thing. He had the cell next to mine, and he
used to sit close to the bars and murmur to me out of
the corner of his mouth.

He was a bad one, this Jigger. He made no bones
of it. He loved badness. He told me of his thefts, his
crooked gambling, the way he had pushed the
queer, the way he had learned to "read the mind of
any lock," as he expressed it, and some of his greatest feats of safe-blowing, how he ran the mold of
yellow laundry soap, how he boiled down the sticks
of dynamite to get the powerful essence, the soup of
nitroglycerin.

I could have listened to Jigger Thompson forever,
with his tales of escapes, hairbreadth adventures of
all sorts and his sessions in jail. He was forty-five
years old, and he had spent more than twenty years
in prison. I asked him if all criminals usually spent
most of their lives in jail, and he said that they did,
but there were a few exceptions, masterminds, fellows who knew how to disassociate themselves
from the atmosphere of crime the moment that they
had worked a successful venture.

These were my companions during the week I
spent in the jail at Chalmer's Creek. In addition
there were visits from some of the biggest miners,
and everyone wished me well and said that
Chalmer's Creek would see me through or bust.

It was a safe and a pleasant way of spending time. I hardly cared how long I had to remain there. But on the eighth day I received a shock, a surprise that took my breath, when down the cell aisle I saw the tall figure of the captain walking, the captain with his right hand gloved in black, using a walking stick in his left hand.

I wasn't the only one surprised. Jigger Thompson, when he saw, caught hold of the bars like a monkey and gaped, and I heard him murmur: "Great Scott, it's the doctor."

I wondered if the captain had ever been a doctor, and where he could have encountered the yegg. But then there was the jailer, unlocking the door of my cell, there was the captain apparently as stern as a drill sergeant, and there was I, laughing with joy because I could see a glint of kindness in his eye.

He went down the aisle with me. He put a hand around my shoulders and walked with his slow, stalking stride. I wondered if he would recognize Jigger Thompson, and I rather hoped that he would, but Jigger had drawn off into the dimmest corner of his cell and was bending his head down as he rolled a cigarette.

We went into the sheriff's office. The sheriff was rather upset and frowning, and he kept looking the captain over in great suspicion.

"You know this man, my boy?" he asked me several times.

I told him, of course, I knew Captain Slocum, and that I had lived in his house in Merridan. Finally the sheriff said that he felt it would be safe enough to turn me loose in the custody of the stranger. He added some advice. "There are scoundrels in this town who want to murder the boy, Captain Slocum,

advise you to get him out of Chalmer's Creek as
quick as you can."

"You are a kind man," said the captain. "You've
taken good care of my boy for me, but, now that I'm
t hand, I shall try to take care of him in my own
vay. I cannot take him from the town at once. You
nay as well let the others know this. I intend to re-
nain right here, in Chalmer's Creek, until the work
or which Don came here is accomplished."

With that, he cut the conversation short and went
ut of the room with me.

"But," I said, "even if we're to stay here, wouldn't
t be better to pretend to leave?"

"It would be safer," said the captain, "but what I
vant is not safety but a capture."

"They'll surely try at me again," I insisted.

"Of course, they will," said the captain. "You're
he bait, and I hope that I'll be the trap that catches
he tiger before he reaches you."

He said it very calmly. But his words raised a
weat on my forehead, I can tell you.

CHAPTER 37

When I came out from the jail with the captain, saw on the sidewalk, holding a pair of good horses no other person than Ebenezer Grey, but so altered in costume that I never should have known him. H wore the clothes of a regular cowpuncher, and, in spite of his pale face, I must say that he looked a home in them. It was a good deal of a shock to se him make his usual little bow, when he first saw me however, and to feel his glance pass in one quive from my head to my feet, viciously searching me.

It occurred to me, as I walked down the steps o the jail, that perhaps he and his wife, and John, the Swede, expected that they would be the heirs of the captain when he died, but, after I turned up on th scene, this hope of theirs was dimmed.

At any rate, it was an ugly moment for me when realized that the old household hatred was stil alive. Grey led the horses behind us, and the captai went on with me to the hotel. He got a room and or dered some food to be brought up for him. I had al ready lunched. His own meal consisted of milk, cheese, and bread. He ate it at a little unpainted deal table, posted in front of the window. As he ate, he was continually lifting his glance so that it passed over the tangled roofs of the town, out across the town to the dusky green of the pine groves, or the flash of the rocks in the sun.

Something was gathering in the captain; I could not tell exactly its nature, but it was a high excitement. He said very few things to me, while I sat there watching him, and hardly once did he look at me.

First, he asked me how I had got on with the Swede. I told him: "Well enough." At that, he smiled and nodded. I wondered how much he was able to guess at, of the troubles I had had with John.

He asked how I handled a gun. I told him, after a moment of hesitation, that I thought I could shoot quite well with a rifle, but that a revolver was my special fancy. I pulled out the gun, and he told me to take it apart and build it together again. I did as he directed, easily. I had done it fifty times before on the march.

He asked if I had ridden Scatter-Gun and the other mustang. I told him that I could ride them all. Then, as he finished eating, he fell to humming, and drummed away at the table with the long, rapid fingers of his left hand.

Finally, he said: "The wounded hand is much better, Don. I am now able to write almost as well as an eight-year-old child."

I had no answer for the remark. I sat like a stick and waited for something to happen, but I was in no haste about it. I remembered what he had said. I was the bait and the captain, with only one useful hand, was the trap.

"I could have used John," said the captain, after another pause. "The fool got himself put out of the way, but I could have used him. Now tell me everything that has happened since you came here."

I began with the meeting with Stingo on the road and told him everything. I never had a listener with such a passion for detail. He made me describe every horse and every man. I was continually squinting in order to get more mental light on my memories. I got through my account of the judge, the jail, the prisoners I had talked to there. I got down to the very remark I had heard my neighbor yegg make, when he saw the captain coming down the aisle of the jail, referring to him as "the doctor" in such a marked way.

The captain made no answer. All he did was to ask more questions. I think I was talking for two or three hours. Then dusk began to fall. Word came up that Cherry, for which we had sent, had arrived and was waiting with Grey in the street below.

Then the captain said: "It's Vickers. That's the key. It's Vickers that we must have, and now I rather doubt that we'll be able to get at the heart of this little mystery unless we find the man. I don't know. We'll have to work up the trail of Vickers. You stay here in the room. Keep your eyes open and your gun ready. Watch the window. Have the door locked."

He left me with that word, and I sat down in that room with my Colt Special across my knees. I could not rest easily. The moment the captain was gone, I was as nervous as could be. So I spent some time looking at various things in the room, at an old chromo on the wall opposite the window, at the doorknob, even at cracks in the wallpaper, at the tops of the four posts of the bed. This silent practice was a thing that John, the Swede, had believed in; I believed in it, too.

Darkness came down over Chalmer's Creek finally. The lights began to shine up and down the main street, which ran beneath my window, and the uproar began to rise like dust to the sky. I sat, huddled, close to the window and watched. The lamp in the room was not lighted. I had refrained from lighting it because I didn't want to give an extra chance to anyone who wished to peer into the room and take a shot at me. But it was rather grisly business, sitting there in the darkness and waiting for the captain—and the unknown.

In the midst of this waiting, something sighed behind me. I dropped out of my chair as though I had been shot. That was a human sound, that sigh. The breath of it touched the hair of my head. And now I squatted against the wall with the revolver shaking in my hand.

A dim radiance came into the room from the street lights. By that radiance I saw that the door to the hall was open, and yet I knew that with my own hands, not very long before, I had locked and double-locked it. I knew what the sigh was now. It was the sound of the draft, as it blew softly into the room from the hallway. What had entered, more than air? I waited one second, then the doorway grew dark.

Someone stood there.

"Nothing here," said a low voice.

"You fool," said another whisperer, "he's got to be here. Ten thousand bucks says that he's got to be here."

"Take that side . . . I'll take the other side to the window," said the first voice.

They separated. I saw their shadows steal down the wall, fainter than ghosts, one to one side, and one to the other.

Suddenly my voice came into me. I tried to speak a sharp challenge, but the words came whistling out in a screech: "Who's there?"

I didn't wait for an answer. I fired at the man to the left of the door. I fired and heard the bullet crash through the wooden wall. The man jumped like a jack-in-the-box.

A gun exploded; the window glass above me was dashed to splinters, some of which showered down into the room. That shot came from the man who had taken the other side of the room. I saw the red tongue of light that flickered out from his gun and switched my aim to him, firing twice at the shadowy figure.

But I felt that I had missed. The two shapes sprang into the doorway and seemed to stick there for an instant. I fired straight at them, half rising. The moment they started to retreat, my own courage returned and grew instantly hot. The gun steadied in my hand, but, before I could fire again, both of the silhouettes were gone.

Then the chief horror came. A form leaped in through the window behind me. I whirled about, but a hard grip seized my gun hand and mastered it.

"It's I," said the quick, low voice of Grey. And he bounded from me across the room.

I leaned against the wall, my eyes dim with horror, and half numb from the shock I had received when Grey jumped in behind me. I saw him reach the doorway and stumble over something there.

He ran into the hall, but, as a noise of footfalls and shouting swept up through the house, he hurried back, leaned over a vague huddle that I now could make out in front of the doorway, and finally told me to light the lamp.

I managed to do that with a shaking hand, then I turned in time to face a throng of armed men who were pouring excitedly through the doorway, the sheriff at their head. At their feet lay the body of a dead man. Suddenly I knew that one of my bullets had gone home—the one I had fired when the two intruders were jammed that single instant in the doorway. I sank into a chair and fairly wilted.

What followed I did not hear or see very clearly, except that I knew, with an infinite relief, that the captain was again in the room, and that the sheriff was reproaching him bitterly with having abandoned me so soon after he had given his promise that I would be safe in his hands.

I remember, also, that several of the men came over to me. One of them leaned over and put his hands on my shoulders and asked me if I had been hurt. I looked up and told him that I'd only been scared to death. He laughed softly, and so did his companions. There was a growl in that laughter of theirs.

"Poor kid," said the fellow who had asked me the question.

After a time, the sheriff asked me to come and look at the body. My knees sagged when I stood up, but I went and stood over the fallen man. He was a short, squat man with a very broad face and a great seam of a scar running down one cheek, pulling his mouth into a crooked grin.

"Did you ever see him before?" asked the sheriff.

I said that I had not.

"That's Walker," said the sheriff. "There's no

doubt now that he and Clark meant murder when they opened fire the other day. That's Smiling Ned Walker, and a good riddance. But, oh, I wish that the man could live long enough to speak two words and tell us the name of the cur that hired him for this work."

"Aye," said a burly miner. "There wouldn't need to be no process of law, I can tell you."

They picked up the body of Walker. He had been shot through the back and the bullet had pierced his heart. I sickened when I saw the red stain on his coat. However, they picked him up and carried him out and the crowd left with them. In the room remained the captain, Grey, and I. The captain locked the door, while I sank down in the chair and supported my head with both my hands. I was half nauseated in the reaction of overstrung nerves. I realized that the trap had been set, and that I had served as bait for the first time. How many other times would they expect me to serve in the same capacity?

CHAPTER 38

The quiet voice of the captain came to my ears, as he was saying: "You failed me, Grey. I told you what I wanted, and you were not here."

Said Grey: "It was bad luck that beat me. When I swung down from the eaves, my coat caught on a nail. You can see the rip in the cloth right here, and—"

"I don't want explanations. I don't want excuses, and you know it," said the captain. "They might have murdered the boy. It's a strange thing that they didn't murder him. And if a hair of his head had been injured, nothing could have helped you, Grey." This he said without in the least raising his voice, but somehow he conveyed an impression that terrified.

Grey attempted no answer. He only muttered: "Yes, sir."

I raised up my head with an effort and managed to croak out that Grey had come in like a hero, in the midst of the firing, and that he had rushed straight at the enemy, but the captain cut me short with a gesture.

"I don't want your explanations, either," he told me curtly.

I was wounded to the quick by these words. In a way, I felt that I had been quite the hero. I mean to say, I felt that way after the fighting had ended.

The captain began to pace up and down the floor in his usual manner, while Grey stood off at the side, looking straight before him like a soldier at a review. Somehow I could tell that he was reeking with a venomous dislike for me, since it was on my account that he had been so severely reprimanded.

"They should have been in our hands," said the captain several times. "One of them should have been ours, taken alive, and out of him we could have squeezed something. But you failed me, Grey, and I'll never forget it. You're not the man you once were. There was a time when I could rely upon you absolutely. The lad, here, is more of a man than you are."

Grey set his teeth and said nothing. I was almost sorry for him. It seemed to him that he had done a most gallant thing, and I still could not understand how he had managed to come flying in at the window.

"Saddle the horses," said the captain to Grey. "Have them ready at once."

Grey left the room, and the captain went on pacing up and down. Once or twice he looked at his black-gloved right hand.

"No fingers, no fingers," I heard him mutter once. "It's almost like having no soul."

It struck me as odd that a man of such a quiet and studious life should miss, so bitterly, the use of his hand. But then I realized that he wrote a good deal

and, of course, to learn over again with the left hand
was a terrific task, and a nerve-racking one.

Finally he paid me a little attention. "Stand up!"
he said harshly. I rose. "Walk to the door and back."

I did as I was told, sullenly.

"You're nervous," he said. "You're as nervous as a
cat. You were frightened out of your wits, just now."

"Yes," I said, "I was about scared to death. I've
said it before," I added, because I wanted to show
that I had not been attempting to pose as a hero.

"I heard your scream," said the captain, looking
me hard in the eye. "It was like the scream of a girl."

He came up to me, still with the unendurable
glance fixed upon me. "What's in you?" he said.
"Have you the right metal? Are you the right temper? Are you the steel that cuts steel?"

I backed away from him into a corner. "Will you
leave me alone for a little?" I begged. "I'm pretty
sick. I'd like to lie down. It looks to me that I've had
about enough for one day."

"You'd like to lie down, would you?" said the captain. "Did you lie down when John, the Swede, put
pressure on you?"

I suddenly was hot all over with anger. "Captain
Slocum," I said, coming out of my corner, "I almost
think that you told John to treat me the way he did.
Did you?"

"And what if I did?" said the captain curiously,
half sneering.

I came up to him with my hands clenched. I felt,
in that moment, all the brutalities, all the sickening
hardships, the falls from horseback that I had endured during the long march. And was it his fault?

"If you told him to do those things to me," I said,
"I hate you from the bottom of my heart. You can

have back everything that you've given me. I won't have anything more to do with you."

He regarded me with the same probing glance, but finally he said: "You may be of the right stuff, after all. I don't know. Get your hat and come with me. And never speak to me again as you've just spoken now."

"I won't budge for you," I told him. "Not until you let me know whether or not you told John what to do to me on the march."

The captain nodded. "What do you think yourself?" he asked.

I thought back to the march, the cruelties, the hideous brutality of the Swede, those constant torments of the morning ride when I was flung to the ground until the heavens spun and turned black above me. I thought of these things, and then I looked at the lean, hard face and the cold eye of the captain. All at once, I felt my face redden and grow hot.

"No, sir," I said, "I don't think that you could have done it. You wouldn't have thought of such things."

"Thank you," said the captain. "Nevertheless, I knew that John would either break your spirit or make a man of you. I wasn't curious as to the methods he would use. I knew they wouldn't be refined, but that they would be thorough. And if you didn't prove to be the stuff out of which men can be made, of what use would you be to me, my lad? Of what use would you be to anyone, as a matter of fact?"

I listened to him with some wonder, but I kept silent. "If I had the use of my right hand," said the captain, "perhaps this would be a good time to shake hands, Donald?"

"Yes, sir," I said. "It would be a mighty good time.

After this, I won't doubt you, sir. But it was pretty hard on me. I could show you bruises that are still a mighty bright green."

The captain's face grew suddenly longer and sharper. "Do you mean to say that the filthy Swede used his hands on you?" he asked me.

"He never touched me," I was able to say. "He never touched Cherry, either." And I added: "He didn't dare."

The captain suddenly smiled on me. "I'm glad of it, Don," he said. "Now, come along with me. There are things to be done, and we will have to start on them tonight. Already we're late. We may be much too late."

I went down to the street with him. The hall of the hotel and the verandah were thick with men. When we entered, nearly everyone looked in our direction. It was a proud thing for a boy to have grown men look at him the way those fellows looked at me. I saw a youth of fifteen or so standing by the water trough and looking at me as though he would be glad to step into my boots. In fact, I had become one of the town sights by virtue of the accidents that had happened around me.

But I was not feeling proud and gay, I can assure you. I felt about as humble as any boy ever felt in the history of the world. I knew somehow that the captain was going to drag me into a current of action so resistlessly swift and so strongly that I would be whirled along with it at a dizzy pace to some great accomplishment, or disaster.

In the street the three horses were waiting. Cherry was one of them, of course, and I felt a bit better when I had my legs over her back, and her dainty head before me. I sleeked her neck with my hand

and she danced a little, to show me that she was ready to be off.

We went on down the street slowly, nearly everyone looking after us.

"Where are we going, sir?" I said to the captain.

"We're going to take a long chance," said the captain. "Tonight, if all goes well, I'm going to force the issue. Before morning, we'll know the truth of this little affair, or else we'll be laid out in three graves, probably shallow graves, Don." I bit my lip. He went on: "First of all, we're going to call on your friend, Judge Carrol."

"He's not in this direction," I said. "He lives back—"

"He's left town today," said the captain. "When he found out that I had arrived and that you were likely to be in capable and kindly hands, the judge took a day off and went out into the country to his ranch. You've been a great nerve strain on him, my lad."

"Yes, sir," I said, "he seemed to take me pretty much to heart, I admit."

"He's a friend of a sort that one rarely finds twice in a lifetime," said the captain gravely. "He's worried so much about you that he wanted to get out into the fresh air to recuperate."

"He's a mighty kind man," I said.

"Look back," said the captain suddenly. "Look back there to the right-hand corner."

I looked and there I saw Aunt Lizzie standing, her face twisted in an expression of really frightful malevolence as she stared after us. It gave me a shudder to see her.

"Yes," I said. "I've seen her before, but I suppose that you're surprised to see her here?"

"Surprised?" he said. "Not in the slightest. This is

actly where I should expect her to be, considering
ow interested she is in you, Don."

He left me to digest this while we jogged out from
e town and into the darkness of the open country.

"Now," said Captain Slocum to Grey, "do you
now the way? Are you sure of it?"

"Yes, sir," said Grey.

"Then take the lead, and ride hard. Satan himself
ay be after us, for all we know."

CHAPTER 39

No man could have lived up to an order better tha
Grey did on this night. There was a moon up, but
was almost worse than nothing to light the way, fc
every now and again the wind blew a drift of cloud
across it, and there were sharp gusts of rain tha
blinded one and made the trail extremely treacher
ous and slippery. Then the moon would shine ou
again, dazzling bright, and set the rocks and th
trees flashing.

Through this confusing weather, Grey kept up a
hard pace all the way; the captain was behind him
sitting straight and tall in the saddle, a masterfu
horseman, and I was last on Cherry. She made th
going easy for me, cat-footed as she was.

We came onto a sort of natural road, finally, an
thereafter the way was not so difficult. This roa
was the shelving shoulder that dropped from a loft
ridge. It was mostly bare rocks, so that the hoofs c
the horses rang loudly on it, but the rocks wer
smooth, not jagged, and gave a sufficiently goo

oting. This natural road was at times wide and at
nes narrow, according to the windings of the
eam that had cut into the hard rocks and paral-
ed the ridge in its course.

It was a mere brook, but, with time and a rapid
rrent, it had clipped its way down through the
ata bit by bit. In places, it was upward of 100 feet
depth, the cañon of that brook, but the lips of the
rge were only from twenty to fifty feet wide. The
lls went sheer down, and in the bottom we could
ar the hollow and mournful voices of the currents.
range to say, on the farther side of the gorge, trees
ew in dense groves up to the verge of the
ecipice, although on the side where we were rid-
g the rock was as bare as the floor of a house.

I remember that the noise of our horses frightened
e. I was afraid, I don't know why, that we might be
erheard, and, when the captain once or twice
rned sharply in the saddle and looked behind
m, I had an idea that the same thought had oc-
rred to him. Or perhaps he was looking back,
ubled by the thought of the demon who might be
lowing us.

As we went on, the way changed—the gorge of the
ook flattened into a valley filled with big trees,
ove whose tops I had glimpses, when the moon was
ight, of a towering, flat-faced ridge on either side.

Presently Grey halted. As we came up to him, he
id: "Now we're near the place. We'd better go on
refully. Anything is likely to happen from this
int on."

"Do you think that they're keeping extra watch,
st now?" said the captain.

"They're keeping extra watch, of course," said
ey, "because they know that you're here. . . ."

"That will do," said the captain sharply.

"Yes, sir," muttered Grey.

He glanced at me, aside. I wondered what it w
that he had left unfinished, and why extra wate
should be kept because the captain was there? The
was a tingle of curiosity in me. Somehow, I kne
that I was close to the revelation of the mystery.

We went on slowly. After a time, Grey di
mounted and led his horse by the bridle. The ca
tain and I imitated his example. With every step v
took, I felt my breath shortening and my eyes sta
ing. The big trees went up like black-bodied gian
on either side of us; an army might be crouchir
there in secure hiding from us.

The forest ended suddenly. At the very edge of i
found myself looking up a ragged cliff, on the top
which was perched a house. The three of us stoc
there on the verge of the woods and saw the hou
above us grow dim in a cloud shadow and the
show glistening windows under the moon again.

In a quiet voice, the captain said: "That place w
a fort and a castle, once upon a time."

"It still is," said Grey. "And it holds a garrison, toc

"You've brought us to the highest wall of tl
place," said the captain. "Why have you done tha
Grey? Couldn't we get around to the farther side?

"We could," said Grey. "That would need a ha
day's march, though, but the important thing is th
they're not likely to expect us from this side. They
not suspect that the wall is scalable. However, it r
ally isn't a very hard climb."

"Can I manage it with one hand?" said the captai

"Yes," said Grey. "There will be some bad chanc
for you, but you can manage it if you want to tal
the risk."

"I'll take the risk," said the captain. "There's nothing remaining to me in life compared with the importance of this night's work."

Grey looked hard at him, but said nothing.

"Another thing," said the captain. "Before we start, I want to tell you that I know how you've served me, Grey. Not entirely for love, let us say?"

"Perhaps not, sir," Grey said very dryly.

"That being the case," went on the captain, "I'm in a position to offer you a perfect reward for your years of labor. If we carry through this night's work, I am going to make you a free man, Grey. I'll relax every hold that I have over you . . . and I'll set you up in a handsomer manner besides."

I saw the breast of Grey rise and fall, and, although a shadow was on his face, I knew that he was tingling with excitement.

"I know you mean it, sir," he said, and his voice was shaking quite a bit.

"I do mean it," said the captain, "and I hope that this won't upset your nerves. You'll have need for good nerves tonight, Grey, and a cool head and a steady hand."

"After what you've promised," said Grey, "I could walk on the edge of a sword . . . I could tear mountains in two, sir."

"And yet," said the captain, "in certain ways I've not been a bad master."

"In certain ways, sir, you have not," Grey stated, very dry again.

"And do you think," said the captain, "that you'll start an entirely new life, you and the excellent Missus Grey?"

"No, sir," said Grey, "the old life is the one I wish to follow."

"And what will your wife wish to follow?" asked the captain.

"Satan, I suppose," said Grey. "He's usually been her leader."

"Very well," said the captain. "Whatever you wish to do, this night will set you free for it. I give you my word, and I believe you will trust in that, no matter how you feel about me, Grey?"

"Your word," said Grey, "has never been broken. I trust it absolutely."

"Very well, then. We start at once up the wall."

"And the boy?" said Grey.

"He stays here, of course, to hold the horses."

"He stays here, does he?" said Grey. "And we—"

"That will do, Grey," said the captain again.

Grey was silent, but I could feel the edge of his hatred well enough.

"Good-bye, Don," said the captain, and strode forward.

"If it's for my sake, sir . . . ," I began, for I had made very little out of the conversation that I had just overheard.

He silenced me by raising his hand, and the next moment he and Grey were climbing up the face of the cliff.

It looked like a precarious business, but, as a matter of fact, the surface of the rock was very much broken with weathering, and they made excellent progress upward. They had arrived almost at the sloping, heavy foundation wall of the house itself when a rock came rattling down the façade and I saw the captain dangling by his arm. Grey caught hold on him, and in a moment they were climbing once more.

That was too much for me, though. I could not en-

ture it when I saw the captain taking such risks
wholly on my account, as I suspected. So I tied the
horses and started up after them. I kicked off my
shoes before I began, and, with both hand and toe
holds to help me, I gained on them very fast. I saw
them swinging a bit to the side, and working up
toward a projecting corner of the building where a
light gleamed behind a window. A moment later
they disappeared, but I made sure that had been
their goal, so I kept straight on in that direction. After only a moment I had reached the window, where
I had the unspeakable comfort and satisfaction of
hearing the voice of the captain inside.

He was saying, very softly: "We don't want to
harm you. We won't harm you if we can avoid it. But
we want a full statement from you, Vickers."

"About what, sir?" asked Vickers in a whining,
shaken voice.

"You can name the subject, I dare say," said the
captain.

"I don't know what you mean," said Vickers.

I got my head to the level of the window sill now,
and I could look into the room. It was a very naked
place. There was another window opening in the
left-hand wall, and the window niches were very
deep, owing to the extreme thickness of the masonry. The furnishings were simply a little table
with the lamp upon it, a wooden cot in a corner, and
two or three magazines lying scattered about, their
gay covers torn and crumpled and the edges of the
leaves turned by much thumbing.

Vickers had squeezed himself back into a corner
and cowered there. Grey was standing near the
door, and the captain sat at his ease in the chair beside the table.

"You know what I mean," the captain insisted gently.

"I don't. I ain't a mind-reader. I can't guess what you mean, or what you want."

"However, I'll give you only one guess," said the captain, smiling in his terrible, cold way. And I saw Vickers shrink and tremble under that glance. "I give you one guess. Tell me what it is I want to know, Vickers."

Vickers moistened his white lips. "It's about . . . it's about Grier," he said.

"Wonderful," said the captain. "What an excellent guess! You've hit on the thing at once. But which Grier, Vickers?"

"Will Grier," said the old man, trembling more violently than before.

"And what about it?"

"The murder of him," Vickers moaned.

"Good, good," said the captain. "And now you can sit down here at the table and write out the full account."

CHAPTER 40

It fell in so closely with my own suspicion that Vickers was the link that would connect us with the truth about the crime, I fairly glowed with triumph and with a sort of savage expectation. Crouching there outside the window, with my toes worked solidly home in a niche between two of the wall stones, I craned my neck to behold and to listen.

Vickers actually got as far as the table, but a new fit of panic got hold of him, then, and he dropped the pen and wrung his hands.

"He'll kill me," said Vickers. "He'll have me torn to pieces and burned, little by little. There's nothing that he won't do to me, when he finds out."

Grey came over from the door. He laid his hand lightly on the shoulder of Vickers and, as Vickers looked up, said: "Do you think that we'll wait very long for you to make up your mind?" He said it quietly, but Vickers forgot his fears for the future in the terror that Grey's pale face inspired in him.

Vickers began to write at once, and Grey, looking

over his shoulder, read off the sentences as they were written down.

In the beginning there was a little formula of legal phrases in which Vickers swore he was about to tell the truth, the whole truth, and nothing but the truth, and then the body of his statement followed:

I had had a fight with my boss in the Rankin mine, where I was working. I quit the job and walked up the valley toward the Grier mine, because I knew that the Griers were good fellows and that they would be pleasant to work for if they took me on.

When I got to the mouth of the little gulch that the Grier mine stands on, a thunderhead came up across the face of the moon, and all in a moment the gulch was filled with rain roaring down and the thunder cracking. I hurried right on to get into the shelter of the mine, but when I got in among the trees, I saw something that stopped me.

The lightning was on the jump. It was so constant and bright that the moonshine hardly counted, even when the cloud split and the moon shone through. As I came in under the trees, I saw the Grier brothers in the midst of an argument in the clearing. They were so hot that they didn't seem to pay any attention to the storm around them. Finally Will Grier grabbed a gun and seemed about to use it, but Hudson Grier was mighty steady and calmed Will down.

About this time, I noticed that I wasn't the only fellow who was watching the argument. Behind the tree next to mine there was the shadow of a big man, and then, by the gleam of the lightning, I had a flash at the face. It was Carrol, the lawyer. I thought it was kind of spooky that both he and I should be there listening to that same argument.

After a moment, it was plain that Hudson Grier was having his own way in the argument. All at once, Will Grier broke out crying like a little boy and admitted that he was dead wrong, begging Hudson to forgive him. Hudson said that he would and that from that minute there would be no shadow between them.

Just then the lightning went rip, rip through the sky, and the thunder nearly put a hole in my ear. I saw Will Grier fall down on the ground and lie still. I saw Carrol, the lawyer, slipping away from his hiding place. And I saw Hudson Grier look about him like a madman.

Well, that was no place for me. I didn't want to be found there by Hudson Grier when he was looking for the murderer of his brother. So I ran as fast as I could leg it and got clean away. Only once I thought that I saw Hudson Grier dashing along behind me through the darkness.

The next day, Hudson Grier was arrested for the murder of his brother. And his lawyer was his friend, Judge Carrol.

That was so funny that I laughed at it. I could see the way the job had been put up. There was a mine in which three people had shares. There were the two Griers, and there was the judge. So the judge murders one man in a way to put the blame on the other, and he gets the other fellow's share of the mine by defending him in the court!

It was so slick and so well thought out that I could hardly believe it. But all at once I started for the sheriff to tell him exactly the truth of who killed Will Grier. On the way, I passed Judge Carrol on the street, and, when I saw how fat and pink, shining and healthy-looking he was, I couldn't help feeling what a pity it would be that a man like that should be rubbed out. Then, besides, all at once it popped into my head how I could live easy the rest of my life and never work any.

It was a mean thing to think of. I'm not proud of it. But I always was kind of sickly; I don't know why. Something wasn't right inside me, about my liver or something. And I hated the hard work that I had to do to get a living, and I wanted to sit around in the shade for a while and watch the others work.

So I stopped Judge Carrol right there in the street, where there were plenty of people passing and where he wouldn't dare to lay his hands on me or pull a gun. Once a murderer, always a murderer, and I wasn't going to give him his proper chance at me, you can bet. I stopped him and just said: "Did you get pretty wet, last night?"

He shrugged his shoulders and started by me, but all at once he seemed to realize that there was something in what I had said. He turned back and gave me a second look.

"What do you mean?" he asked.

"I mean, there at the Grier mine, in the gulch, during the lightning and thunderstorm," I said.

I thought that he'd pull out a gun and shoot me down, from the look of him, but I was wrong. He hung fire for a minute and began to look a little sick about the gills. Then he said: "Now, Vickers, you're a good fellow, and I see what you want. We'll just come to terms!"

Well, we settled on terms on the spot. I got $100 a month, and I haven't done a lick of work since. But I want to say that life hasn't been so easy. My stom-

ach went back on me, and I had to use stimulants a lot, because nothing else would sit on my stomach very good. Then, along come the time when Hudson Grier was in the death house, waiting to get hanged, and that was a mighty hard time on me, too. But I got through it, because I had given my sacred word of honor to Carrol that I wouldn't tell.

When he came to the end of this strange document, I had barely strength of will to keep from leaping into the room and jumping at his throat. I wanted to choke the life out of him. He had been the murderer of my father almost as much as Judge Carrol.

But what kept me from attacking that weakling and beating him to death was the thought of the judge himself. When I thought of his big, fat, soft, shining face, such a fury came up in me that all of my senses were drowned in the rage.

The memory of my father rushed back across my mind, and love for him and hatred for the scoundrels who had ruined him worked in me at the same moment till it is a wonder that I didn't tumble from the wall.

The captain, having read over the document, signed it below the name of Vickers, and he had Grey sign the paper, also. For my part, I suddenly wondered how Grey had been able to learn so much about Carrol and Vickers during his short stay in Chalmer's Creek. But now I prepared to get down the side of the wall before the captain and Grey should appear at the window. I had been ordered to hold the horses below, and I had not done my duty.

At that moment I had a most frightful shock. As the captain finished folding the confession into a small and compact size, the door of the room soundlessly opened, and a veritable host of rifle barrels were thrust in, as it seemed to me. No, there were only three. But one of them was that same fellow with the long, red neck and the small head who had tried to murder me before this—Clark. Beside him stood that celebrated fighter, Stingo, and there were two other men who I never had seen before.

Most important of all, behind the others, safely to the rear, was the fat, glowing face of Judge Carrol, and beside the judge was my companion from the Chalmer's Creek jail, Jigger Thompson.

Take them all in all, they looked to me like a picture of the end of the world.

CHAPTER 41

was like a charge of infantry, the way those people
ame through the door. The captain and Grey re-
:ted in different ways. The captain jerked the
olded piece of paper that contained the confession
f Vickers behind him and sent it sailing through
ie window just past my head. I saw it flutter down
ke a swooping pigeon out of the air. But my atten-
on was riveted on the room, where I saw Grey pull
vo guns in a flash. But the captain dropped a hand
n his shoulder, and Grey laid his weapons on the
ible before him.

The judge dominated the scene at once. He came
1, pressing past his armed men, and saying: "Very
ell done, Captain Slocum. Very well and snugly
one. This prevents immediate trouble. If your rash
oung friend"—nodding at Grey—"had fired a sin-
le shot, you would both have been dead men."

"So it seems," said the captain, as calm as you
lease. "As it turns out, we have a chance to sit

down. I don't know whether I should invite you to
sit down, or if you should invite me."

"Why, Captain," said the judge, "I dare say that
I'm the host and should do the honors. Sit down, sir.
Since there don't seem to be enough chairs to go
around, sit down and I shall take the other chair.
Your younger friend appears the athletic type, and
you see that flesh is heavy on my bones?"

The scoundrel was perfectly at ease. So was the
captain, I must say. He took out a package of cigarettes and offered them. When they were refused, he
lighted one, and calmly looked through the smoke
at the men before him.

The tenseness had gone out of the air. Two men
guarded the door. Others were posted in the corners. I only wonder that no one occupied the window, thereby probably discovering me. To this day
am astonished that I did not start the descent. In
part, I was afraid that I might betray myself by the
noise I might make in climbing down, and, in part,
curiosity held me there, peeping from time to time
over the sill of the window and listening with all my
ears. Curiosity was a force in me as terribly strong
as the impulse that urges a man to hurl himself from
a height.

Then there was a strange rage in me when I
looked at the face of Judge Carrol. I could not see
enough of that face. The smiling pinkness of it infuriated me, and yet fed a well of poison in me. I
wanted to level a revolver across the window sill
and fire a bullet into his flabby throat and stop that
lying, hypocritical voice forever. That was my
thought.

"So here we are, not all of us complete strangers,

ger Thompson, here, is an old acquaintance of
urs, I believe?"

Jigger Thompson advanced with a grin.

"Why, how do you do, Jigger," said the captain. "I
ought that you were in jail."

"Only takin' a rest," said Jigger. "Mighty glad to
e the doctor again."

"It seems that you have several names, sir," said
e judge, with his oily smile.

"One gathers names, if not moss, in a long and
ling career," said the captain.

"You got the moss, too, I guess. I know something
out your deals, Doctor," said Jigger Thompson,
utside of the ones that I figgered in. There must've
en a hundred grand in that job you done on the
ells Fargo."

"You flatter me, Jigger," said the captain.

Not until he replied this time, did the truth pene-
te me like the thrust of a knife. I almost lost my
ld and fell from the wall. The truth was the cap-
n was a criminal. All at once I could understand
s departures from the town, his long absences, the
ig business" with which the town gossip vaguely
plained his trips. Indeed, everything was clear.
rs. Grey, Grey himself, even John, the Swede, they
re all the criminal subordinates of the captain,
d his rock-strong hold upon them was simply the
mplete knowledge he had concerning them and
e dominance of his more powerful brain.

I was stunned. I clung to my place, gasping for
eath. Here was my fairy tale dissolving into the
ost acrid dust of the commonplace. Yet something
d and wistful in the nature of the captain was un-
rlined. He was not all bad. He had shown me

what he could mean as a friend. Oddly enough
think that after the first shock, I had a greater affe
tion for him than I ever had felt before.

"One picks up trifles, here and there," said tl
captain. "Autolycus was my predecessor, somewh
removed in time."

"What guy was that?" Jigger Thompson asked.

"Interesting man. Sorry you haven't heard abo
him," said the captain. "Sorry, also, that I find you
a hostile camp today, Jigger."

"Well," said Jigger Thompson, "you know tl
way that it is. A gent takes his bread any way that .
finds it, so long as the butter side is up."

"Of course," the captain said. "I was not
proaching you."

Jigger turned to the others with a grin. "I to
you," he said. "Slick, ain't he?"

"Very, very," said the judge. "I only wish, Ca
tain, that you and I could have met under more au
picious circumstances."

"Why, sir," said the captain, "as a matter of fa
I'm afraid that no circumstances, fortunate or othe
wise, could have possibly made us friends."

"Now, what do you mean by that?" asked t
judge.

"Common murderers," said the captain, "I've
ways detested, and robbers of children."

I thought that the judge would die of a stroke
hoped that he would, as I saw him swell and tu
purple.

"Is that your tune?" he said.

"I have no tune for creatures like you, Carrol," t
captain stated in his calm way. "I only have t
truth, more or less naked."

"Listen at him," said Jigger Thompson. "Rare, n't he? I always said that he was rare, didn't I?"

The judge could not speak for a moment, and dur-g that interval I saw Stingo advance a step or so d lean a hand upon the edge of the table. Steadily, iietly he stared at the captain. He looked him up d down. He seemed to be reading a printed page. made me a little sick at heart to see that brilliant llow, with his strength and manhood, enlisted on e side of a villain like the judge. Yet Stingo seemed art from the others, untouchable, far removed by s personal beauty and a sort of gloriously shining ergy. It was as though nothing he did could be an equate or real expression of his mind or soul. Ac-n was to him incidental, purely. But now he found the captain a star worthy of his consideration, d how gravely and deliberately he reviewed the an. He maintained the same unvarying posture nile he stared.

Now the judge recovered himself enough to burst it: "I don't know whether you're mad or a fool!"

"I don't expect you to understand me," said the ptain. "I'm of a different class and above your mprehension, Carrol."

"A thief, a safe-blower, a yegg . . . above my com-ehension," the judge said.

The captain made a judicious pause. "Yes," he id, "quite above it."

The purple grew richer in Carrol's face. "I under-nd," he said. "You see where you are, and you want sting while you can. Well, you can't sting me!"

"I have, though," said the captain. "You have a ick skin, of course, but now you are writhing.)wever, these other people see you for what you

are . . . a fat, vain, mean-hearted cur, Carrol. That
your nature, and all the world sees it. Much mo
than you can ever guess. A hypocrite burns on
once, but then he is consumed to the very bones!"

"Go on," panted Carrol, attempting to smile. "Y
haven't long for it. Go on and talk some more.
amuses me. But you see that I've got the plate
cream, and you've got . . . what you can guess."

"You won't have the plate of cream long," said tl
captain. "There's one outside of your net who w
spoil your game."

"There's nobody outside my net," said Carr
"You lie and you know that you lie!"

"You forget the lad," said the captain.

"You mean the Grier brat?" the judge said.

"That's the boy I mean."

"You mean that a half-fledged little fool like th
will be a difficulty?" exclaimed the judge. "Let n
tell you, Slocum, that I've pulled the wool cor
pletely over his eyes. He believes with all his hea
that I was the greatest friend of his father."

"Let me tell you this," said the captain. "He's a
ready on the verge of the truth. When he hears
he's the mouse that will gnaw your heart, Carrol."

The judge laughed angrily. "If I can handle you
he said, "don't you think that I could handle him?"

"You can't, because you can't handle the asser
bled manpower of Chalmer's Creek," said the ca
tain. "Come, now, Judge. You've lived longer in tl
far West than I have. But you don't understand the
people. You don't really know their hearts. Your tv
contemptible attempts on his life have roused tl
men in Chalmer's Creek. If once they dream th
you're the fellow who hired murderers like Walk
and our friend Clark, yonder . . ."

But Stingo slowly turned. He faced Clark.

"Clark," he said, "did the judge hire you?"

"It's none of your cursed business."

Stingo crossed the room and stood close to the tall man. "Clark," he repeated, "did the judge hire you?"

"Don't pay any attention to him," Carrol declared, writhing uncomfortably in his chair.

But suddenly Clark gave way under the pressure of Stingo's near presence. "Maybe he did," he muttered.

Stingo turned and slowly came back to the central table. He no longer looked at the captain, but at the judge.

"The fellow's out of his head," said Carrol to him. "As a matter of fact . . ."

Stingo raised his hand, and the judge was silent.

"Chiquita was right about you," he said. "She's always right. You're a dog, Carrol."

CHAPTER 42

It was a second stunning blow for me, a stunning blow of joy this time, however. The judge heaved himself out of his chair.

"You know who you're talking to, Stingo?" he demanded. "You know what I mean to you and Chiquita?"

"Yeah. I know," drawled Stingo. "I was just adding it up. You mean poison. That's what you mean. You mean dirty hands. You're a dog!"

"Boys," the judge said with a wonderful calm that showed the strength of his mind, "let Stingo go out of the room. He's lost his head. I know the boy. There's good in him, but his crazy temper gets away from him. Stingo, you can go, safely enough."

"And what if I stay?" Stingo asked.

"Things are going to happen in here that you may not like to watch," said the judge.

"You'll knife the captain and Grey, will you?" Stingo asked.

"What else is coming to them?" demanded the

udge. "They've come here asking for it. They're go-
ng to get what they're after. It's fair. It's the game as
hey're playing it."

Stingo stepped lightly back from the table. In his
ands were two big revolvers. I cannot tell what
movement he made to get them out. They simply
prang into the grip of his fingers. He held them
arelessly, low, hardly hip high. He made no attempt
o draw a bead.

"Stingo!" snapped the judge. "What on earth are
ou up to? What do you mean? Don't you see that
ou're helpless, even if you side with them?"

"I don't know," Stingo said in that same quiet,
houghtful voice. "I think that I'll prefer going down
vith them. But, mind you, I'll be shooting even
vhile I fall."

Well, there was a very definite meaning in that. If
e was shooting while he fell, riddled with bullets,
ther men would be falling, also. He had wedged
imself into a shoulder, so that the entire room was
efore him.

"And you drop first, Judge," he said. "I'll have
ou dead before the party even begins."

Judge Carrol moved slowly backward toward the
oor. He took in the situation. His voice rang sharp
nd high as he said: "No foolishness, boys! Stingo
as lost his mind. Let's get out of here and let him
tew in the same juice that will boil the other two.
3ack up, friends!"

He reached the door. The others surged after him.
\s the door closed, I heard him shout in a sudden
renzy of rage and excitement: "Get into the two cor-
er rooms! Then sweep the walls under the tower.
Ve've got them like rats, and we'll eat them by de-
rees, and Stingo with the rest!"

That was clear enough. To either side, I could see the windows that commanded the face of the tower wall. And that moment I began to climb down with a frantic haste.

I saw something above me, as I went down. It was the silhouette of a man's head, leaning out the window, and I thought that it was the head and the shoulders of Captain Slocum. Then a rifle rang from a side window and the head of the captain disappeared.

This showed that they were watching the window and not looking far down the wall to where I descended. I began to have more than a ghost of a hope that I might escape. So down I went, biting my lips in a desperate haste, cutting the skin from fingers and toes as I gripped the rough masonry, and then the rough surface of the cliff below.

A blinding shower of rain passed over. Through it I could hear the regular explosion of guns above me, and I could guess that the besiegers were keeping up a steady fire upon the window through which alone, the besieged might escape.

The shower passed. As the moon came out in a silver flood, I looked down and saw that the base of the rock was not twenty feet below me. Joy and surety filled me; in another moment I would be on the back of Cherry and flying toward Chalmer's Creek to bring all the armed succor that would follow me back to the scene of action.

Then something struck down through me. It pierced my left shoulder and angled across my back. It struck me with the weight of a hammer. I felt, I actually heard bones break inside me, as my grip was torn from the crevice where I held and I rolled limply to the bottom of the rock. I lay there as dead

Another bullet struck by my head and cast a shower of stinging sand and gravel in my face.

This spurred me to get to my hands and knees. I crawled toward the shadow of the trees, dizzy and sick. Another rifle bullet cut through my left thigh, turning it numb and dropping me on my face again. The whole heavens seemed roaring above me with gunfire; bullets struck in a noisy shower all about me.

But it is not easy to strike a mark when one shoots down from a height. I got to my hands and knees and crawled safely to the shelter of the blackness under the trees.

A shameful moment followed for me. I was hurt beyond belief. I knew that I was going to die, and, like a weakling, I got to Cherry and fell flat, threw my arms around her slender, iron-hard forelegs, and lay there sobbing like a baby, twisting and writhing in my agony.

Then I felt the hot breath of the mare puffing down my neck and my back as she sniffed at me, and somehow a sort of shame came into me and gave me a kind of strength.

I felt my wounded leg as I sat up. It was wet with running blood. So I tore off my clothes—literally tore them off, and, out of half my shirt, I made a bandage and wound it tight about my thigh. In a patch of moonshine that shimmered through the leaves, I saw the pulsing flow of the blood die away. So much for that.

The nauseating ache that filled my body and my soul was not from the thigh wound. That was a stabbing-knife pain. The other was the deadly matter, from the bullet that had struck my shoulder and ranged sideways across my body. With my hand I felt the naked small of my back. There was very little blood trickling.

I remember thinking that the men from the house of Carrol would soon be down to stamp the last spark of life out of my body. Meanwhile, my heart and my lungs, at least, had not been touched by the first rifle shot. There was a ghost of a chance in flight. There was none in staying writhing on the ground where I had fallen.

So I got up, untethered Cherry, and dragged myself upon her back. Sickness, faintness swept over me, but my feet were lodged in the stirrups at last. I reined Cherry through the woods and down the trail. At the same time, I heard riders calling to one another and sweeping behind me down the same trail—sweeping at a gallop, in spite of the dimness of the trail, and its rocky, root-encumbered earth.

So I called to Cherry. As she swept away in a gallop, she lurched, and this bent me back and seemed to break me in two just above the hips. I shall never forget that blinding pain, nor how the red sparks flew out across my sight. Only gradually, my hands pulling at the pommel, my teeth set, did I manage to pull myself erect and, just as I came upright, a branch struck me full in the face and knocked me completely down again.

I should have fainted then, I dare say. Only some miracle supported me, chiefly the miracle of fear that galloped behind me, sliding through the patches of moonshine that fell down between the trees. As I lay sprawling back, I turned my head in my pain and saw them coming like demons behind me, four riders at full speed.

So I pulled myself erect a second time, and then slumped forward over the pommel and called on

Cherry in a gasping voice. Ah, what an answer she made! There was no hand on the reins to check her as she raced. She had to choose her way, and she chose the right way, the way by which she had come to that place.

The pursuing noises dropped away from me. But, the instant that they diminished, the frightful pain struck up into my brain from my wounded body. Only terror could compete with that agony.

Gunfire sounded behind me, single shots, repeated. They were signals, I knew, for no bullets crackled through the branches above my head. What signals? I hardly cared. My brain was numbed. Otherwise, I should have halted Cherry and slipped to the ground and lain flat there, but I could only think of one thing at a time, and what mastered me then was the problem of keeping erect in a saddle slippery with blood.

We left the trees. We bolted out under the bright, cruel light of the naked moon, and the wind clipped sharp and cold through my body. I had thought that I had endured all the pain that the body could suffer, but biting wind found new corners of my being to torture.

We fled on, and the way before me was an infinite distance. Each stride meant a new pulse of suffering. How many strides to Chalmer's Creek?

We turned a corner and before me I saw the answer to the gun signals that I had heard to the rear. Three men were jogging toward me, their rifles balanced across the pommels of their saddles. When they saw me coming, bloodstained, half naked, I heard them shout. The leader threw up his hand, commanding me to stop.

I should have stopped, if I had been in my right

wits. But fear is the great master. No sane creature would have thought of attempting to escape, no sane creature except a hero, and a hero I was not. But when I saw the three, and their ready rifles, I did not even pause. I turned Cherry to the side and drove her straight at the chasm that I have described before, the gorge that hemmed that natural road against the side of the cliff.

I remember how Cherry saw the thing and chopped her stride, shortening it, until I screamed out in my agony to her. Her ears went back, when she heard me. She shuddered through all her beautiful body, and then, pricking her ears forward, she dashed forward straight at the jump.

As out of a great distance, I heard the horrified shout of the three who had blocked my way. They did not fire. They left the chasm to do their work and gather me in.

That gulf opened before me as we raced up. It seemed infinitely wide. Hardly a bird, I felt, could have winged across it, and the mournful voice of the waters beneath welled up into my ears. Then I slanted my body forward, ready to be dashed to my death, and Cherry, gathering herself mightily, flung high up and forward above the abyss. Beneath me, I saw the glint of the water. The moon struck its flat face to silver, and here and there white lips were curling and snarling about the rocks. Then came a shock that almost cast me from the saddle. We had struck the opposite rim of the ravine! There we hung one dreadful instant, poised between life and death, before Cherry gathered herself once more and clawed her way to the easy slope beyond.

The horrified yells of the three men had died out. Shouts of astonishment followed. Then, as we drove

nto the sacred and sheltering darkness beneath the
rees, bullets began to crackle like fire through the
branches.

Not one of them struck us. The suddenness of the
hing, which it has taken so many words to describe,
had put those marksmen off balance, so to speak,
and in a moment we were away, and galloping
hrough the shadows of the woods. For the very first
ime in the ride a real hope came to me. Not that my
suffering was less, but that I felt the kind fates
would not bring me through so much in order to
dash me down in failure at the end of the effort.

But I still was far from my goal, and the stream
hat I had leaped would have to be crossed farther
down. Might not the three horsemen speed down
he bank and cut me off from Chalmer's Creek?
Aye, unless Cherry could outdistance them. She
had dropped one party of pursuers before. She
might drop these as well. So I called on her, and
she responded.

We raced on the verge of the trees. I saw the gorge
of the stream widen into a valley, and far back, on
he other rim, I saw the riders fading back into the
noon mist. So fast did the mare go, the breath
seemed to be blown from my lungs. I tried to catch it
back, but it would not come. I seemed strangling—
ny head spun—and suddenly I knew that I was
fainting. The dread of that froze my poor brain. It
was already giddy enough with the endless, the
soul-filling pain, and with the loss of blood. But I
forced myself to act. Leaning forward, I took off the
stout straps that connected with the nose band of
Cherry. I bound part of the reins around my body.
The other part I lashed securely to the pommel of
he saddle. And we galloped on into an increasing

darkness, into an increasing suffocation of lungs and brains.

My consciousness left me until the cold sting of water roused me. I found that Cherry was crossing a broad stream of water. Before us was a swarm of lights, dancing like red and golden bees. *Was it the town of Chalmer's Creek*, I wondered drowsily. The current swished beneath us. I hung limply and heavily upon one side, the grip of the bridle rein preventing me from falling.

I made a vast struggle. But it was no use. I could not pull myself up into the saddle again. There was no good in the trying, it appeared. So I hung there, the rein encircling me with a narrow band of fire. All the nerves of my body were gathered there under the red-hot touch of torture. That pain had roots in my whole being, but it flowered where the cruel leather sank into my bare flesh.

At least, the agony burned the shadows from my brain. Then I found that we were no longer in water, but climbing a slope, and behind me men were rushing on horses, shouting to one another.

I called to Cherry. At a soft gallop she went forward, her head turned to watch over me. We entered the region of the lights. They spun and whirled before my eyes. Sometimes I felt that I had ridden straight into a vast conflagration, and the pain I felt was the licking of the flames. But the shadowy horsemen had not followed me. Then I was aware of voices and the white gleam of human faces. Hands laid hold upon me and wherever they touched my body they gave me new torture.

The illusion of the fire was still upon me; I combined it with this new picture and told myself that I was in the region of eternal torment, brought there

for my sins. I was dead, and my naked soul was now
to begin an endless anguish.

Then the grip of the reins no longer held me.
Many human arms upheld me. I heard voices raised
in fury, shoutings, callings, and the lovely head of
Cherry close to me, her ears pricking, her eyes like
great, dim stars.

Cherry would not leave me, I thought. *Not even in
perdition.*

"Go slow," I heard them saying. "Don't stumble . . . don't you see the poor kid is dying?"

It was odd, I thought, that they could not see that
I was already dead, being there among them, in torment. Was there human kindness, even in the infernal regions?

Then I heard a sharp, high-pitched voice, and,
looking up, I saw the face of Chiquita. She was weeping. "Oh, Chiquita," I said, "are you here before me in
perdition? Go back to earth. Find Chalmer's Creek.
Tell them that Judge Carrol is a murderer. He killed
Will Grier. He'll kill the captain and Stingo."

My mind became a blank. Then I was aware that
voices were crying out in an agony of anxiety:
"Where? Where?"

"The house on the ranch of the judge . . . up the
creek," I whispered.

Then it seemed to me that a thousand faces withdrew from about me, and afterward there was a
sound of thunder and of shouting.

CHAPTER 43

That was not all a delusion. There was a shoutin
and a thundering through the streets of Chalmer
Creek as nearly every able-bodied man in the tow
mounted his horse and spurred out to take the tra
up the valley. They went like a storm, and the
found the house of the judge on its crag.

Some of them guarded it from below; some c
them climbed to the higher side to take it on its les
lofty front. But before they gained the height, al
sound of gunfire had ended. As they reached th
upper level, there was only a sweep of riders rush
ing away. They had been warned in time.

Only one man lagged behind the rest, a ponder
ous and clumsy horseman. His mustang began t
buck under the great weight of the rider, and tha
was why a volley of half a dozen bullets found th
body of Judge Carrol and dropped him, lifeles:
upon the ground while his horse galloped off.

Afterward, Stingo, the captain, and Grey cam
out from the house, and they were escorted like he

es back to the town. Heroes they were, too, in my
ense of the word.

I did not learn of these things at once. Between
ss of blood, which left little fluid in my body for
e heart to pump, and a fever that followed the
ain and the exhaustion of that ride, I was out of
y head for a long time. But the wounds were no
eat matter. That through the thigh was as clean as
whistle, and the first rifle shot had clipped my left
oulder, cracked a couple of ribs as it ranged
ownward, then plowed through the flesh to the
all of my back, where it lodged just under the
in. A mighty painful wound, but not the slightest
nger unless infection should set in. No, I had suf-
ed more from shock and fright than from any-
ing else.

When at last my wits cleared and I found myself
ng in bed as weak as water and with a sort of
ldness of spirit blessing me, I found that first rifle
ll lying on a saucer on the small table beside my
d. When I turned my head, I saw Grey sitting in a
air in the corner.

He got up and came to me. "How goes it, sir?" he
d.

"Why, it goes fine," I said, searching his cold face.
But the coldness disappeared; a flashing smile
nsformed him.

"Now, thank heaven," he muttered. He disap-
ared. Then he came again, and the captain was
ore him, taking long, eager strides, and there was
sardonic face above me, scowling down.

"Well," he said, "I hope that this is the end of this
ursed nonsense."

"I hope so, sir," I agreed.

But I grinned at him. He never would frighten me

again with his gruff ways. I had seen his great hear
and understood.

At one of his shoulders stood Grey, at the othe
was John, the Swede, and both of them were grin
ning broadly. The smile of John, in fact, made hin
look like a half-wit.

"Now, then," said the captain, "scatter out of th
room, the lot of you. You might wake poor Chiquit
and tell her that he's come around. She'll sleep a
the better for knowing, and the child needs slee
You can tell Stingo, too, but tell him that, if h
whoops, I'll cut his throat."

They left the room; the captain sat down beside m

"You seem to have found your own people, Don
he said.

"Yes, sir," I said, "I hope that I've found them."

"Well," he said, "it's a good thing for a lad, I da
say, when an entire town adopts him. I think that a
of Chalmer's Creek would go barefoot for you, Don

"Why, sir, those were not the people I meant."

"No?" he queried, raising his brows in a fier
and sudden manner. "Then who do you mean?"

"I mean John, sir," I informed him, "and Gre
and you yourself, if you please."

"Ha?" said the captain. "I never heard such no
sense! Your people, indeed. The three of us." He g
up and paced the room with his stalking stride agai
"Do you know what the three of us are?" he sai
halting beside my bed and speaking very quietly.

"I was just outside the window and heard ever
thing," I told him. "And I know that I want no bett
friends."

"You were outside the window?" said the capta
"You climbed up behind us?"

"I couldn't help following," I said. "I didn't mean
eavesdrop."

"And you want such fellows for friends, do you?"
said as fiercely as ever.

"Yes, sir," I said. "They'd do me forever, if I'd do
r them."

"It's the rash judgment of a giddy boy," he said.

"It's out of my whole heart, sir," I said.

He made a pause, for a moment. At last he said:
onald, as I've said before, my right hand is no
od, and I don't believe, ordinarily, in using the
t hand. But on this one occasion, I shall have to try
make it do, if you are willing."

So he held out his left hand to me, and I gripped it
bly, and so we remained for a long time, silently
d gravely looking one another in the face.

ABOUT THE AUTHOR

ax Brand is the best-known pen name of Frederick
ust, creator of Dr. Kildare, Destry, and many other
tional characters popular with readers and view-
s worldwide. Faust wrote for a variety of audiences
many genres. His enormous output, totaling ap-
oximately 30,000,000 words or the equivalent of
0 ordinary books, covered nearly every field:
ime, fantasy, historical romance, espionage, West-
ns, science fiction, adventure, animal stories, love,
ar, and fashionable society, big business and big
edicine. Eighty motion pictures have been based
his work along with many radio and television
ograms. For good measure he also published four
lumes of poetry. Perhaps no other author has
ached more people in more different ways. Born in
attle in 1892, orphaned early, Faust grew up in the
ral San Joaquin Valley of California. At Berkeley
became a student rebel and one-man literary
ovement, contributing prodigiously to all campus
blications. Denied a degree because of unconven-

tional conduct, he embarked on a series of adventures culminating in New York City where, after period of near starvation, he received simultaneou recognition as a serious poet and successful auth of fiction. Later, he traveled widely, making his hom in New York, then in Florence, and finally in Los An geles. Once the United States entered the Secon World War, Faust abandoned his lucrative writin career and his work as a screenwriter to serve as war correspondent with the infantry in Italy, despi his fifty-one years and a bad heart. He was kille during a night attack on a hilltop village held by th German army. New books based on magazine seria or unpublished manuscripts or restored versior continue to appear so that, alive or dead, he has ave aged a new book every four months for seventy-fiv years. Beyond this, some work by him is newl reprinted every week of every year in one or anoth format somewhere in the world.

RIDERS OF PARADISE

ROBERT J. HORTON

Clint and Dick French may be identical twins, but Clint's wild ways contrast sharply with his brother's more sophisticated tastes. But then Dick decides to share his brother's responsibilities at the family ranch—and ends up sharing his enemies as well. When notorious troublemaker Blunt Rodgers mistakes Dick for Clint, the tenderfoot looks to be doomed. Three shots are fired, Blunt ends up dead, and the sheriff doesn't need evidence to peg Clint the killer. And once word gets back to the infamous outlaw Blunt rode with, a whole gang of hardcases will be gunning for *both* brothers.

SBN 10: 0-8439-5895-2
SBN 13: 978-0-8439-5895-9

MEDICINE ROAD

WILL HENRY

Mountain man Jim Bridger is counting on Jess
Callahan. He knows that Callahan is the best man
to lead the wagon train that's delivering guns and
ammunition to Bridger's trading post at Green
River. But Brigham Young has sworn to wipe out
Bridger's posts, and he's hired Arapahoe warrior
Watonga to capture those weapons at any cost.
Bridger, Young and Watonga all have big plans for
those guns, but it's all going to come down to just
how tough Callahan can be. He's going to have to
be tougher than leather if he hopes to make it to the
post...alive.

ISBN 10: 0-8439-5814-6
ISBN 13: 978-0-8439-5814-0

HEADING WEST
Western Stories
NOEL M. LOOMIS

Noel M. Loomis creates characters so real it's hard to believe they're fiction, and these nine stories vividly demonstrate his brilliant storytelling talent. Within this volume, you'll meet Big Blue Buckley, who proves it takes a "Tough *Hombre*" to build a railroad in the 1880s and "The St. Louis Salesman" who struggles with the harsh terrain of the Texas prairie. Most poignant of all is the dying Comanche warrior passing on the ways of his people in "Grandfather Out of the Past," a tale that won Loomis the prestigious Spur Award. Each story sweeps you back in time to the Old West as it really was.

ISBN 10: 0-8439-5897-9
ISBN 13: 978-0-8439-5897-3

BLOOD TRAIL TO KANSAS

ROBERT J. RANDISI

Ted Shea thinks he is a goner for sure. All the years he's worked to build his Montana spread and fine herd of prime beef means nothing if he can't sell them. And with a vicious rustler and his gang of cutthroats scaring all the hands, no one is willing to take to the trail. Until Dan Parmalee drifts into town. A gunman and gambler with a taste for long odds, he isn't about to let a little hot lead part him from some cold cash. But it doesn't take Dan long to realize this isn't just any run. This is a...*Blood Trail to Kansas*.

ISBN 10: 0-8439-5799-9
ISBN 13: 978-0-8439-5799-0

NIGHT HAWK

STEPHEN OVERHOLSER

He came to the ranch with a mile-wide chip on his shoulder and no experience whatsoever. But it was either work on the Circle L or rot in jail, and he figured even the toughest labor was better than a life behind bars. He's got a lot to learn though, and he'd better learn it fast because he's about to face one of the toughest cattle drives in the country. They've got an ornery herd, not much water and danger everywhere they look. The greenhorn the cowboys call Night Hawk may not know much, but he does know this: The smallest mistake could cost him his life.

ISBN 10: 0-8439-5840-5
ISBN 13: 978-0-8439-5840-9

To order a book or to request a catalog call:
1-800-481-9191
This book is also available at your local bookstore, or you can check out our Web site **www.dorchesterpub.com** where you can look up your favorite authors, read excerpts, or glance at our discussion forum to see what people have to say about your favorite books.

THE LAST WAY STATION
KENT CONWELL

As soon as Jack Slade and his partner, Three Fingers Bent, arrive in the small Texas town of New Gideon, they know no one wants them there. There's been some rustling in the area, and folks aren't taking too kindly to strangers. But things don't get any better when Slade and Bent move on. The two don't get far before a posse from New Gideon rides up, accuses Bent of murder, and takes him back to face a judge. Slade knows he won't have much time before his partner hangs on a trumped-up charge, and there's only one way he can save his friend—he'll have to find the real killer himself!

ISBN 10: 0-8439-5928-2
ISBN 13: 978-0-8439-5928-4

MAX BRAND®

TWISTED BARS

He was known as The Duster. Five times he'd
been tried for robbery and murder, and five times
acquitted. He'd met the most famous of gunmen
and beaten them all. Before he gives it all up, he's
got one battle left to fight. The Duster needs a
proper burial for his dead partner, but the
blustery Rev. Kenneth Lamont refuses to let a
criminal rest in his cemetery. The Duster knows if
he can't get what he wants one way, there's
always another. And this is a plan the reverend
won't like. Not one bit…

ISBN 10: 0-8439-5871-5
ISBN 13: 978-0-8439-5871-3